Servant of the Jackal God: The Tales of Kamose, Archpriest of Anubis

Servant of the Jackal God: The Tales of Kamose, Archpriest of Anubis

by Keith Taylor

In-house editor: Darrell Schweitzer

Fantastic Books
1380 East 17 Street, Suite 2233
Brooklyn, New York 11230
www.FantasticBooks.biz

ISBN 10: 1-5154-2360-3
ISBN 13: 978-1-5154-2360-7

First Edition, 2012
Second ISBN, 2018

Contents

DAGGERS AND A SERPENT

I.

The raiders came out of the desert like a sudden storm that whirled against Anubis's temple. Despite its high walls and pyloned gateways, it was no fortress. The Libyan savages swarmed over the walls of the outer court in moments, avid for plunder. In a moment more they had opened the bronze-hinged cedar gates. The guards who sought to stop them were speared or clubbed down, and their blood flowed in dark streams.

Other raiders rushed through the open gates to join the desert men. This second group sweated in ribbed horsehair corselets and padded caps with swinging tassels. Better disciplined than the naked tribesmen, they trotted forward under the weight of a long bronze-headed ram. From above, on the walls, their ram looked like a stiff-bodied centipede with sixty fateful legs.

Wheels rumbling, a war-chariot drove into the public courtyard. Its naked driver reined the horses back, while his passenger raised a hand and shouted orders. Lean, forceful, he wore a red pleated kilt and headcloth. The bearing of a prince marked him out—but a prince of bandits.

His soldiers swung back the ram, then heaved it forward to crash on the gates of the roofed inner court, which was not accessible to climbers. The whole building boomed like a drum. Within, priests, priestesses, servitors, and scribes milled in confused terror. Most hardly believed it was happening. Temples were not attacked in Egypt... it never occurred.

The second set of gates burst in. Libyans and men-at-arms charged together, yelling. The soldiers had been drugged with a potion that excited them to fury, as well as numbing their souls to fear of the gods; and they had been brutal men before drinking their lord's potion. Here was slaughter, the smell of new blood. Here before them lay victims and loot. The Libyans had their own gods, and in any case were outright bandits to whom anything in Egypt was fair plunder. They would slay and rob their present allies joyfully if a chance ever came. Surging through the smashed gates, they all behaved alike.

Wide-bladed spears sank into bellies, to be twisted and yanked back, spilling gore. Axes swung down on shaven heads. Eyes bleary with sleep and wide with consternation bulged in the horrified realization of death, then saw nothing. The priestesses and other temple women suffered worse. Their screams rose on the night wind and were silenced in the end by knives.

Bloody excitement stirred the man in the chariot as he watched, though he tried to conceal it beneath a haughty bearing. His father had impressed upon him firmly that this was business. He decided, reluctantly, that these creatures had enjoyed themselves for long enough. Driving among them, he swung a long-lashed whip and called harshly for discipline. Soldiers and Libyans alike shrank from the lash as though it was something immeasurably more dreadful, pressing against the courtyard walls to avoid it.

"Empty the store-rooms," the man commanded loudly. "Strip the place of gold and precious stones. I will see to the shrine."

The captain of soldiers saluted. "Yes, lord."

They scurried to obey. Stepping down from his chariot, the leader stalked through the temple's vestibule, a tall figure muscled like a hunter of lions—which he had been from boyhood. Of lions, and women, and power.

At the entrance to the inner shrine, he did not even hesitate before parting the rich hangings.

Murals of Anubis covered the walls. Here he embalmed a body with meticulous patience, there he performed the ceremony of restoring the senses—"opening the mouth"—on an upright mummy, elsewhere he guided the soul to the afterworld. These were his functions as god of the dead, the Lord of Tombs. The man in red smiled scornfully.

His glance moved to the diorite image of Anubis, with its golden kilt and jewelled trappings. The Announcer carried daggers. Around his forearm coiled a viper, the ancient instrument of death for a Pharaoh. His head, traditionally, was that of a jackal, with snout and pointed ears.

Before the image stood a lean old priest. He peered like a mole in the yellow lamp-light. The intruder supposed there was little chance of this one recognising him, despite his noble rank, not that it mattered. Probably all he saw was a blurred figure.

"You are doomed beyond hope," the priest said in a surprisingly steady voice. "Do you not fear?"

"What? This?" The bandit leader waved an arm at the jackal-headed image of black diorite. "None of it has moved me since I was a boy, old priest. I should fear to strike against a temple of Amun-Ra, since he is revered by the Pharaoh, and holds the great power of being in fashion. Likewise Osiris, who is both royal and beloved. But the jackal? No one remembers him while the blood runs hot, only when their time comes to die—and his Archpriest is not close to the circles of power. I have no fear."

"Then as well as a murderer, you are a fool. The Archpriest of Anubis is the greatest magician in all of Kheml! I do not pity your doom; you have earned it. But I pity your ignorance."

"Indeed." The man in red smiled mockingly—but his eyes flashed with stung conceit. He was young.

He shook out the lash of his whip and struck with it. Cubits of thin braided leather coiled around the old priest's body. The intruder uttered the words of a spell that made his throat vibrate, brief though it was. Then he loosened the whip with a motion of his arm and pulled it back.

The priest made a ghastly noise. Worse ones followed, though they did not issue from his mouth. His head began to twist inexorably on his neck. He tottered, then fell, as his legs turned around in the same way, with the hideous cracklings and tearings of complete dislocation at the hips. Muscles stood out in distortion through his skin.

After an excessively long while, he lay still on the floor of the inner shrine. His eyes stared at the dark ceiling, and his skinny toes pointed in the same direction, yet he did not lie on his back. His knobbed spine and shrunken buttocks faced upward, while his belly pressed against the floor, in a disconcerting and abhorrent reversal.

Traces of revulsion even touched the man in red, though morbid curiosity and the thrill of lethal power were far more strongly felt. He worked his shoulders back and forth as though to release tension. Then he briskly tore headdress, armlets, collar, belt, and golden kilt from the statue of Anubis. Quenching the golden lamps, he tore them down, thrusting them into a sack with his other plunder. Leaving, he ordered a minion to take the precious hangings from the doorway.

A plain massive barge waited at the water-side to receive the loot. The brigand-noble supervised the loading to be sure that no one cheated. His whip trailed freely from his hand.

"Greatest magician in all of Khem," he repeated, smiling ironically. "Yes, I have heard that, Kamose, you whom sots and fools call Satni-Kamose. I have heard that and other rumours, too. But what charlatan does not make such claims?"

The barge sat low in the water as it moved out from the temple quay. People who might have come running from nearby villages chose to hide their heads and see nothing. The barge moved down a well-maintained canal towards the Nile. Looking back, the man in red saw the Libyans moving into the desert by the light of the temple's blazing gates. He dryly commended them to the care of their father Set.

A good night's work. My father plans the attack. I lead it. The Libyans, conveniently out of reach, take all the blame but a lesser share of the plunder. Let the upstart Kamose find the truth, if he is such a master of the sorcerous arts.

II.

"Shape of the black crocodile! May their bodies be accursed! May the destruction of Set fall upon them! They shall eat no food in the afterworld, their names shall be expunged from life, they shall belong to the Devourer!"

The outburst of passion ended. Kamose, Archpriest of Anubis, returned to his ebony chair and sat brooding in anger. His linen robe hung in two parts from his upper body, he having torn it to the waist when he heard the news of the temple sack. The messenger who had brought those abominable tidings remained kneeling, discreetly quiet.

Kamose repressed his fury to a contained seething. *"Who?"*

"Savages from the west, holy one. Desert men. Libyans."

"So." Kamose looked again at the written report he had been given, his eyes and mind now intent; rage gained nothing. It made a man a fool. "Those children of darkness."

The missive was not in formal hieroglyphs. Kamose deigned to read it anyhow, a sign of his outrage. He twice studied the passage which described the condition of his subordinate priest's body, with the head and legs twisted backwards.

"You may leave," he told the messenger. "Say to my major-domo that I command food, drink, and raiment for you, after a bath."

Sitting alone, he considered the atrocity. Kamose was tall, with an air of sombre but great vitality, muscled more like a soldier than a priest. His hands and skin, however, were definitely those of a scribe. He carried Syrian blood from his grandmother; it showed in his blade of a nose and narrow, somewhat tilted eyes. Kamose shaved his head and observed all the other strictures of his priestly station, except for a little pointed chin-beard. He supposed it was his Syrian strain that led him to prefer it. Besides, it saved trouble. Ritual prescribed a false beard of like size and shape in any case, for certain occasions.

Frowning, he walked out on one of the terraces of his mansion. All around him lay fanes of gods and mortuary temples of former kings, with cemeteries of huge extent in between. Abdu was more a great necropolis than a town. At its western side, among the low desert hills, lay the dark granite temple of Anubis. It was far larger and older than the temple at Bahari which had been looted, but no more sacred to the jackal-headed god, Foremost of the Westerners. That was to say, Lord of the Dead.

Kamose administered all such temples. In addition he held charge over the graceful mortuary temple of Pharaoh Seti, the Ramesseum itself, and many others. Their endowments were immense. Having them in his control had made him a number of jealous enemies, such as the entire priesthood of Thoth. Kamose wondered if some of them could be responsible for this horror. The first step in a scheme to discredit him?

Shrugging the torn robe back upon his shoulders, Kamose went thoughtfully to his own chamber. There he found Mertseger, and she was restless. Instead of discreetly keeping to the form of a tall, supple woman, she had let her legs merge into the mottled tail of a large serpent, while her forearms had grown scaly and taloned. Yet the sight was not horrible. A lethal, ancient fascination invested her, springing, as Kamose well knew, from the most lurid fancies of man.

Half lifting from her couch in the rags of a purple gown, she looked at her master from ophidian eyes and greeted him with a kiss.

"Such transformations are ill in this house," he said harshly. "You know that. I prefer that my servants imagine you to be a mortal woman."

"Then set me free!" Her tail lashed about, found a leg of the couch arid coiled in frustration around it. "To offend me by holding me captive so far from my home is a fatal thing, magician."

"To threaten me before you are able is foolish, too. Freedom? I think not, O Mertseger. Having delivered Buto from your haunting, and increased my fame in the Delta thereby, I would undo my credit if I allowed you to return. Besides," he added, "your needs are too malign, as wives and mothers bereaved can attest."

"What do you care for those mortals?"

"Little, perhaps, and yet I had a wife and children once."

The lamia hissed in mockery, running a forked tongue out between her delectable human lips. The contrast would have appalled a normal man; Kamose felt amused and aroused. Being a magician, he knew that Mertseger's perverse allure was her means of drawing victims to her embrace, and knew equally how they ended, but he stood in no such danger. Rather, peril to the lamia attended *him.* And she could assume a completely human shape when she willed, a socially advantageous power not shared by Kamose's other leman, the she-sphinx Nonmet.

"Once," she said. "As mortals reckon time, it was long ago, Satni-Kamose. You have changed much."

"While you have lived many times longer than I, and in all those millennia changed not, nor learned a thing." He ignored her use of the erroneous nickname bestowed on him by the vulgar.

"I am content," Mertseger answered, coiling. "And you? Did all that you learned from the Scrolls of Thoth increase your felicity?"

A smoking anger kindled in Kamose's eyes. He held his features impassive. "Daughter of serpents, don't seek to provoke me. You might have the misfortune to succeed. Transform!"

She hissed again.

"Transform, Mertseger, or I deal with you harshly."

Scaly forearms softened. The talons became feminine hands. Mertseger's deadly tail shrank and bifurcated.

Kamose nodded. "You may be able to sate your appetites again. Men have sacked one of my temples with slaughter. When I learn who—"

"My good lord." Mertseger looked melting. She curled her human legs under her, posing in purple tatters. "I regret the gown. But your own robe is conveniently rent."

"So it is."

Kamose took her in his arms. Even Mertseger's serpent-tongue was now human, pink and flat, as the occasion proved perfect for him to discover and appreciate. With the increase of her pleasure her tongue reverted to the ophidian, not that Kamose minded greatly. Later still, her lower body changed back to the coils of a glittering snake, writhing and undulating. This presented her lover with a greater challenge. However, it was not his first experience of that, and he proved equal to the situation. But prudence dictated, even to him, that he should not sleep beside Mertseger. He stayed wakeful while she drowsed until the morning.

In the grey hours, memories bummed around him like gnats. After the tragedies of his youth he had travelled widely, learned to extend his life span, and on returning to Egypt, lived as an ascetic hermit for years—but he had wearied of that, finally. Again he entered human society, became a priest and archpriest (with a great deal of hidden sardonic amusement) and turned to sensuous pleasures once more (though not quite of the ordinary sort).

Egypt had come to lamentable days. Kamose was not disposed to shudder and wail over this, since he knew how transient are both good and unfortunate times. Still, lawless plunder did not suit him; he had immense estates and wealth in his charge that might be ravaged by such action. He also had a dreadful patron in the shape of the mortuary god, to whom even he must render an account.

The stars grew pale. In his aspect as Khepri the Regenerate, the Sun appeared across the Nile. Mertseger awoke, stretching sensuously. She heard Kamose say firmly, "We travel to Badari, daughter of serpents. Prepare."

"Badari. Is that where—?"

"Where the temple was despoiled, yes."

Mertseger hurried. Kamose had half-promised the villain responsible would be her prey, once he was exposed. Her heart beat like a young girl's.

III.

Kamose bowed low before the desecrated statue of Anubis. Although he knew well that gods were not perfect beings, and further that many of their attributes and legends were made by the men who worshipped them, he had long been bleakly aware that they existed and held fateful power. The jackal-headed lord of death at least was fair; he treated everyone alike.

Kamose had fasted and ceremonially washed. He wore a robe of seamless linen. In his hands he held a silver bowl filled with Nile water, which he placed on the bare altar.

"O Foremost of the Westerners, Announcer of Death, you who foresee destiny, reveal to your servant who hath done this impious crime! Let judgement and retribution befall them."

Kamose bent forward, staring into the transparent water. Incised at the bottom of the bowl was a picture of Anubis. Under Kamose's unwinking gaze the picture stirred, moved, and walked forward across the surface of polished silver, to vanish from sight and be replaced by other gods in procession. Horus the Living Falcon, son and avenger of Osiris; Sekhmet the Lioness, fierce, unpitying, armed with the scorching heat of the Sun; Isis and Nepthys, the mistresses of magic and mourners of Osiris; Osiris himself wrapped as a royal mummy but with skin green as the verdure of renewed life; Thoth, vizier of the gods, ibis-headed divine scribe. Kamose's skin prickled coldly as he beheld that limning. Thoth was an even greater lord of magic and prophecy than Anubis, but Kamose had been out of favour with him for many, many years—ever since, as a youth hungry for knowledge, he had stolen from a tomb the master-scrolls of magic which Thoth had written.

Contempt changed the shape of Kamose's mouth as he remembered that young man—a dreamy, studious fool. He was gone now, perished as Crete, lost as Troy, and good riddance. Thoth had punished that theft in full measure. Kamose had to control a boiling of rebellious hatred even now, almost a hundred years later.

The water clouded. Shapes moved murkily through a mist of blood. Libyan tribesmen in tall head-dresses slew, raped, and then plundered. Soldiers of Egypt burst the temple doors. An arrogant figure killed the priest unpleasantly with one light lash of an enchanted whip. His face appeared clearly. Behind it loomed another face, considerably older, austere, cynical, and tired, yet resembling the younger man's to a marked degree.

The water grew transparent again, and for a moment, cut on the bottom of the bowl, Kamose saw a number instead of the formal depiction of Anubis—the number thirteen. The water rippled, the number was gone, and once more Kamose saw a jackal-headed figure bearing daggers and a viper.

"My thanks, great one," he murmured.

The revelation had been clear. Two nobles were the culprits, one senior, one young, very likely related if that strong resemblance was a guide; and the younger had led this blasphemous raid in collusion with Libyan bandits. Thirteen could only mean the Thirteenth Nome—the province of Sawty.

Treading slowly, a deep scowl on his forehead, Kamose went out through the roofed courtyard and the broken, leaning gates. Though the temple had been cleansed with water and sand, it still smelled of blood. The sacrilegious reek stung his nostrils.

Men shall die, and worse than die, for this act.

With an executioner's look in his eyes, he left the temple and went to the nearby house of embalming. Rows of cadavers which had been his priests and priestesses lay there, desiccating in beds of dry natron. Kamose examined them. He took particular notice of the chief priest's body. The embalmers had turned his wizened head the right way around on his shoulders once more. They had also seen fit to amend the reversal of his legs and fit the dislocated femurs back into his hip-joints, but the torn, distorted muscles told their story to Kamose even before he questioned the undertakers. He remembered what he had seen in the divinatory bowl.

"The whip of Selket," he said aloud. "Very few such lashes exist. When I find one—belike in Sawty—I have found my murderers. But first let me deal with that desert scum."

Kamose kept a vigil in the plundered temple that night, before the statue of Anubis, that would have seared another man's soul to ashes. Holding a viper and a dagger in his naked hands, he invoked his jackal-headed lord. Also, he addressed himself to other gods of the dead: Neith, Wepwawet, and the slain and resurrected Osiris, "He Who Makes Silence." But Thoth's name he did not speak.

A black night wind blew through the outer courts and into the shrine. Bats and owls flew above the roof. Ghouls crept out of their lairs in ancient cemeteries to stare with purulent eyes at the temple, though they dared not come too near. Something they sensed or foresaw seemed to amuse them; now and then, one gave a shout of hideous laughter.

At midnight, a little golden jackal appeared. After circling the temple several times, it came padding through the burst gates, shrinking with each forward step. It showed no fear of the ghouls, which was strange. Nor did one of the vile grey shapes molest it. They allowed it to pass, and it almost crept on its belly through the inner court, whining as though summoned on a journey it would rather not make, by a power it could not resist.

"Welcome, little brother," Kamose said, turning.

Bending, he seized the jackal and raised it towards the plundered statue of Anubis. The beast gave a piteous yelp of terror and twisted convulsively in Kamose's hands. He held fast. The statue's red eyes seemed to glitter with awareness.

In an instant, the jackal became heavy as granite. Kamose quivered with the effort of holding it. With reverent dread he set the little beast back on the floor. It slunk out. Something dreadful, which it carried now like a burden, had possessed it.

It vanished like a shadow through the pylons of the outer gateway. No one reported seeing it again, but its tracks, unnaturally deep, led into the western desert before the wind brushed them away. It travelled deeper into the wastes, night after night, resting by day, neither eating nor drinking.

Long after it should have perished, the jackal reached a large Libyan camp. Music, singing, and festive laughter came to its sharply pricked ears. Looting the temple of Anubis had made these people prosperous. They celebrated freely. They feasted and danced. The jackal crept closer until the firelight gleamed in its eyes.

Then it rushed the camp. A horrible cry of release burst from its throat, enough to make the stars quiver. Asses and other cattle fled wildly into the desert as the jackal raced from hearth to hearth, but not one human creature fled, although there was much screaming. And all human voices in the end were silent.

The jackal was not seen by mortal eyes again.

IV.

"O my father, let us repeat this action!" The young man's eyes glittered with anticipation as he swigged beer, the rich dark beer made from barley and dates. "There are temples and to spare, the land abounds in them. Half belong to outworn gods, ill serviced and guarded; and the times are lawless. Who will suspect us? We can do as we please."

"Not yet, my son." Watab, Prince of the Thirteenth Nome, smiled like a crocodile. "There is a war to fight with our accursed neighbours. Have you forgotten that we needed the temple gold only to hire mercenaries? The plunder of the whole Twelfth Nome is more than the wealth of any temple, and we can pass off this private campaign as loyalty to Pharaoh. Our old foes have been indiscreet at last. I have waited and planned for this longer than you have been alive."

"I yearn for the day we will make an end of them!" the younger noble said. He was not wearing red now. "Let's hire the mercenaries, then. Kushite bowmen. Shardana sworders. I'll drive my chariot through their gardens in the high blaze of noon!" He drew the lash of his long whip through his fingers.

"All that and more." His father pointed to the whip. "However, leave that toy behind, Paheri. Its effect is too distinctive. You performed your raid well, except for that one thing. Using the whip of Selket on the priest was an error."

"No doubt. I had a concern that I might encounter magic and need some swift magic of my own, but there was none." Paheri shrugged. "So much for the powers of Anubis."

Prince Watab's mouth drew downward in a bitter, weary expression. "I ceased to believe in the powers of any god long since, my son—or at least in their care for the actions of men and women. Clearly they have deserted us. Weak successors of the mighty Usermare contend for the Double Crown, and leave us princes and chiefs to battle likewise. Justice is no more than a feather in the wind. We cannot afford principle. We can only secure the future for our descendants in such ways as are left, and hope that for them there will be better times. This is ill, but it must be. Remember that. Always be cunning, ruthless, wary—but feign virtue well." He held out his hand for the whip. "And do not leave your signature upon any crime you commit."

"I'll remember that, father." Paheri showed a cheerfully cruel smile as he handed over the whip of Selket. "However, if I take alive any of those Twelfth Nome curs who slew my uncle and my brothers, I shall ask for that whip again."

"And shall have it."

"Falcon of the Sun!" Paheri exclaimed suddenly. "A ship is making for our quay! A prince's ship, by its appearance—or—"

Prince Watab shaded his pouched eyes and squinted. From the roof garden, he could see over the high walls of his mansion all the way to the river, though poorly. Years, and the bright sun of Egypt, had impaired his sight. Not until the ship glided closer did he recognise it as a small galley with its sail spread to the wind. Except that its hull seemed dark, he could not perceive detail. However, his son owned sharp vision. Paheri discerned the emblem of a black jackal couchant upon a pedestal, displayed upon the galley's sail.

"Father," he said with seeming coolness, "a messenger from the temple of the dog presumes to visit us."

"So?" The prince's visage became like a formal mask. "Let us receive him."

Watab sat in haughty state to receive his guest, shaven head bare, body robed and jewelled. Paheri stood arrogantly behind him, bare to the waist except for collar and armlets. His military kilt of stiffened linen hung short on one side, long behind the right leg, in the royal fashion to which strictly speaking he had no right, despite his descent from a Pharaoh. A sheathed sword lay nearby on a table. Two women with fans flanked the prince's chair, and a scribe with pen and papyrus sheets sat below the dais. Impassive soldiers guarded the door.

Watab's major-domo, a large and sonorous person, announced the visitor in a voice that cracked unprecedentedly.

"The Most Reverend Kamose, Archpriest of Anubis, lord."

Kamose entered, erect and saturnine. The soldiers at the door grew somewhat less impassive as he passed between them. Their eyes shifted uneasily to regard the priest-magician, as though guilt and foreboding had touched their spirits.

Kamose's own gaze remained fixed on the prince's dais. Robed in pleated linen, Kamose did not wear the full regalia of his office that day, neither the artificial leopard-skin nor the gemmed apron; only a broad collar, belt, and armlets of jet and gold. He carried a jackal-headed staff of black wood. Behind him walked lesser priests and scribes—and Mertseger, in spurious human form, robed as a priestess, the image of dedicated beauty. Paheri looked at her with lustful interest, and drew his own conclusions as to why she accompanied Kamose.

The lecherous foreign dog, he thought.

Kamose looked at the two nobles. Paheri's rashness and pride was easily read in his bearing. Watab covered his feelings better. His visage, slack-skinned, gashed by lines of disillusion, still expressed authority and resolve. Father and son both had the symmetrical features of native Egyptians whose every remotest ancestor had been Egyptian too.

Their disdain for this upstart priest with a Syrian grandam was so complete they took it for granted. As the fact that they breathed air. Kamose had long been accustomed to that attitude. It amused him now. Even from criminals.

Watab said, "I make you welcome, holy one." Kamose's tomb-black eyes held an implacable glitter as he regarded the prince. He answered grimly, "Thy welcome is rejected. I bring thee the judgement and condemnation of the lord of sepulchres, even Anubis. The reason is thy plunder and desecration of his temple, thy murder of his servants. I travel to the Delta now in order to place proofs before Pharaoh. Therefore I bid thee and thy son Paheri to relinquish thy places in the world, and to accompany me in chains."

His words echoed from the stucco walls as though from the stone slabs of a deep grave-chamber—and the air seemed to darken. Paheri stared in amazement for a long time, then laughed contemptuously. His father's jaded, unscrupulous face showed a surge of furious blood.

"Madman! Will you slander us to the Living Horus? That shall mark the end of your priesthood."

"And perhaps of you," Paheri said, sneering.

"I have more proof than I require," Kamose said. "The least of it stands here. This woman is the priestess Mertseger, who survived the vile attack upon the temple wherein she served, and recognised thy son as the leading perpetrator, with his red garments and lethal whip. Also, divination bears out her testimony. The Libyan barbarians who were thy allies shall be brought manacled to witness against thee. Denial, therefore, cannot spare thee the consequences of thy blasphemous carnage."

"You are indeed mad," Watab repeated. "What, the testimony of savage brigands against a nomarch of Egypt? What are the divinations of a priest, one bribed no doubt by my enemies? Your journey to the mouths of the Nile would be fruitless even if you were to arrive."

"Not that you shall," Paheri added. "Your journey ends here, *holy one.* Your witness, the woman, shall witness to nothing. Not you nor this retinue shall be seen again. Look around you. We keep many soldiers, O Kamose, and they answer to us, not to you or even to the Living Horus.

These are evil times, wherein the power of the Double Crown is weak. The worse for you."

"But your enemies in the neighbour nome are strong," Kamose said calmly. "They will be glad of a pretext to attack you. If my galley comes to this port and goes no further, they will have their justification."

Paheri laughed aloud. "We have our own plans for those curs of the Twelfth Nome. Their treachery, not ours, is now established. Let them justify themselves if they can."

"Your galley will proceed downstream," Prince Watab said harshly. "Men dressed as you and your retinue will be seen on her decks. She *will* vanish before reaching the Delta, O fool, but not in my domain. You and your folk will sink with her. Meanwhile you may have accommodations in a strong storeroom. Take him away."

Two soldiers taller and stronger than Kamose converged upon him. He did not even glance at the hands that gripped his arms. His sombre gaze never left Prince Watab's face.

"Instead, depart with me and confess before Pharaoh. You would be wise. I make this offer once."

"Twice, as I reckon, now," the prince answered ironically. "You wasted your breath to say it even once."

Kamose disdained a reply. He allowed the soldiers to remove him. As they departed, he heard Paheri say mirthfully, "I will attend to the woman."

V.

Kamose sat composed in subterranean darkness. He set his back against a great jar of oil. No light entered this cool store-room below the foundations of Watab's mansion. Still, Kamose sensed the progress of the Sun with his sorcerer's perceptions. Twilight had passed, the stars had shone in the sky for a full hour, and Kamose sat in the dust of the storeroom as though at ease in one of his own temples.

His vessel, undoubtedly, had been overrun by the prince's men-at-arms shortly after Kamose had been cast into this dim prison. The priests and acolytes of his retinue would be lying bound in some similar place. Kamose smiled derisively as he thought of it. These rascals had something to learn.

The prince's son would surely be with Mertseger. He had boasted that he would attend to her. He! Attend—to Mertseger? Kamose's smile grew wicked.

The time was ripe.

"O great one, Anubis, Foremost of the Westerners, Lord of Tombs, Announcer; Restorer; God who Opens the Way, send against this house the ones who have endured your retribution, even the Libyan robbers allied with Watab the Accursed. Send them now, out of the West that is thy realm. Kamose, Archpriest of thy temples, calls upon thee. Be it so."

The darkness in the shut storeroom could not have increased. Nevertheless, it seemed to thicken until it pressed on Kamose's skin. Baying from a vast distance, he heard the cry of a titanic jackal. Time flowed by like barely warm pitch. Kamose waited.

With his mind's vision he saw everything that transpired above. Loping, padding shapes moved through the night, standing more or less upright, anthropomorphic yet not human. They prowled through the grain-fields. Reaching Prince Watab's walled mansion, they began to clamber over the walls, just as other shapes had done at the doomed temple. A dozen skulking forms converged upon the gate-lodge facing the river. Kamose could imagine the choked cries, no doubt a wild shriek or two, and then the mortal silence.

I daresay I will soon enjoy release from this storeroom, he thought peacefully.

The door crashed wide before he had drawn another twenty breaths. Armed soldiers bearing lamps and weapons filed among the great sealed jars, the lined storage pits, and Watab himself followed. Rage and consternation warred in his face. Behind both, to Kamose's eyes, lay the beginnings of a ghastly fear. He struck Kamose twice in the face.

"Swine and progeny of swine! What have you done? What have you brought upon me?"

"You have brought it upon yourself. Let us go and see."

When Kamose walked from the storeroom, no one laid a hand upon him, but rather drew back from his presence. None mocked his appearance, either, though stubble had grown on his shaven cheeks and dust thickly fouled his robe. One of Watab's soldiers whimpered, "Holy one—have mercy—" Watab struck the soldier down, and thrust Kamose violently ahead of him. The priest laughed. They reached a portico that looked out upon Watab's cool gardens, with their fish-ponds, flower-beds, and costly foreign blooms. They brought no satisfaction to the prince now. He looked on them with bulging eyes and frothing lips, those walks of his that an hour ago had been secure pleasaunces.

Corpses floated in the nearest pond. Others sprawled across crushed iris and asphodel. Monsters with scarlet jowls, red of hand, moved towards the house. They walked bipedally, having the bodies, arms, and thighs of men, but their heads were the heads of golden jackals, with scavenger jaws able to crack heavy bone; and their legs below the knee, also, were as the hind legs of jackals, so that they leaned forward for balance as they came.

"It appears, Prince Watab, that just as did the functionaries of a certain temple, you are receiving guests you did not invite," Kamose observed.

"Send them away, or you die!" Watab brandished the whip of Selket for emphasis. "You control those devils, do not pretend otherwise."

"You should recognise them," Kamose said. "These are the Libyan warriors you paid to cover the deed of your soldiers. The Lord Anubis burdened a jackal with the power of his curse and sent it to deliver his judgement. Here it is. They, with their women and children, and all their descendants, shall wear the forms you see. Now they answer his summons, to wreak his will on their former comrades."

"Send them away!" Watab's voice sounded scarcely human.

Kamose shook his head.

"Refuse," the prince whispered, "and before they can advance another step, your whole retinue dies. Look behind you, demon."

Kamose turned around with an expression of polite but small interest. Soldiers along the portico held daggers to the throats of his priests and acolytes. Sighing like a man wearied with foolish behaviour, Kamose clapped his hands sharply.

The veiling illusion that had cloaked his retinue vanished. Watab's soldiers recoiled with yells and shudders from standing, ancient mummies. Buried in the desert sand beside clay pots of food and their weapons, long before the first pyramid was raised, they had been kept from decay by dryness only. White ribs showed through flesh like ancient leather. Their eyes had become void pits. Long teeth glinted dry in their jaws, and their hands were claws of bone.

Kamose said ironically, "It is my turn to advise you to look."

Howling, Watab swung his lash at the saturnine priest. One of the mummies stepped between them with dreadful quickness, its bony heel clicking on the tiles. The whip curled around it. Ancient tendons burst as its head and legs turned backwards. Two more liches seized the prince and wrested his whip away. He shuddered uncontrollably in their dead grasp, while his eyes acquired a disordered stare. Kamose took possession of the whip of Selket, coiling up the supple lash with distaste.

"If I required more proof against you, it is here," he said like a judge pronouncing doom. "Your son Paheri partook of your crimes, and he too must answer. Is he hiding?"

Watab said nothing. His mouth had become as numbed as his mind. He looked like a man floundering in a poisoned swamp where soon he must drown.

Kamose looked at him closely. "Ah, yes. He boasted that he would attend to the woman, as I remember. Belike he's oblivious. Let us go and find him."

He turned his back on the gardens, to lead the way through the prince's house. Watab followed, escorted by two lipless corpses, while a third walked behind with a splayed, grotesque gait due to its legs being dislocated and reversed. It seemed to grin with malevolence.

Watab lurched and stumbled as though his will no longer governed his own legs. To him it appeared that what had been his mansion was, in the space of an evening, annexed to hell and overrun by demons. Behind him, the transformed Libyans advanced through corridor and chamber, their jaws seeking the throats of his soldiers. Kamose walked before him, never looking back. Grey dust fell from his robes as he trod. To Watab's half-blind gaze it seemed like the long accumulations of the tomb.

VI.

Kamose knew what they were likely to find when they intruded upon the lamia and the prince's son. He felt untouched by pity for the latter. The harvest of Paheri's own deeds had ripened.

Yet Kamose felt haunted by a sadness which arose from the humanity he had never been able to eradicate, despite his direst efforts. He too had been a father, and lost wife and children to the vengefulness of a god. Each one of Prince Watab's dragging steps behind him was a heavy reminder of grief. He ground his teeth. Curse human feeling that could survive even decades of traffic with demons, and return to haunt him with misgivings!

He halted at the entrance to a chamber from which a sound of low moaning issued.

Kamose shackled every natural response. They would have included grey skin, sweat, and a twisting belly. Instead, he turned an implacably harsh face towards the prince.

"See," he invited.

And Watab saw.

Head hanging limply over the edge, his son lay on a couch strewn with oryx skins. One arm lolled slackly towards the floor. Paheri had lifted the other to touch, to caress as though enthralled, the half-female monster that arched over him. Her long ophidian tail moved on the floor.

Worst of all was the hideous pliant softness of Peheri's ribs and thighs. They were broken as though in the pulverizing coils of a python. Despite those fearful injuries, Paheri continued to embrace the lamia even as he shuddered and died.

Kamose watched coldly. His natural horror at the sight faded, sinking into the past where it belonged, dead and buried with the scholarly youth of a century before. Let all temple-defilers meet such a fate. He stared with contempt at Watab, Prince of the Thirteenth Nome.

Who shook and babbled and clutched his head. "Fool!" Kamose said. "I offered you a journey to Pharaoh's palace in chains. A kindly proposal. You should have accepted."

Watab turned shuddering away from the sight in the chamber. He began weeping, rough wild sobs that jolted his body in spasms. The withered mummies watched him impassively.

Jackal-headed creatures still bounded and loped through the chambers of his house, killing the last of his soldiers while red pools crept across his floors. Watab's sobs became gulping laughter that rose madly higher. Yes he would threaten no one any longer.

Turning, Kamose strode from the house, through the garden and the gates, towards the stone quays by Prince Watab's private canal. He preferred not to bid Mertseger follow him. She might join him aboard the galley when she was—satisfied.

He could wait.

EMISSARIES OF DOOM

I.

The land of Egypt was overthrown. Every man was his own guide,
they had no superiors. The land was in chiefships and princedoms, each
killed the other among noble and mean.
—Papyrus of the late Nineteenth Dynasty

"The noble Tayo, emissary of the King of Kush, brings submission
and tribute to the Living Horus!"

The Kushite retinue hardly did honour to the Living Horus, Setekh-
Nekht, Pharaoh of Egypt. Among the many courtiers, officials, scribes and
priests who watched it approach, none was impressed.

The southern ruler had sent an offering so scant it amounted to a direct
insult.

Among the greater priests, but a little aside, stood a tall man with
narrow Syrian eyes and a pointed chin-beard. His pleated, folded robe of
snowy linen was the conventional vestment. Above it and across his chest,
he wore a black garment which imitated the pelt of a jackal, the beast
sacred to Anubis.

For two hours he had been using considerable discipline not to yawn.
Now it appeared the tedious routine might be broken a little by a display
of Pharaoh's anger.

He was right.

Setekh-Nekht's eyes flashed beneath the Double Crown. He said
wrathfully, "Take this trash away! Let the savage return alive by my
grace to his master. Tell him Pharaoh bids him send gold from the
mines between the Second and Third Cataracts. Egypt's ministers will
inform him of the amount. Egypt's Viceroy in Kush will see to its
collection."

Tayo stood upright, his eyes burning with a malevolent, prideful glare.

The bearded priest shook his head, very slightly.

Seven feet tall and muscled like a lion, he had many times the physical presence of Setekh-Nekht, but those watching reckoned him foolish to display it. His voice boomed like a conch. "O mighty Pharaoh! The Viceroy appointed by you died on the day I left Mi'amh. Another, it seems, must be set in authority over Kush. My master and I will revere him—" Tayo paused, and went on with an open sneer, "—as we do the Living Horus."

The man wearing the stylized jackal-pelt released a tiny sigh. This savage was foolish indeed. His chances of living out the day grew smaller with each word he uttered—with each haughty look.

Setekh-Nekht sat like a carven image for a moment. The real carven images on the back-rest of his throne, the goddesses Nekhebet and Wazt, vulture and cobra, protectors of the king, seemed to wait on his sacred words.

He soon uttered them. "Take this Kushite and beat him with rods! That he may bear Egypt's commands to the King of Kush, let him live, yet beat him most soundly. Pharaoh has spoken."

Six soldiers converged on the barbarian giant. Roaring like the beast he resembled, he broke the arm of the first with his ebony sceptre of office. Seizing another by the throat, he lifted him into the air and hurled him at two more, while courtiers darted back and additional soldiers rushed forward.

The bearded priest remained where he was, amused at this latest show of men's madness. Then a flash of concern crossed his lean face. Rameses, the Crown Prince, had taken a sword as though to subdue the lunatic in person. The Queen stretched out her hand and called him back.

The priest, being closer, closed his own hand on the prince's strong arm. "Be guided. Great One. Egypt needs you, and see, there is no reason for you to dirty your hands."

Young, soldierly, and deeply aware that he carried a great name, Rameses would not have listened, but the priest's touch rooted him to the floor somehow. Tribute fell from the hands of the Kushite retinue, and its bearers wailed on their bellies. An elephant tusk crashed to the floor, logs of black wood bounced and rolled, and a curious red-haired ape scuttled for safety. The keepers of two fine leopards alone held to their wits—and the leashes of the snarling animals, since letting them loose in the throne room would mean dying in quicklime.

Three soldiers dove for the envoy's legs and pulled him down. Two more gripped his arms. Another two levelled spears at his sweating chest. It required the whole seven to hold him quiescent.

Setekh-Nekht said harshly, "Impale him! When he is dead, send his head back to Kush in a sack of salt."

Taking advantage of the uproar, the bearded priest spoke softly to his attendant, a young lesser priest. "Go. Observe the execution and describe it to me later."

"Yes, holy one."

Frowning, the man in vestments of Anubis watched the envoy hustled from Pharaoh's presence. His somewhat oblique eyes widened in speculation. Prince Rameses was looking at him in much the same way, as he noticed in a moment.

"Pardon my meddling, O heir to Pharaoh."

Rameses said dryly, "You did not merely meddle. You presumed to use sorcery on me, Kamose, for I could not stir in spite of wishing it. I shall ask you to explain that later. For now—tell me why you are so interested in how that man will die."

"I think he is more than he seems, Great One." The priest named Kamose tugged pensively at his chin-beard. "And I should like to know if it is true that the Viceroy of Kush died on the very day this Tayo set forth. Also, *how* it happened."

Prince Rameses shrugged. "This is the first I have heard of it."

"And I."

A quarter-hour later, the one Kamose had sent to observe the Kushite's death came back. His forehead and cheeks dripped sweat. Soldiers came close behind him. Eddies of gossip and surprise whirled through the packed courtiers, to be quelled at once by the ancient habit of gravity in Pharaoh's presence. The news, whatever it was, travelled as far as the feline-faced Royal Secretary and Butler before he stopped it. Kamose's ears and brain extracted three significant words from the murmurs.

Kushite… magician… escaped.

The second word touched him most sharply. Kamose himself was widely known as Egypt's greatest magician. Some of those who said it were even

fit to judge. Certainly, if there were other contenders, their names escaped
him. To their jealous fury, even the priests of Thoth could supply none.

"Is that true?"

"Yes, holy one."

"Tell me everything later."

"Tell me with him," Prince Rameses added grimly.

He mounted the throne-dais again, to stand beside his parents.
Protocol swallowed embarrassment. Although Kamose behaved with the
rest as though nothing had happened, his thoughts were seething—and
they reached deeper than sensation or outrage. These events had
significance.

The affront from Kush was not astonishing in itself. When Egypt lay
divided, or beset by foes from elsewhere, the Kushites had always taken
the opportunity to revolt. This time around, they seemed to be testing the
spirit of Egypt first. The envoy had provoked Pharaoh's anger on purpose.
He had expected to be condemned, and he had expected to escape
Pharaoh's justice. That appeared clear.

The important thing was to learn what further plans he had made.

II.

*The advance which thou hast made towards the House is a
prosperous advance; let not any baleful obstacle proceed from thy mouth
against me when thou workest on my behalf.*

—The Overthrow of Apep

Although he came rarely to the royal court, Kamose stood well in
Pharaoh's favour. Thus he had been granted apartments of his own in the
palace. He summoned his shaken acolyte there to question him.

"Tell me what happened, as the gods live, with no vapouring."

Two other persons were present; the Crown Prince, Rameses, and a
well-shaped woman in the robe of a priestess, seated to one side on a
couch, demure and silent.

The acolyte gulped. A rotund young man named Serkaf, he did not
easily withstand shock or surprise. Being careful in duty, though, he
applied himself to tell the story as his master ordered.

"Holy one, they took the Kushite out to destroy him, even as Pharaoh said. He was bound with strong cords and surrounded by spears. Then he spoke words in his devilish tongue, and the spears became lethal snakes! They turned on the men who held them! Being bitten, they fell down, writhing, and shortly they died. Then the serpents attacked the other soldiers, and in the confusion, the Kushite magician vanished. He was free of his bonds when men saw him last."

"Vanished?" Kamose said angrily "He's seven feet tall and the hue of dates! However he escaped, he will not stay hidden long."

"Is that sure?" Rameses asked. "Clearly he's a magician of some power."

"Oh, Great One." Kamose softened his voice in respect. The prince might be a valiant soldier, but like most men of action he was too easily impressed by magic. "Clearly. Yet changing staves to serpents is not a monstrous feat. The priests of Thoth can do it. Serkaf here, my greenest acolyte, can do it. I'll have him demonstrate, if you wish."

"There is no need." Rameses drank wine cooled in the palace lake. "Well, was there more?"

Serkaf nodded jerkily. "A thing foul to repeat, mighty prince. Before he disappeared, the Kushite shouted threats against your sire, the Pharaoh. He declared the Royal Falcon would—would fly to his horizon—within the month."

Rameses hurled his wine-cup across the room with a blistering curse. "Words! Bluster! Vile and blasphemous, yet nothing but bluster! Who is this Kushite pig?"

Kamose nodded, bleakly speculative. "That is what I should most like to know, Great One. Who is he? Not a fool. He staged that outrageous brawl in the throne room so that none should forget him, knowing he would escape later—and he spoke words that none should forget, also. How if, unthinkably, he does plot the death of Pharaoh? And if it came to be? All would then know his end came from Kush."

"It must not happen!" Rameses had turned pale. "This miscreant—can he be human? Perhaps he is a demon, O Kamose."

The woman in the background lowered her eyes. Her lips moved in the shape of a smile.

"Mortal or demon, he must be found quickly," Kamose said, "and thy father, Great One, must be protected day and night until that is achieved."

"What spies and bronze swords can do, will be done," Rameses vowed. "But you, wise Kamose, can you defend him with magic, if he should come under attack by magic?"

"That is a fearful trust to bear, Great One," Kamose said, "yet I will undertake it. If you and Pharaoh are prepared to calm the priests of Thoth for me. They will have fits with their legs in the air when they hear."

Rameses laughed shortly. "We will deal with the priests of Thoth, believe me."

When priest and acolyte had gone, Kamose sat scowling, barely noticing the cup of wine the woman placed before him. She seated herself and watched him from formidably deep black eyes. At last he stirred and tasted the wine.

"Guarding the Pharaoh against a wizard," she observed, "is a dangerous charge. One might fail."

"The priests of Thoth would like that." Kamose smiled darkly. "So might you. If I were destroyed, you would be free, lustful and voracious one."

"I'm sufficiently content in your service. I have lovers enough, and victims enough. That organisation of tomb-robbers—" She smiled. "Perhaps I can help in this matter too? You must discover where the Kushite hides, and I know the Delta well."

"You were its haunting terror until I curbed you, Mertseger. No, this I shall do without your help. It brought me much credit to rid the Delta of your depredations. I do not wish rumours to spread that the lamia has returned. Keep to your human shape and be discreet—or I shall be angry."

"This man changes rods into serpents," Mertseger said, and laughed a little. "I could show him a serpent." Opening her lovely mouth, she extruded a long forked tongue and hissed loudly.

"Do not so," Kamose ordered, adding ironically, "You are human, a priestess, and a woman of virtue. No, others may search for Tayo. I shall devote myself to protecting Pharaoh from whatever petty spells the Kushite may use against him. Two demon-spirits from the Duat whom I control can do that best; the Green Flame, and the Bone Breaker."

"Set them to stalking the palace halls and Pharaoh will surely die," Mertseger said maliciously, "not of spells, but of horror."

"Oh, they shall walk unseen," Kamose said, "and chase baleful influences from the Pharaoh's vicinity, since other beings of darkness fear them. Nearly all others," he amended, "as they in turn fear me."

Mertseger did not deny it. "What is the Living Horus to you, that he should continue living?" she asked idly. "You know he is not a god. You know the Nile would rise each year without him."

"The men who work the land do not," Kamose answered, "and there is too much disorder in Khem now. I dwell here too. My footsteps have been printed in enough foreign countries."

III.

"You cannot escape me for I am your fate! There is only one means of escaping me and that is if you can dig a hole in the sand, which will remain full of water, and then my spell will be broken. If not death will come to you speedily, for you cannot escape."
—Story of the Doomed Prince

Kamose's eyes glittered with impatience and irritation. The man facing him also wore the vestments and regalia of an arch-priest, though not the conventionalised black jackal's pelt which characterised the Temple of Anubis. On the contrary, he carried a gilded staff with a carved ibis-head. Despite the dignified finery, his face expressed little character, its most memorable feature being a soft, heavy mouth, on which rested a smug expression.

"You are a fool, Beba," Kamose said sourly. "You, and most of your priests of Thoth. But clearly you have gained the ear of Pharaoh in this matter, so if that is a triumph, enjoy it. I only beg that you will waste no more of my time."

Beba chuckled. "You may indeed have little left, O Kamose. If so, it is well. Did you suppose you could hide your evil magic from me, the chief servant of magic's ibis-headed lord? Long ago, unlawfully, you gained your own knowledge by stealing the scrolls written by Thoth himself! For that you were punished, and yet you learned not—"

Kamose took three forward steps, his face black with fury, and caught Beba's throat in the fingers of his right hand. Very softly he said, "Little man, do not speak of that again. You might find out what punishment is."

Beba pulled himself free, choking and alarmed. He retreated from his rival and answered between coughs, "Yes, you speak—like a man of violence, a worker of evil. You summoned demon-spirits into this palace! Why, unless to harm the Living Horus? But now he has commanded that you remove them. Your scheming has come to naught in the face of the servants of Truth, Kamose."

Kamose said harshly, his anger still blazing, "You serve Truth badly. Fools always do. The Green Flame and the Bone Breaker walked the palace for days, at my command, and invisibly, so as to cause no fear. If I meant harm to Pharaoh, it would have been done by this. My purpose with them was to banish and frighten other demon-spirits who might approach, sent by the Kushite. But none have come. It appears he was a petty conjurer from a savage land, a braggart, a liar, and no threat to Pharaoh. Therefore I have removed those demon-spirits as needless presences."

"You had to." Beba reminded him swiftly. "Pharaoh commanded it."

"At your persuasion. Consider that you have the better of me, then, be gleeful and revel in it. I have said already that you waste my time. If this is all—"

"It will never be all," Beba said vindictively. "You will be removed from your priestly office and brought low, Satni-Kamose."

"Not to your level. It is a measure of your soul that you use that vulgar nickname. Be gone."

Kamose brooded in the priest of Thoth's absence. The soft frog had overstepped indeed, when he dared mention the god's vengeance on Kamose for stealing his scrolls of magic from a hidden tomb. So long ago. All of a century ago. And still Kamose could scarcely think of it, how his wife and children had died, how—

Enough. He rejected the thoughts bitterly The matter of his two demon-spirits called for attention. To invoke them, summon them from the Underworld, the Duat, and give them earthly substance, had been a dire, dreadful action. Even though the possibility of a threat to Pharaoh's life had justified it, that possibility seemed a mirage now. The Kushite "magician" had done nothing, which fairly well argued that he was not able to, beyond conjurer's tricks like turning rods to serpents.

The obvious course was to dismiss the demons wholly from the earth, not merely from Pharaoh's palace. Let them return to the caverns of night in the Duat. They were better there than in the realm of the living. Should they escape his control, they would either destroy him, or innocent fools for whose lives the law must hold Kamose to account.

Still, the situation was not yet wholly clear. It might not be as simple as he had represented it to Beba—who in any case could only grasp simple issues, and not all of those. Kamose might still have tasks for the demon-spirits, before this affair ended. The risks involved in sending them away and then bringing them back once more, if he should require to, made even his blood thicken, as with the deadly effect of hemlock.

Two things were sure. Because of Setekh-Nekht's dictum, he might not bring them to the palace. Nor might he allow them to roam at large, idle. However, there were temples of Anubis in the Delta, as in every place which boasted tombs and necropoli. A chapel existed even in this city of Pi-Rameses.

At midnight, within the chapel's walls, Kamose called the two by the light of bronze lamps shaped like dog's skulls, wherein burned oil mixed with powdered mummy from a traitor grave. He drew blood from his arm with a copper knife. Raising it high, he then traced in the air a hieroglyph more antique than the pyramids. Its meaning was *relentless*.

The spirits responded.

The Green Flame appeared as a shape of emptiness, a shadow with thickness, somewhat human in outline and a bright, blazing emerald in colour. With it came a fierce dry heat more desiccating than the desert at noon.

Although the Bone Breaker did not scorch by its presence, it wore a form still more grotesque to behold. Also manlike, more or less, it had grey dead flesh as hard as leather and wore its bones on the outside, like partial armour. Its head resembled a malformed, snouted skull with eyes and a tongue. If possible, its hands were less lovely still.

"Welcome," their master said ironically.

"What would you?" the Green Flame asked in a hissing, crackling voice. The other uttered the same question from a throat clogged, apparently, with putrescence.

Kamose had no wish to hold lengthy conversation with these beings. He said curtly, "Somewhere in the Delta a dangerous man is at large, an outlaw from Pharaoh's justice. He has murdered; what else I am not yet sure. Find and destroy him."

Both demons expressed pleasure. Kamose added repressively, "*This man only,*" assured them of the pains they would suffer if they exceeded his command, and then described and named the Kushite envoy. The demons demanded to know how even they could find one man in the vastness of the Delta.

"Have I not told you that he is no Egyptian? Have I not described him? Few men could be more conspicuous! Yet he has some cunning, and so—where does a man hide a leaf, if he is crafty?"

"Upon a tree," the Bone Breaker answered in its husky, phlegmy tones. "Among other leaves."

"Yes. Among Pharaoh's soldiers there is a corps of Kushite archers and another of spearmen. For the most part they are tall. Seek him first in their barracks, but remain unseen, and neither harm nor frighten any that is not the man I designate."

"How shall we tell him from the rest?" the Green Flame asked in scorn.

"He's a magician, or what passes for a magician in Kush. You will smell sorcery on him. Besides, he is noble, not common—again, by Kushite reckoning. If he be not concealed among the soldiers, then seek him more broadly, but find him! I am not concerned to do your work for you!"

Raging with unvoiced hate, they departed. Fiercely and long though he had striven to leave normal human emotions behind—and the pain they caused—Kamose felt relieved by the demons' absence. The gods knew he had other things to do.

Counter the poison being poured in Pharaoh's ear by the priests of Thoth, for instance; they would be busy against him. How fortunate, he thought, that he enjoyed Pharaoh's favour to a degree, and that of Prince Rameses even more. But to become complacent about royal favour constituted a great step towards losing it. Even Egypt's greatest magician might not safely ignore politics.

IV.

That which is an abomination unto me, that which is an abomination unto me, let me not eat. Let me not eat filth, and let me not drink foul water; and let me not be tripped up and fall in the Underworld.

—Papyrus of Nu

Setekh-Nekht, Pharaoh of Egypt, writhed on his couch and fought to breathe air grown hot and stifling. The pleasure lakes around the palace brought no cooling relief. Hideous dreams assailed him. Runnels of sweat poured from his skin; his fingers twisted the fabric beneath him.

Wildly, in his dreams, he looked for his royal protectors, the goddesses who warded the king. He found them, but not as they should have been. The Vulture hunched brooding on a plinth, her great wings folded, not outspread in guardianship.

Groaning, he turned in search of Wazt, his active defender, the Cobra who turned her burning eyes on his foes and shrivelled them with her glance. She coiled on the floor, head lowered, the hood flattened against her neck rather than distended in wrath. Malformed things crawled in the shadows.

"Help me! I am the Son of Ra! Let me not perish on account of my enemies!"

Tiye-merenese, the Great Queen, mother of his heir, heard and awoke in distress. "My lord, I am here! What—"

His eyes opened, but he did not wake. Nor did he see her. For Setekh-Nekht, a naked figure huge in height strode from the shadows, strong past his power to resist, the shapes of evil pressing behind him. A dark hand closed on his shoulder and dragged him from his bed with such force that he screamed in pain. A long black corridor like the passage of a tomb opened before them. His assailant hauled him along like a child until they reached a chamber hewn from rough black granite.

"Do you know me, Lord of the Two Lands, you who made the brag that you are Lord of Kush as well? Do you know me? You condemned me to be thrashed with rods, and then to die impaled, but now it is I who sentence *you*!"

"No! Nekhebet, Wazt! Strike him down!"

Neither goddess answered, and the huge dark shape laughed in contempt. "Fool! Your protectors have gone! You yourself dismissed them at the urging of that other fool, the Archpriest of Thoth! The hour of your fate is here!"

There was a heavy rod in his hand. Setekh-Nekht remembered his divinity, his kingship, and his manhood. Rising: to his feet against the awful strength of the hand that held him, he struck once, twice and again, strong blows that went home—*without effect*. Then the rod rushed down and snapped the bones of his arm. Further blows flattened him to the chamber's granite floor.

The terrified queen in Setekh-Nekht's bed heard the bones break, saw his forearm hang distorted from the couch's edge. She saw nothing else, no presence that might account for the injury, and he seemed to struggle against nothing, on a bed of tasselled linen. Yet huge wealed stripes appeared on his body. Bruises that bled, such as are caused by impact against rock, flowered on the Pharaoh's legs and back. One by one his ribs broke. The queen fought free from her trance of horror, and shouted for help with all her voice.

The Pharaoh seemed to hear. Briefly his eyes cleared, and he whispered, "Tiye..." Then he croaked further words.

They were his last. Some unseen force hauled him into a standing position and thrust him against the wall. Fearful impacts lashed across his taut belly, as from a smiting baton, breaking the organs within, liver, spleen and stomach.

The force holding Setekh-Nekht released him. Spewing bile and dark blood, he collapsed across the couch. Queen Tiye-merenese shrieked and shrieked. Even when her attendants rushed into the chamber, and guards clattered behind them, her screaming continued, rising higher.

By morning, all the city of Pi-Rameses knew that Pharaoh had died. As the Kushite threatened, Setekh-Nekht had flown to his horizon, sent there by loathsome murder. And considerably within the month.

V.

As concerning the fight hard by the Persea tree in Annu, it concerneth the children of impotent revolt when justice is wrought on them for what they have done.

—Papyrus of Nebseni

Kamose made obeisance before the throne of Egypt, his dark eyes burning like anthracite. The Pharaoh's throne stood empty. Queen Tiye-merenese sat in the other, her face and bare breasts gashed in lamentation, looking at the Archpriest of Anubis with haunted eyes. Rameses stood beside her throne, resting a hand on her shoulder. He looked appalled and bewildered, but with his magician's eyes, Kamose saw the seeds of huge anger sprouting in his heart.

"My lord spoke before he died," the Great Queen said like a stone image; except that stone does not bleed. "These were his words. '*The priests of Thoth have failed me. Send for Kamose.*'"

Despite his sardonic, self-contained philosophy, Kamose felt a rush of relief. Dying in such torment, Setekh-Nekht could hardly have known what he was saying. He could as easily have raved curses against Kamose for letting him die.

"I am here, Great One."

"What should we do?"

"The Kushite, Tayo, is a stronger magician than I believed. He has taken the earthly life of Pharaoh. The new Living Horus—" (Kamose bowed to young Rameses) "—must be guarded against his malice, before any other consideration. I shall surround him with spells and charges so potent that nothing can prevail against them."

"And the murderer?" Rameses asked.

"My demon-spirits are seeking him now. Soldiers, of course, with all the vizier's spies and agents, are combing the Delta. With reverence, Great One, this vile savage's apprehension can wait. Your divine life must be made safe at once."

"Yes." The queen's voice shook. "Listen, my son. Your father's *ka* was dragged from his body and thrashed to death in darkness. It must not happen to you!"

Kamose laboured nine days and nights, and nine more, and another nine, to ensure that safety. He kept strange terrible vigils, and invoked the Pharaoh's protecting goddesses anew, to watch over Rameses. He sacrificed a great bull hippopotamus to Set the Defender. At the end he vanished for three days, and returned gaunt, weary, sunken-eyed, the mark of great talons furrowed across his chest, but with a look of dark triumph stamped on his face.

"You are safe, Pharaoh," was all he would say. Rameses, who *was* now officially Pharaoh, and the third to bear that name, looked into Kamose's eyes, and believed, and could scarcely resist a shudder.

"The magician of Kush has not yet been found," he said. When Kamose blinked, swaying on his feet, Rameses said quickly, "My friend! Forget I am a god, and rest before you fall!"

Thinking as best he could, with a brain that should have been shattered by his late experience, Kamose muttered:

"So? He laid his plans well. Perhaps he even had help from traitors. In his place—I should have quit the Delta—taken ship down the Red Sea."

"In due course we shall have him," Rameses said fiercely. "Let not your heart trouble, for I shall order the new Viceroy of Kush to bring him to justice."

"As Pharaoh speaks, let it be written," Kamose said hoarsely. "Well—if we cannot find the magician at once—we know where to find his master, and the one—who sent him on his mission."

"The King of Kush?"

"Yes."

Rameses felt the duties of a Pharaoh and a son pulling in different directions. "I cannot send a host to Kush, much less lead it, not even to avenge my sire! That would leave Egypt unguarded."

"In these days when it has no union." Kamose closed his eyes. "Grant me time to recover, Great One. Then leave Kush to me. When I have finished, they—will take no more liberties here."

Kamose's recovery filled most of a year. The Nile rose and receded, the harvest was sown, ripened and reaped, before he was quite himself again. However, he did not wait that long to do as he had undertaken. He waited only days. He considered the King of Kush owed him a debt, and there were beings he could send with that message, his own sort of emissaries; beings who could not be made to wait indefinitely like soldiers in barracks, either. He commanded them and dispatched them.

They travelled by night. Dogs howled in the Delta as they passed. Soldiers on the mighty white walls of Hikuptah felt a cold wind blowing. At Abdu of the Pilgrimages, and at Thebes where mighty Amun-Ra was worshipped in the greatest temple on Earth, evil dreams troubled the inhabitants. The demons came to Elephantine by the First Cataract, upper boundary of Egypt, but did not linger there. They travelled straight across the desert within that immense bend of the Nile where the gold of Kush was mined, by convicts and traitors. Their existence was torment, and death a happy release. The demons observed their pains, and in the night the miners heard them laughing. Then they went on. The journey was arduous—even for such as they—and they came to the palace of Kush filled with harsh rancour.

The monarch of Kush slept in his domed chamber, watched over by warriors who would walk into a furnace at his bidding, rich in beasts, gold and pride. No evil dreams troubled his sleep, as they had the Pharaoh of Egypt. First he awakened, and *then* his nightmare began.

Above him loomed a face of leering bone, and on his other side a blank head like a shape carved from the vacant air, burning emerald in hue. The king's warriors lay around him. They did not move. The nearest had a strangely shapeless head, as though his skull had been pulverised without one drop of brains or gore spilling forth. This the king saw in a passing wild glance, but gave it no notice or thought. His mouth stretched wide to scream.

Fingertips of blunt grey bone closed on his throat, and squeezed with a kind of obscene delicacy, crushing the larynx just enough to prevent any sound above a whistling whisper. Air still reached his lungs. Breathing was not much impaired. The King of Kush in his demented terror failed to make this discovery for some time.

When he did, it brought him no joy.

His slaves found him at dawn. Every bone in his body had been broken, the large ones splintered lengthwise, the small ones crushed as in a press. Not one fragment protruded through his skin, which was neither torn nor broken anywhere. But his flesh had been desiccated dry, as though by days in the scorching desert air. His eyes, like grey pebbles sunk far back into his skull, yet seemed to stare appalled.

Words were seared in the plaster wall as though by fire. Written in the hieroglyphics of the Two Lands, they said: EGYPT'S ANSWER TO THE MURDER OF EGYPT'S PHARAOH.

Far away, the new Pharaoh leaned on a balcony of green malachite, looking over gardens and stone-quayed harbours. Kamose stood beside him. He now carried a sky-blue fan made from a single ostrich plume. This, a sign of great royal preferment, went with the title Fan-bearer at the King's Right Hand.

"My messengers have no doubt reached the King of Kush by now." he said. "No other will blaspheme against the life of a Pharaoh again. Or should they dare, you are protected, Lord of the Two Lands."

"That accursed envoy escaped," Rameses said. "He may have returned to Kush by now."

"Such is my hope."

"Your *hope!* Why?"

"The vile Kushites bury a king's greatest servants alive with him, to serve him in the hereafter." Kamose's smile was a chilling thing. "His magician and royal envoy should qualify as a great servant. It were fitting if Tayo should be given such a part in his king's obsequies."

AUTHOR'S FOOTNOTE: Abdu of the Pilgrimages, where the body of Osiris was said to be buried, is modern Abydos; Hikuptah is Memphis; and Kush is the modern Sudan, more or less.

HAUNTED SHADOWS

Grant me splendour in heaven, power on earth, and acquittal in the Netherworld

—Hymn to Osiris

"O Ganesh, it was effective! *The spell worked!*" The speaker was not quite shouting in his excitement. Still, his idea of restraint seemed to end there.

Since Ganesh the Jeweler employed about twenty people in his workshop, and they could all see this young fool gesticulating and babbling, Ganesh suggested they speak in his private back room. He led the way.

What a young fool this Amenufer was! All his royal kinship and training in the Temple of Thoth could not conceal it. Slender, shaven of head and body, clean to fastidiousness, he could not have been the more obvious type of a young scholar-priest. He could hardly have formed a greater contrast to the bulky, shaggy-haired, bearded jeweler, either.

"Don't talk of spells so freely, young lord," Ganesh advised. "No harm done, yet. It's known that all lector-priests are magicians, and that I dabble in such things. But we do not wish more than that to get out! Anyhow," he added, "which spell did you mean? The papyrus fragment I gave you has five written upon it."

"Yes, yes. Four achieved nothing. I suppose they were wrongly copied. But the one, the one that confers understanding of the speech of birds—it succeeded!"

"Succeeded?" Ganesh echoed. "You have the gift now?" He did his best to sound astonished. In fact he considered that the level of Amenufer's wits should always have given him a special affinity with birds.

"Yes," Amenufer said, answering his question. "From the cackle of geese to the blood-lust of hawks! Oh, they say little worth hearing, their minds are tiny, but it is a wonder, O Ganesh. And it provides proof that the other spells, at the original source, must have been effective also. To open the earth! To divide the sea! To find hidden treasure! To behold the Afterworld!"

"In short," Ganesh said indulgently, "to realize all the night dreams of boyhood. The original source, as I heard, is best left alone."

"The original source is the Scrolls of Thoth!"

"One should take care," Ganesh rumbled, "how one speaks that name. The original source is—hidden. None knows where."

"It's rumoured that one man does." Amenufer leaned forward and said in a whisper, "Kamose, the Archpriest of Anubis! When he was young, he too sought the Scrolls of Thoth. He found them in some ancient tomb. He learned all that was in them. At last he returned them to their place, or so it is said."

"It is said."

"It is true!" Amenufer insisted, with the vehemence of pure wishful thinking. "A man can lengthen his days to thrice the normal span by the knowledge in that writing. Kamose has done it! It is denied, but still well known, that he is a son of Rameses the Great, and was Archpriest of Ptah in this city in former times. He—"

Ganesh snorted. Moved beyond manners, and even beyond caution, he said bluntly, "Nonsense! I know more about the Archpriest of Anubis than most. I have been forced to do his bidding now and then. Yes, he is a mighty magician, and he has lengthened his days beyond the common, but he was never a son of Rameses the Great, or a priest of Ptah, either. One named Khaemwese was both. Vulgar legend has confused him with Kamose."

"And why should they not be the same man?"

"Because it is a matter of record that Khaemwese died before his royal sire. Bah! His tomb stands outside this very city! Young lord, I speak with rude scorn, I know. It is unfitting. But how can you, a priest yourself, be unaware of this?"

Amenufer was nettled. "Then who is Kamose? Surely you who know so much, and boast of your dealings with him, can tell me!"

"Boast?" Ganesh shook his shaggy head. "Not I. No man in his right mind boasts of dealings with *that* one. Except that I am sometimes of use when he wishes to find egregious defilers of tombs, he would never notice me." The bulky jeweler shivered. "And I should be happier."

"Words!" Amenufer sneered.

"Words? Listen, young lord, for I do know something of this priest-magician. Not that I dare tell it but in cups of the strong black wine he once gave me for a gift. I have the last jar here—"

Ganesh unsealed it, and poured two chalices full. Despite his spoken scorn of the jeweler's fear, Amenufer did not refuse the drink, and cousin of Pharaoh or not, he swallowed deeply. Only after emptying the cup did he prompt Ganesh to continue.

"Yes, Kamose. He's certainly no son of Rameses the Great, for he was born before him, in the time of the Pharaoh Ay—"

"A hundred and thirty years ago?" Amenufer broke in. "Who speaks nonsense now?"

"Yourself you said it. He has lengthened his days to three men's span. Or five, or seven, who knows? But this I do know. The Archpriest Kamose was young, even as you, in the reign of Djeser-Kheper-Ra, Horemheb the Commoner—young and foolish. He was a junior priest, and a scholar in the Temple of Thoth. Although young, he was married, with two small children, and his wife breeding yet again.

"He must have been a fool in those days. Greedy for knowledge, he thought knowledge and learning equalled wisdom. Always he studied the writings in the temple libraries, even those which were banned to him—and that, with his priestly training, was his beginning in magic.

"He found references to the Forty-Two Scrolls of Thoth. Just like you, young lord. The distorted, partial, or ineffectual copies are many, and in Kamose there grew a craving to find the originals."

"Just like me," Amenufer said impatiently. "I take your point, jeweler. Spare me the homilies! Did he find them?"

"Spare me your impetuousness, young lord," Ganesh advised. He scratched in his beard. "Listen to this story. It could save your life."

"I listen," Amenufer said condescendingly.

"Without interruption?"

"Agreed."

Ganesh continued, after he had stared at the young fool for a long moment.

"This Kamose of long ago was green as just-sprouted barley. One morning, a man he had never seen before approached him at his studies. His shadow fell across the papyrus Kamose was reading, and he said mockingly: 'Why do you waste your time studying these writings which will never bring you closer to that which you desire? For a price I will show you the place where the Scrolls of Thoth are.'

"Kamose's hackles rose. The stranger was gaunt-faced, with sunken cheeks and eyes, his very manner a challenge. He wore judge's vestments, of a strange, antique sort. Kamose supposed he must come from some backward district.

"He demanded to know where the Scrolls were. The stranger said—well, it is no matter what he said, for the present."

"Interred with a great official named Khuywer," Amenufer supplied promptly, and showed a smug smile when Ganesh looked startled. "Yes, it's known to me. Khuywer had them sealed in his tomb a thousand years ago. I seek those writings, as you know; and I have made progress."

Ganesh thought bleakly, *A dangerous amount of progress.* He hadn't imagined that Amenufer knew so much. This changed things. His quest had to be taken seriously now.

"Of this Khuywer I have heard," Ganesh said, understating somewhat. "In whose reign did he live? Where is his burial place?"

"The reign of King Unas, or so it seems. His burial place I do not know. Yet. I am certain it lies above this city in the ancient necropolis, but that scarcely helps."

"No," Ganesh agreed feelingly. "The tombs of Hikuptah are multitudinous as the fish of the Nile, from ancient times until now; and many of the older ones have been removed or built over. Also, records were lost when times were lawless."

Amenufer agreed sweetly. "It does make rich tombs difficult to find in order to rob, does it not, jeweler? But you are resourceful in these matters. You will have to be. We cannot ask the Archpriest Kamose to tell us."

Ganesh shuddered. "That's no jesting matter, young lord."

"He dare not offend me. I am a nephew of the royal house. What did the convenient stranger say to him of the Scrolls' hiding place?"

Ganesh answered with sweat on his thick cheeks and his eyes shifting. "He said, 'If you obtain the Scrolls of Thoth you will have all power and knowledge, and my price is that you will then grant me one thing—and that must be whatsoever I ask.'

"Kamose made no promise, then. But after hearing these words he had no peace of mind, barely knew in what part of the world he was, and could not apply himself to anything, for yearning after the Scrolls of Thoth.

"His wife saw the change in him, and like all wives could not rest until she had made him tell her the cause. Greatly alarmed, she begged him to forget the Forbidden Scrolls, and have no more to do with the stranger. (Truly, she was the wiser of that pair.) And Kamose did strive for a while to forget all about it. He asked to be given more practical duties, and spent less time in the libraries.

"Then the stranger appeared again, to repeat his offer, and all Kamose's longing for the Scrolls of Thoth returned, but tenfold stronger. Without hesitation, then, did he promise the stranger what he desired. He swore to it by the greatest oaths. The stranger led him by night to the necropolis outside the city, to that tomb where the Scrolls of Thoth were buried, the tomb of Khuywer.

"It was hidden and closed, no doubt, but Kamose was even then a magician. He uttered a spell to make the earth open for him, and having done so, he descended to the burial chamber. Khuywer's mummy lay there in a granite coffin. Beside it stood a limestone one, empty.

"There were furnishings, and statues, and accouterments, but only the Scrolls of Thoth concerned Kamose. They lay in a chest of cinnamon wood inlaid with gold, forty-two of them, and they shone with a light that filled the burial chamber.

"The stranger, whom Kamose had forgotten existed, spoke beside his ear. 'These can be read at any time you wish,' he said. 'Look at the paintings on the walls.'

"He pointed to one. It showed Khuywer, at the gate of his temple, hearing cases—*a gaunt man, with hollow cheeks and sunken eyes, even as the stranger.*

"Then Kamose blanched, for too late he felt afraid. The stranger said, 'Now I will tell you. I am Khuywer, that ancient judge; I am the *ka* of Khuywer. I have brought you to my tomb by the lure of the Scrolls of Thoth. As you see, I did not lie. You may take them for my part, though you would be a fool. I obtained them, long ago, even I, and the god Thoth was angry; he sent his Shadow Eaters to destroy my wife Neshemet, and then me. For further revenge he caused us to be buried in tombs far apart, and because I have shown you the Scrolls, you must bring her mummy here and lay her in this limestone coffin prepared for her, beside me.

"'Be warned by me. Should you remove the Scrolls, the Measurer of Time will be angered, and his Shadow-Eaters will come to destroy you.

Perhaps he would recall them if you were to repent, and relinquish the Scrolls, but even then the god would require that you bring them back one by one with a forked stick, all forty-two, wearing a lighted brazier on your head. Save yourself grief and pain! Leave the Scrolls here.'

"Kamose answered, 'I will bring the mummy of Neshemet, and lay her in the limestone coffin, and I will take the Scrolls of Thoth away and master their contents.'

"And he did," Ganesh finished, washing down the words with another deep draught of black wine. "He did. He carried the cinnamon-wood chest away, and—one must suppose—never looked back to see shapes like the shadows of maned baboons loping across the earth behind him. Do what he would not, young lord. Forget those accursed Scrolls."

Amenufer, unmoved, asked, "Is that all the story?"

"It's barely the beginning. But there should be no need to recount more."

Amenufer emptied his cup. "I shall take my leave. Listen, O Ganesh. Discover more written spells—effective ones—and you will find me generous. Above all I desire that spell which opens the earth."

"I wonder why," Ganesh said sourly. "Then no doubt I will see you again in my poor workshop."

"No doubt."

Amenufer departed. Lifted on his pole-chair by the brawny arms of four servants, he did not notice a hunched black shadow prowl after him—a shadow apparently cast by nothing. *He*, preoccupied, did not notice it. But Ganesh did.

II.

Now Thoth was the god of wisdom, and his Scrolls contained all that was known in the world, and anyone who read them could enchant the sea, and enchant the sky, and enchant the earth, and understand all that the birds said, and the animals, and could control everything by his magic power.

—The Story of Satni-Kamose

"My nephew is a young fool," said the Lady Yati with precision.

Ganesh tried to respond tactfully. Because the Lady Yati and her nephew were both of Pharaoh's kin, while he was a shifty jeweler (of foreign descent, at that) who dealt routinely in looted gems and gold, to make any answer at all required tact. But he was used to dealing with her by now.

"I am sure he's less wise than his aunt," Ganesh flattered. "Many young men are foolish. He may gain sagacity as a few years pass."

"Amenufer? I doubt it." Yati held a length of fine aquamarine linen against her body, then a scarlet one, trying to decide. She was giving a banquet that night. "And however that may be, he is showing no sign of sagacity now. Is he?"

"I fear not," Ganesh admitted. "Even as you declared to me, lady, he has been searching out secret and arcane writings, and now haunts old tombs to copy and peruse the inscriptions therein. That pastime is one step from contraband and tomb-robbing. It is taking him into bad company."

"Such as yours. I implore you to keep his feet out of quicksand, O most cunning Ganesh."

Ganesh knew very well that "implore" translated as "command" on the Lady Yati's lips. He watched her discard the fabric and return to the low stool before her dressing table. She sat straight-backed, a plump, short-limbed woman, but voluptuous in shape and remarkably firm for one who had borne four children.

"He seeks something," she said pensively. "I don't care what. It may be best if I do not know. You will be admitted to this house again tonight. Amenufer will be here. The pair of you may as well intrigue in comfort."

"Just knowing he is under my wing keeps most tricksters and thieves at a distance, lady."

"They think you have marked him for your own meat," the Lady Yati answered cynically. "Swindle him a little if you like. The lesson will do him good. Only remember he must not suffer harm."

"As you command, it will be."

Ganesh presented himself at the porter's lodge that evening, and was duly granted ingress. The banquet had begun. Hummocks of smoking food filled the air with appetising odors. Scented oils on the bodies of Yati's guests added a sweetness that pleased the nostrils. Cones of unguent atop the women's plaited wigs still kept their shape, for it was early yet; they would melt with a vengeance later in the evening, releasing their perfume, dripping down to the wearer's shoulders and breasts. They would very likely have discarded their gowns by then, this being one of the Lady Yati's banquets, and lie embraced with lovers.

Such feasts were nothing out of the way in Nineveh or Crete. In sedate, responsible Egypt, they were rarer. But not unheard-of. The debaucheries of Yati's circle formed a source of appalled delight to the gossips of Hikuptah, who exaggerated them to the limits of their highly creative fancy.

Bulky Ganesh the Jeweler, sweating in his robe, appeared as incongruous among these lightly-clad elegants as a bull hippo among herons. A thinly smiling major-domo led him to a lesser chamber.

Amenufer awaited him, wearing a kilt of intricate pleats and folds with a jeweled collar and belt.

"Peace, young lord."

"I greet you. Will you eat with me?"

Ganesh was willing. Although a light repast compared with the plenitude in the main dining room, this food had been produced by the same cooks, and was no less delicious. He ate from dishes of fish, goose, and beef. The dessert was black figs cooked in honey and wine, with a soft, creamy cheese of delicate flavour mounded beside them.

"Rumour avers," Amenufer said, "that some truly virtuous wives in this city, with a craving to shine as hostesses, have abandoned their virtue to my aunt's friends for the secret of some of her recipes."

"Worth it," Ganesh said, and belched contentedly.

Distaste made the young scholar-priest suddenly abrupt. "We spoke of a spell that opens the earth. You have not found it?"

"Not yet. Surely some of the senior priests in your temple must be cognisant?"

"Of course. But they will not tell me."

"Neither will I, perhaps. I did not come here tonight to help you find what you seek, but to try, again, to persuade you that it is better not found."

"A waste of breath."

"Young lord! You do not know what befell Kamose! Listen, I beg, to more of his story and you may decide otherwise."

Amenufer made a sudden, impatient gesture, then paused in calculation. Ganesh could almost see him thinking that he might gain a clue to his quest if he paid attention. After all, the jeweler was an associate of the Archpriest Kamose, if a lowly one.

"You may tell me."

Ganesh leaned forward. "Wise. Hear me, then. Did I break off the tale when the young Kamose had left Khuywer's tomb with the Scrolls?"

"Yes."

"He took them to a safe retreat. As safe as any place can be, when one has such perilous treasure. He studied the Scrolls as a glutton gorges." (The glisten of Amenufer's eyes said that he would do the same, given the slightest chance.) "He committed the spells and lore to mind by copying them in wizard's ink, barely sleeping until the task was done—and it was lengthy. Then he washed the ink from his copies with pomegranate wine, and drank the wine after strange rituals. Then he knew forever all that was written in the Forty-Two Scrolls of Thoth.

"None of this was done easily, or without danger. The Shadow Eaters of Thoth came to Kamose's retreat, and very hardly did he hold them at bay until he had finished his procedures. But the knowledge in the Scrolls themselves gave him the power, so that the Shadow Eaters went away balked and frustrate.

"Then Kamose set about keeping the oath he had sworn to the judge's *ka*. The judge's wife, remember, had been buried far from her husband, at Per-Bastet in the Delta, city of the cat goddess, where she had yielded her life. So Kamose travelled there. Because he now knew all the secrets of magic, he had no need to hire or ask for a vessel.

"Before doing this he did have the grace to return and visit his own wife. I know little about her, not even her name. Clearly he neglected her. The pursuit of magical knowledge must have meant more to him than she did, but I gather she was honest and faithful. And she had given birth to their third child, a girl, while he was away.

"Upon learning what had happened, she was much afraid of the god's vengeance. He comforted her, and said that he could well protect himself, and her, and their children. He realized that he must keep them at his side to do so. Thus they all accompanied him on his journey to Per-Bastet.

"Kamose fashioned a small ship from refined beeswax. He gave it a mast, sail and oars. Also, he filled it with little carved images of a captain, a steersman, and rowers. Then, placing the wax ship in the river, he pronounced the spell to make it real and bring its sailors to life.

"Now Kamose's wife must have dreaded the anger of Thoth, but as she sat beneath the awning on the deck, and looked at the sailors brought to life from images, who worked the ship and never wearied or spoke, she may have feared her husband more. She feared his long absences, I would say; she feared what he had become; she feared their present errand.

"In all three she was right.

"Without fuss, then, without portent, an ibis flew over the awning and perched on the ship's rail. It fixed its gaze on Kamose's wife. Her face grew blank. Saying no word, she came from under the awning. She walked across the deck to the ibis as it fluttered its wings. Then, as she reached it, still holding her baby, the bird flew up. Kamose's wife fell forward across the rail. She and her daughter went straight down into the green water, to sink like anchors.

"How Kamose shouted to his unnatural crew! How he seized his remaining children and held them back from the ship's sides! How he ordered the silent captain to turn, and sent half the sailors diving after his wife and infant! Then he bethought him of magic (for although he now possessed the power, he was not yet accustomed to using it, and this disaster had him distraught, I should not wonder). So he made the river to rise up on each side like a wall, leaving the bed of the stream dry and open. Then he descended to the bottom, and found his wife and child, but they had drowned, and he could only retrieve their bodies."

Ganesh halted in his story for a moment. His voice was hoarse. Reaching for the beer-jug, he irrigated his hairy throat. Amenufer seemed unmoved by the tale, and said only, "This does not affect me. I have neither wife nor child to put at risk."

Ganesh lost control. His black eyes flashed with bull-like wrath. "Whelp! be quiet and listen! There is enough and more than enough that may befall you, even though you have no family to suffer!"

Upright, on his feet, blazing, he no longer seemed only a dishonest tradesman. Amenufer felt the impact of his massive physique, and also, it may be, the weight of more experienced manhood. For that moment he felt that he was a mere conceited stripling, royal connections or not, and he was quiet.

"Kamose arrived in the city of the cat goddess," Ganesh resumed. "He did what he had to. First, he arranged for his wife and daughter to be embalmed. Then he made offerings to the goddess and sought her protection for his other children.

"He kept them beside him, watching them always, while he found the tomb of the judge's wife, Neshemet, and made arrangements to remove her mummy. He was afraid, now; as his wife had been. He dreaded to leave Per-Bastet and the protection of its goddess. He dreaded to travel again upon the flowing Nile.

"With all his new power, he did not know what to do. In any case, he could not leave until his wife's funerary preparations were complete, which would take the usual seventy days. It occurred to him that it might be best to remain in that city, even though it is notorious for licence. There are worse things.

"One afternoon, he was walking in the precincts of the Temple of Bast with his children. A woman approached him. Very beautiful, dressed richly, with taste, she was an obvious courtesan, yet quiet and well-mannered. She seemed accomplished.

"She made no crude advances. Kamose, bereaved and tormented, might have rejected them with contempt if she had—or availed himself desperately of the offer. Sometimes a man takes wine to forget his troubles, and sometimes a body. But after what had happened, I think he feared to let his remaining children leave his sight for a moment.

"The woman treated them kindly. She was indeed a courtesan—but a temple courtesan, a priestess of Bast. Kamose spent time in her company while trying to decide on a course of action. Once she invited him to the marshes for a picnic and a day's fowling—she had two cats trained to hunt water-birds—saying that he might bring his son and daughter. But Kamose declined. There were crocodiles in the marshes. He neither dared to leave his children, nor take them to any place of dubious safety.

"The moon approached the full for the second time since he had entered Per-Bastet, and his mind grew more haunted still. His enemy among the gods was—is—the Lord of the White Disk and Master of Magic. His power grows as the moon waxes. Fearing this, Kamose confided in the woman while dining with her, while his children played with her cats in the sunken-floored room just beyond, and the moon rose over Per-Bastet, brilliant and gibbous.

"She received the revelation unshocked. She uttered no empty words of comfort, either, but advised him to placate the Ibis-Headed One by giving back his Scrolls at once. Then, perhaps, he would be content and exact no further toll from Kamose for his presumption.

"'Have you made offerings to Thoth and sought his pardon?' she asked as she poured perfumed wine.

"'I have not,' he answered grimly. 'Do you suppose it would profit me?'

"'Perhaps,' the priestess said. She touched his hand. 'Think. If you offer prayers and undertake to return the Scrolls, he may grant mercy.'

"Kamose thought about it. 'I am grateful,' he said. 'It's worth an attempt.'

"'It is,' she agreed, and looked upon him gently. 'Remain here tonight. Rest in my house, you and your children. Do what must be done tomorrow. Else I fear you may indeed suffer what the *ka* of Khuywer forebodes, and be forced to bring back the Scrolls with a forked stick, and a lighted brazier on your head.'

"Kamose slept with his children beside him and his arms about them. That moonlit night, as on many other nights, his sleep was murky and disturbed. In his dreams he became enamoured of the priestess, and found no joy but in her company. Longing for the friendship of her thighs overwhelmed him. He neglected his wife's obsequies, and heeded their children's safety less. Always, he looked for the priestess's favours. The more obsessed he grew, the less kind she became, and flaunted her lovers before him. Wholly enamoured and foolish now, he pledged her his possessions. She tempted him with promises of delight to come, and had him assign his property to her, bit by bit, in writing, duly witnessed. Even the wealth set aside to maintain his wife's tomb he made over. (And though it was a dream, it seemed most real.)

"Tossing restlessly on his couch, he dreamed that the priestess said, 'No, this will not do. What if your children cry out, when they are grown, that I have taken their inheritance, and seek a judgement to regain it? Perhaps they could succeed. You must destroy them, Kamose.'

"With his dream turning now to the foulest of nightmares, Kamose saw himself protest, and plead, and then weakly accede. He saw himself rise to advance upon his children, who now shrank from him, crying. He saw his wife cursing him from the Country of Osiris. Yet in his dream he struck down his small son and daughter as the courtesan had asked. He saw them lifeless, and cried out in horror.

"He awoke sweating coldly.

"His eyes were bleary, young lord. His head swam. But gradually he saw that moonlight filled the chamber where he slept. Crouching in the moonlight were black shadows uncast by any fleshly bodies, shadows shaped like maned baboons. Kamose's hair lifted in horror. He had magically guarded the chamber against the Shadow Eaters' approach, yet they were present. That meant treachery. Someone had undone his safeguards; it could only be his hostess.

"He called his children's names. There was no answer. The moonlight showed him their shapes on the floor. He flung himself upon them, and they were void of breath, flaccid. The specters had come in the moonlight and done that which their name implies—eaten the children's shadows, so that their lives departed.

"*While he slept!*

"Kamose turned upon the Shadow Eaters and cried out against them the most tremendous curse in all the Forty-Two Scrolls of Thoth, but it achieved nothing; they had come at the bidding of a greater Master of Magic. Then he uttered a potent spell of dismissal, and this had effect, since their ghastly errand was done.

"Kamose laboured long hours to revive his son and daughter, with all the magic at his command. In vain. Not until dawn, by which time he had abandoned the task in despair, did he so much as recall the existence of the priestess. He went seeking her with yearnings of dire and fell revenge.

"He found her. She was a faience statue, inlaid and gilded, painted with consummate skill. Her carnelian mouth wore a smile.

"The plainer statues which had been her servants stood around the house. Now he saw. If Kamose, mortal, young and foolish, could crew a ship with transformed images, the god of all magic could surely give the semblance of life to a woman's image, to speak, and cajole, and comfort, and deceive.

"She—it—had even suggested the god might relent if he returned the Scrolls. She, speaking as the god directed. While all the time the god had intended—this!

"Before leaving the house, Kamose smashed the priestess's image into a hundred pieces. They were worth the contents of a king's tomb. He left them for any passer-by."

After Ganesh finished his tale there was a considerable silence. He looked down at his thick hairy hands in something like embarrassment.

"I have been long-winded," he said finally "Young lord, forget the Scrolls of Thoth."

Amenufer answered stubbornly, "No."

"I will not help you find them! Or Khuywer's tomb! I do not want the displeasure of a god. The Archpriest Kamose's either, come to that."

"As you wish, jeweler. I need no help from you. I believe I have found the tomb of Khuywer by myself. Besides, all this story (long-winded, as you say) I have been hearing from you—I do not credit. It contains more detail than you would know unless the words were placed in your mouth by someone. Who but Kamose? You told me he makes use of you. Well, I am a nephew of Pharaoh's own house, and I stomach no interference from you, or the Archpriest of Anubis. Say so to him from me! Farewell."

Clearly; this was dismissal. Ganesh had tried his best, but by all the gods of Egypt and Canaan both! this young fool was pig-headed! And his boast of having located Khuywer's tomb might be more than wind.

A possibility highly displeasing to the Archpriest Kamose...

III.

Follow thy desire and thy good,
Fashion thine affairs on earth after the command of thy heart.
That day of lamentation will come to thee, when the Still of Heart
*   does not hear:*
Mourning does not deliver a man from the Netherworld.
                                    —Harper's banquet-song

Amenufer smiled smugly as he walked in the colonnaded outer courtyard of Horemheb's temple-tomb. That commoner from Ninsu who became a general, a power behind the throne, and in the end Pharaoh, was not buried in it; when he wore the Double Crown, he had a new sepulchre made. But both his wives lay here.

"Tonight," Amenufer exulted, "the Forty-Two Scrolls of Thoth will be mine! All sorcerous and mantic knowledge will be mine! One truthful thing that rogue told me; the power of Thoth is greatest by moonlight. But tonight is moonless. And despite Ganesh and his master, I now have the spell that opens the earth!"

He did not realize he had spoken aloud until a heavy bass voice answered him. "I know you do."

Amenufer spun around. He was alone, serving a month of duty as custodian of this temple-tomb. His royal connections had made it easy to amend the roster, and the other priests on duty would not come to serve until sunrise. However, it was no priest who had spoken. Amenufer knew the voice very well.

"Ganesh, you scoundrel! Begone."

The jeweler ignored the command. With a ponderous stride he came in through the pyloned gateway. Bracketed torches gave a shaking orange light to the courtyard. Ganesh looked around with feigned wonder. Then he looked at Amenufer, the young fool.

"Why are you here? This is not the tomb of Khuywer, where that which you seek is buried. Khuywer died a thousand years ago."

"Do not play with me!" Amenufer snapped. "I know this is Horemheb's tomb. Yes, and he demolished much older tombs to prepare its foundations, a thing you hoped I did *not* know! Over there—" He pointed dramatically to the north-west corner of the courtyard. "—below the paving, lies a deep shaft plunging down to Khuywer's resting-place, where the Scrolls are hidden. Because Kamose *did* bring them back, did he not, after Thoth punished him?"

Ganesh shrugged with weary patience. "Would you believe me if I denied it? But there is time and to spare before dawn. All I told you was true. I would finish the tale before you rush into more trouble than you know."

Amenufer also shrugged, but insolently. "It's your breath, jeweler. Waste it if you wish, but I warn you I am armed. And priests subordinate to me sleep nearby."

"Then I shall keep my voice low." Ganesh came further into the courtyard, among the pillars with their carved reliefs. He seated himself at the base of one, sighing. "At least you had the wit to choose a night with no moon."

"Of course."

"Of course," Ganesh echoed ironically. "You are far too clever to do otherwise. Kamose thought himself clever at your age, and—no, *he* did not pay, others did."

"I have no family, as I said."

"No more had Kamose, when the Lord of the White Disk was done. And he was demented with anguish and rage. He vowed the god should never have his Scrolls again. He travelled back to Hikuptah with five embalmed bodies for company; those of his family, and the mummy of Khuywer's wife, Neshemet.

"He kept his promise to lay her beside her husband. Horemheb still lived and reigned as Pharaoh in those days; then as now, his tomb was built above Khuywer's, and to meddle with it was perilous. For that Kamose cared nothing, and he possessed spells to open the earth as well as close it again—so access to Khuywer's tomb was easy."

"Be more concise," Amenufer told him, "or stand out of my way; jeweler. I'm eager to begin."

"More fool you," Ganesh retorted. "You do not recognize a last chance to desist. Well, then. To be concise as you require, our Kamose stood in the burial chamber of Khuywer again. The judge's *ka* witnessed while he placed the mummy of Neshemet in the limestone sarcophagus, and spoke the proper rites above it.

"'My gratitude is yours,' said the *ka* of Khuywer. 'Because I am grateful, I will advise you soundly. Bring back the Scrolls of Thoth and place them here. Else his vengeance will pursue you.'

"'It has,' Kamose answered with a half-mad laugh. 'There is nothing more he can bring down on my head, O Khuywer. I can deprive him of nothing *he* values—except the Scrolls, it appears. But that I shall do.'

"'He can do much to you yet. To me, nothing; I am dead, so that no god but the Still of Heart may touch me. Bring back the Scrolls.'

"'I will not,' Kamose answered. 'I go now to burn them.'

"The *ka* of Khuywer cried out, and vanished. As for Kamose, he went away, to his retreat where the Scrolls were hidden. There he tried to make good his threat, and set a torch to them. They would not burn. When he tried to rend them, they would not tear. Then he bethought him of the spells of annihilation which were contained in the Scrolls themselves. Those ought to be effective against their own source, he reasoned, and made ready to speak them, but the chance was not granted him.

"YOU HOLD WHAT IS MINE, a voice said.

"Kamose looked, and saw the god Thoth, ibis-headed, with the white disk of the moon on his headdress and a notched palm-branch in his hand.

"GIVE BACK THE SCROLLS.

"Even in his hatred, Kamose felt awe, yet he stiffened his spine and answered savagely, 'I will not. If you could take them without my giving them up, you would have done so. If I cannot destroy them, I can consign them to a dung-pit until it is filled, and lime it, and cover it, and leave your precious Scrolls therein!'

"The god said calmly, YOU WOULD NOT BE WISE.

"Kamose was chilled to the soul, and thought of all this being might do to him. The Measurer of Time seemed to see him thinking. He let Kamose think, and then spoke again.

"IF YOU MUST RESIST LIKE A CHILD, THEN PLAY A CHILD'S GAME WITH ME. HOUNDS AND JACKALS, BEST OF THREE. WIN, AND I RELINQUISH THE SCROLLS. LOSE, AND YOU MUST YIELD THEM. WILL THAT CONTENT YOUR ANGRY PRIDE?

"Kamose was mortal, and just wise enough, even in his madness, to be afraid. He consented. The god produced a game board of white crystal and jet, bound in a gold frame, with matching pieces. The pair of them played a game. The god won easily.

"GIVE ME THE SCROLLS.

"'I will not,' Kamose answered defiantly. 'It is the best of three.'

"Once he had spoken, all feeling and power left his legs. He looked beneath the table and saw that they were turned to black diorite. The god said inexorably, THEN YOU MUST PLAY AGAIN.

"Kamose played again, and he lost again. The god demanded the Scrolls a second time, and still Kamose refused. With that, his body became stone even to the breast-bone, so that no part of him lived but his head, shoulders and arms, and the heart and lungs within.

"THEN YOU MUST PLAY AGAIN.

"He did, and lost a third time. Again the god repeated his demand. Kamose yielded, choking on his capitulation, and promised to return the Scrolls to the tomb of Khuywer. The god said that his body would be restored when next the moon was full. Kamose sat with his thoughts until then. When he could move, he restored the Scrolls to the tomb.

"Afterwards, he vanished from the haunts of men for years. Some say he sojourned in the desert with no company but vultures and jackals. It is agreed by most that he left Egypt, to travel long and widely before he returned—but what is agreed by most, and what is true, are seldom the same. It matters nothing. What matters is that all I have told you should change your mind."

Amenufer stood silent for a long while. Ganesh began to hope he was convinced at last. However, he shook his head, obstinately.

"What are these but words? Words planted in your mouth by your master Kamose, I have no doubt, and likely untrue. He wishes none to equal his power. Go back to him. Tell him the Scrolls of Thoth have been taken by another—for I shall take them."

Ganesh rose terribly to his feet. "Tell Kamose?" He tore away his shaggy beard and wig. The bulky, padded robes followed, exposing a body of lean, tense muscles in a plain kilt and sandals. Cloth pads emerged from the thick cheeks, making them flat and changing the voice. "Tell Kamose? Young fool! I am Kamose."

"And I am Pharaoh's cousin," Amenufer replied, though he started first. "Archpriest of Anubis, do you think to frighten me in this manner? Why come disguised as the jeweler?"

"I always was the jeweler. There are several such identities I maintain and use in Egypt. That is by the way." Kamose's harsh, vehement voice seemed to cut like a scimitar. "Because you are Pharaoh's cousin, as you say, I have tried to dissuade you from this mad course, and even been free with confidences from my past to do so—more than you deserve."

"It was all true?" Amenufer stammered.

"Indeed. Presume to pity me, whelp, and I shall destroy you. That callow priestling who read the Scrolls and lost his family thereby has not existed for a hundred years. Still, I remember. Open Khuywer's tomb, remove the Scrolls, and I know how their maker will respond. Desist. It's an honest warning."

"You desire no man to rival you in sorcery!"

Even to Amenufer, his words sounded like childish bleating. To Kamose, they must have done indeed. He laughed like the clash of a bronze sword on rock.

"You are late come to do that! I am more than a hundred years your elder, practised and seasoned beyond your power to overtake. Because you are of Pharaoh's kin, I make you an offer. Join the Priesthood of Anubis and *I* will instruct you in magic."

"A paltry offer!" Amenufer said. "Promise to teach me as much magic as *I* desire, and as quickly, and—it may attract me. Otherwise, stand aside."

"Those who know me, even Pharaoh's Majesty, do not tell me in curt accents to stand aside."

Kamose began pulling at his hands, finger by finger. The large calloused paws of Ganesh the Jeweler came off like gloves, which they were, made of tanned and pliant monkey-hide with a skill which deceived the eye. The black hair that pelted them thickly also helped hide their artifice. Kamose's own hands, thus revealed, proved lean and sinewy, with large tendons. The disguise had been complete.

"I have an argument left," he said. "The *ka* of Khuywer gave me a warning, which that false priestess repeated in Per-Bastet. Both declared that the god would force me to return his Forty-Two Scrolls one by one, in the end of a forked stick, with a lighted brazier on my head."

"Yes," Amenufer said, and now his voice held an uncertain note. "I remember."

"He did."

Kamose swept off his soft, closely-fitting skullcap. The torchlight flickered on a scalp of lumpy scarring and thin membrane over seared bone. How the brain within had escaped broiling, strokes, or permanent madness was more than Amenufer could conceive. He shrank back.

"I will not invade the tomb!" he promised, shrilly. "Put back your cap!"

"Surely," the Archpriest said acerbically. "I prefer to. It does not please me to stand here as an exhibition."

He replaced the skullcap.

"Forgive me," he added, "if I doubt that your sudden attack of sense will prove lasting. It appears unlike you. I shall remain until morning—and you must enter the priesthood of Anubis as I said, so that I may undertake the tedious duty of control over you. Otherwise—" Kamose drew a complex glyph in the air with his hands, and uttered a Word. "See what would have come to you had I not been here."

Like one whose eyes have suddenly been opened, Amenufer saw what had been invisible to him before. Shapes like deeper shadows in the moonless dark lurked between the pillars of the colonnade. Much as they resembled large maned baboons, they also differed from them indescribably. They had gathered, Amenufer knew, to swarm upon him if he dared enter Khuywer's tomb. They would have devoured his shadow; that part of a man's spirit without which he could not continue living.

Amenufer felt ill. Watching the beings lope and shamble away, he felt grateful as never before for the Archpriest's sardonic presence. Turning his back on the gateway, leaving the court, he trod through the tomb-temple's statue room, and the second courtyard, to the chapel at the rear. Kamose walked beside him.

Stripped of conceit for the present, Amenufer felt like a child in the company of a dreaded guardian to whom, none the less, he looks for protection.

Kamose, as he had declared, had too much experience to think that this chastened and grateful state would be lasting.

THE EMERALD SCARAB

I.

The Archpriest Kamose at the best of times had an austere, sardonic presence. This was not the best of times. Haggard from grim vigils and sorceries, eyes reddened and sunken, he glared at the stone desiccation table on which lay a Pharaoh's corpse. It neither impressed nor awed him; he had seen other dead Pharaohs—greater ones.

Besides, and strictly speaking, the body could *not* be seen for the heaps of powdered natron covering it over. Kamose noted the hue and texture with an expert's eye. Frowning, he rubbed a little of the granulation between his fingers.

"How long since this was changed?" he demanded.

"Ten days, holy one."

Penma'at spoke, the Second Prophet of the Temple, a thickset, conscientious man. Although he made an able subordinate, he would have done poorly as the Archpriest. In Kamose's absence, he had directed the embalming process. Now he watched apprehensively as his master lifted the corpse's arm out of the greyish-white heap. Turning swiftly, he raked his underlings with a baleful stare.

"You sacrilegious swine! This is a *Pharaoh,* and you prepare him for the tomb as though he were a Libyan spearman! Ten days, you say? I cannot believe this natron has been changed at all!"

"Yes, holy one!" Penma'at bleated. "Each ten, or sometimes seven, days! I saw to it!"

"If that's true, it was not fresh. Either you hoped, with the spirit of a sand-flea, to pare cost—or you are so wholly incompetent you did not even know. Remove this excuse for natron! Take it hence! Let me see how much of your witless damage I can undo."

They obeyed, bowing out backwards, one or two of the minor priests even stumbling in the face of their master's ire. Penma'at kept his usual pompous poise, though appalled to have been rated before his inferiors in such a fashion. Old Djeseret looked vaguely distressed, and the young lector-priest (whom Kamose did not know) seemed amused if anything. Certainly his air of self-love did not lessen. Well, it wasn't astonishing; he had noble, if not prince, written all over him.

Alone in the *wabet,* the place of embalming, Kamose swept the natron to the foot of the sloping stone table. Setekh-Nekht's eviscerated, eyeless body looked almost prepossessing when one considered that he had been thrashed to death with a heavy rod. Curved ivory splints and gold wire braced his rib cage within. His right arm, broken in two places while he strove to protect himself, had been neatly bound in straight splints.

The fractures were not fatal. It had been savage blows across his abdomen, one after the other, that truly made an end of Setekh-Nekht. Nothing could have been done for the ruptured stomach and spleen (and almost pulped liver) except, when death came, to dry them, preserve them with spices, and cover them with layers of resin before they went into the mortuary jars. Sinking to one knee, Kamose studied the four such jars ranged on a shelf near the floor, with their varied stopper-lids, one each for the lungs, liver, stomach and viscera.

All appeared in order. It should be. Worthy, predictable Penma'at would never allow anything less than what was wholly proper. Setekh-Nekht's existence in the hereafter depended on the presence and condition of those internal organs. Penma'at believed it, and so did the Pharaoh's kindred.

Kamose smiled at the thought—a mocking, blase smile. All this careful art, perfected down the generations, to preserve a corpse intact in the belief that the spirit could not survive without it—and the first step in the process was to scrape out the brain and discard it like rubbish! Could there be a finer example of the power of tradition to immobilize the wits?

Doctors knew the various effects of blows to the skull and brain injuries. They knew them well. Medical scrolls which listed the symptoms dated back to Imhotep's time. Surgeons even opened the skull to relieve the pressure of bleeding or a depressed fracture, and the result—on occasion, at least—was a wondrous benefit. Yet established lore said the heart was the seat of mind and spirit, so even those with the strongest reasons to know otherwise, took it for granted.

So be it. Kamose did not intend to correct the error. As Archpriest of Anubis, jackal-headed lord of the mortuary and embalming arts, he controlled vast estates, properties and endowments because of that fatuous belief. Let him contradict it, and his enemies would swarm over him like gleeful crocodiles. Even the queen-widow and her son, Prince Rameses, heir to the Double Crown, would turn against him. At present they were his friends.

Setekh-Nekht, I'll see you embalmed and coffined, and preside at your funeral, since your survivors command it. But assuredly it is a step down for me. I performed the obsequies of Usermare. You reigned a scant three years.

Leaving the *wabet*, Kamose paused a moment in the hard, hot sunlight beside his pole-chair and four brawny servants. For that moment, his brain spun and his legs felt weak. Betraying no sign of indisposition, he climbed into the pole-chair and ordered his bearers to proceed.

"The Temple of Amun-Ra."

He wasn't himself, he thought grimly. After the stresses of his recent sorcery, he would be lucky if he was himself again in two seasons. His physical vitality had worn thin, his temper become raw, his control over it uncertain, and his sight dimmed on occasion. He carried the slash of a demon's quadruple talons across his chest beneath his robe to remind him of an almost mortal mistake. And his enemies must not know it, which meant, of course, that Kamose's few friends must not know it either, for once they did, his enemies soon would.

He'd been foolish to go about the city in a pole-chair, when he normally travelled by chariot or his black galley. Chariot, next time, with a great show of vigor, no matter how wearing it might be—and once the Pharaoh was duly entombed, a request to be allowed a retreat to his mansion at Abdu. Even though his enemies might gain political ground, Kamose could regain it when he returned, especially with his greater life span. Politics, to him, was a tiresome necessity, not sport or a serious affair.

From such political necessity, he paid his respects to the local chief priest of Amun-Ra. Minor though this Delta edifice might be compared with its immense mother-temple at Thebes, still it was rich, still a fane of the most powerful priesthood in Egypt. Even Kamose took care to stay on amicable terms with them. (He enjoyed the never-failing enmity of the Temple of Thoth, and one priestly feud was enough.)

Kamose proceeded to the treasure room. Penma'at arrived and joined him shortly. The various substances and appurtenances needed to complete the preparation of the king's body, once it came out of the natron, had been stored here awaiting use. The largest temple of Anubis in the Delta was neither large enough nor secure enough for such a purpose. Having been appointed Controller of the Mysteries (chief embalmer, in plain speech) by royal command, Kamose must now take inventory and arrange to transfer it all to the *per-nefer,* the "house of beauty", where the embalming process would culminate.

Oils, balsams, spices, and resins took a good deal of space, along with myrrh-filled cloth pads for stuffing the body cavity. Despite their immense cost, they were cheap beside the array of amulets meant for planting within the royal corpse or wrapping between the layers of mummy bandage. Casket after casket Kamose opened, under the watchful witness of two priests of Amun-Ra, to record the contents after he had noted them against a master-list. Golden *djed* pillars, scarabs winged and plain, sun disks, Eyes of Horus, lions, bound gazelles, couchant jackals, little figurines of at least twenty gods, stylized papyrus columns, horizons, paired feathers, and more and more, in gold, electrum, and gemstone, were taken out, itemized, and meticulously packed in their caskets again. The least article in the array would set a man up comfortably for life—and, if he were caught stealing it, cost him a less than comfortable death.

The greatest talisman lay within a box of jointed ivory. There was no visible lid or hinge. Two of its five hidden catches had nothing to do with opening it; they merely released poisoned needles, and breaking it would unleash a fine dust deadly to breathe. Even Kamose, who knew its secrets, placed bronze stalls on his finger-ends before touching it.

Closely nested inside blazed the Pharaoh's heart scarab, an emerald the size of a man's two fists, carved in the shape of the beetle of resurrection. Heavy gold clasped the base, on which was engraved a prayer.

Kamose repressed a scornful smile, unmoved by the jewel's splendor. It was supposed to prevent the Pharaoh's own heart from testifying against him in the judgement hall of the gods. In that respect it had about as much power as a pebble, to Kamose's certain knowledge; and besides, a few generations at most after Setekh-Nekht's funeral, it would have been taken by robbers.

Briefly, then, the Archpriest's face and eyes altered. He bent over the emerald scarab once more. Lifting it in his sinewy hands, he stared at nothing for a space, seeming to brood like a vulture high in some burning sky; intent on a portent below that only his eyes could discern. Then he replaced the gem in its box with a steady hand.

"Let this be taken to the *per-nefer* under no ordinary guard," Kamose ordered. "Twenty warrior princes will suffice. Only porters of our temple, who have served long, are to bear it, and you and I will accompany them, O Penma'at. Then the divine body of Pharaoh is to be carried there—after cleansing, as always."

Penma'at bowed. "As you command, holy one."

He spoke a little stiffly. Kamose supposed his language to the man in the *wabet* still rankled. He would concede it had been ill-advised, especially before underlings, but he had a larger matter on his mind than any grievance of Penma'at's. A discovery just made had briefly brought him close to panic, as though he were a normal mortal man.

The emerald scarab was false as a harlot's affection.

II.

Mertseger laughed, a rippling susurration like wind in dry grass, the mirth of the serpent she was.

"Oh, no! Indeed? This great gem is nothing but paste?"

Kamose smiled with her. It was rather a joke, for those who could appreciate it, and he had found the lamia to be among the few able to share the blacker depths of his humour. Jesting with her of course was dangerous. That had to be borne in mind.

"The great gem is real. There has been a substitution. Malachite and gilded lead, not paste, if I may be laboriously exact. One cannot tell the difference by sight because the thief has cast an illusion of similitude over the counterfeit. He must have placed them side by side to do that."

"That might have been anyone, at any time, my lord," she said pensively. "Even the temple artisan who carved the jewel, if he knew magic—and if he did not, any priest down to the most minor would have been able to supply his deficiency." She ended in a tone fit for discussing the most remote abstractions, "There *are* corrupt priests."

"Even priestesses," Kamose replied just as gravely. "Now hear me, marvellous one. The risk alone means this can be no ordinary theft. The robber chose to chance his act's being noticed before the scarab was hidden forever inside a king's carcass. One supposes he must be daring, bold, without scruple, and confident—even over-confident, reckless. The qualities of youth."

"And greedy. Or desperate."

Kamose agreed. "I have such a fellow under my eye. He's the lector-priest taking part in the mummification, and I have not known him before. He's some sort of cousin to Prince Rameses. Wenching, betting, and racing his chariot are his chief delights; he gives as little time as possible to priestly duties. It shows, I may say. His knowledge of the rituals is slipshod. I'd confine him on a plain diet and have him study day and night until he was perfect—not in any hope of making him devout, my serpent, but to teach him that I expect my priests to be meticulous, at least. It cannot be done because he's royal. The Vizier at Hikuptah appointed him to this task. I wish—quickly—to learn if he pilfered the emerald."

Mertseger stretched, smiling. "For that he must run free."

"He might be desperate for wealth. His favourite pleasures are costly. Assume the guise of a courtesan, O Mertseger; and cross his path; learn if he is guilty. But that is all! Control your deadly appetites where he is concerned! He's not to be harmed, nor is he to guess what you are. I will deal with him if he is the thief." Kamose looked her in the face with a gaze more lethal than her own. "Flout this command and I turn the blood in your veins to vitriol, serpent."

He could do it, and would. Mertseger knew it beyond doubt. In her human shape as a priestess, she was a tall woman, supple to the point of seeming boneless, and here in Kamose's private quarters she had cast off her temple robe to be easy in her skin, unconfined. But as anger possessed her, that skin colored in herpetoform mottlings, black and yellow, while actual scales broke out in places. Her fingers tensed.

"Vitriol?" she said fiercely. "To hold me captive, even for you, Kamose, is to keep vitriol in a tube made of unwaxed reed. Have a care to *your* flesh!"

"I shall. Meanwhile, go fascinate this youthful lector-priest—or lecher-priest may be more appropriate. His name is Reni."

The ophidian patterns faded from Mertseger's skin. She said woefully, "Will you allow me nothing in the way of pleasure?"

"Of your own peculiar pleasures, from this man, no. He's highly connected. And I cannot always find traitors or criminals for you, O

Mertseger. Discover all there is to know about Reni, and I make large effort in that direction."

Mertseger departed, seething, but intent on her task and hopeful. Kamose experienced a certain relief. She would do as he ordered, and do it well, but in all likelihood there was no need. The young lector-priest did love chariots and fine horses, and exorbitant wagers; but such was his skill that he generally won. He was unlikely to be the culprit. This, Kamose had already ascertained.

He preferred, though, to have Mertseger occupied, and at a distance from himself. Let her discern his current weakness, and there would probably be no choice for him but to destroy her. Holding her under his control, just as she said, formed a circumstance of extreme peril, but until he did so her depredations had imposed terror on the entire Delta. By bringing an end to that, Kamose had vastly increased his own reputation. Besides, the lamia made a fearsome weapon when his enemies overstepped the mark or some criminal—tomb-robbers in particular—grew too egregious. And she was a remarkable lover.

Kamose's expression became bleakly amused. Until he recovered, it was fortunate that he possessed elixirs and potions which could renew a man's vitality even at the point of extinction. Although they could not be taken too often, he would assuredly never conceal the truth from Mertseger without them.

She had shrewdly said that the emerald might have been stolen at any time since it was carven. Still, Kamose had his own reasons for thinking the theft a recent one, and the motive other than greed. The emerald scarab being his responsibility, the most likely reason for stealing it (almost the only one to justify such immense risk) would be to discredit him. Kamose knew numbers of folk who dreamed longingly of such an outcome.

So. Recent theft reduced the number of suspects. Reni, though not eliminated yet, ranked among the less likely. Any of the half-dozen lesser priests involved in embalming Setekh-Nekht had had opportunity. They might be desperate on their own account, or the compelled tools of a greater man's scheme. Kamose had given secret commands already, and meant to know everything there was to know about all of these men within three days.

That left, in positions of far greater trust and authority (and therefore opportunity), Penma'at and Djeseret. Both possessed more than ordinary integrity, Penma'at in addition valued his honours as Second Prophet more than any conceivable wealth, while Djeseret had always been removed from worldly matters to a nearly grotesque degree, wholly steeped in religious concerns. Besides, he was growing senile.

Penma'at did have a large family, though, and if one of them should be in serious trouble or threatened with disgrace—*that* would make him vulnerable to pressure, honest as the Second Prophet was. No. Penma'at could not quite be discarded from consideration as a thief and traitor. Both Penma'at and Djeseret possessed more than the modest degree of magical ability needed to perform the theft. For that matter, most of the lesser priests probably had it.

Kamose pondered. It would be interesting to solve this riddle by his own knowledge and wit, not by divination or the aid of spirits. Simply giving the culprit enough rope for his own noose might provide the answer.

He began early next day in the *per-nefer.* Unlike the *wabet,* a closed and heavy vault, this place admitted air. Little square windows near the high ceiling let in light while keeping out oppressive heat. The plaster walls carried bright paintings. While their subject matter was solemn— embalming rites, funeral processions, the judgement of souls—one wall showed happy spirits in the Afterworld, and all were decorated in vivid hues.

Even the mortuary bench was very different. Procedures in the *wabet* had been carried out on a heavy stone table, sloping and channeled to drain away fluids. Here the royal cadaver lay on a magnificent lion-headed bier.

Kamose, washed and purified, entered in his ceremonial vestments as Controller of the Mysteries. A black jackal-mask with crystal eyes covered his head. He wore a kilt of many intricate pleats and a sort of linen corselet to his armpits. It almost hid the lacerations of the demon's claws. The fresh red scars just showed. His collar, armlets, belt, and short oblong apron glittered with crusted jewels. From behind the belt a long black tail hung down.

The lector-priest Reni came late, and through the mask's eyes Kamose saw that he looked somewhat worn and wilted. Flagrantly against the ritual purification rules, and the sanctity of the rite in which he was engaged, he had been wenching and carousing the night before, and Mertseger—abroad in a rich litter—had contrived to catch his attention.

She worked swiftly. Kamose had heard her description of events when she returned an hour before dawn. The lector-priest assuredly did not behave like a man with aught on his mind but merriment.

Kamose rebuked him sharply for lateness. The rituals began. Setekh-Nekht's gutted corpse had been washed clean of natron before Kamose's minor priests carried it to the *per-nefer*. Much shrunken by the desiccation process, it stared from empty sockets while the minor priests rubbed milk, wine and juniper oil into the skin—all but the face, which had already been covered with a thin coating of resin.

Kamose's part began. Personifying Anubis, he chanted an invocation. That complete, he removed the temporary stuffing which had filled out the bereft body cavity until now. The lesser priests placed it aside in a basket. Kamose, each movement slow and solemn, began to restuff the body with linen pads containing fine sawdust, powdered myrrh and cassia. He had to reach in through a deep slanting cut above the groin to accomplish it.

"O royal falcon, Setekh-Nekht, go forth into heaven as the lion-god Ra, who has eaten the thigh and divided the carcass. Be justified; inherit eternity. Your heart shall speak for you, it shall be found true."

Kamose reached out his hand. The lector-priest took the great scarab in a grasp that trembled. Its green blaze illumined his face. He appeared distinctly out of sorts. Passing over the jewel, he intoned the prayer engraved on its underside, working hard to speak clearly.

"O my heart, which I had from my mother! O, my heart of my coming into being! Do not stand as a witness against me. Do not contradict me with the judges, or be my enemy in the presence of the guardian of the balance…"

Kamose took the scarab, watching his subordinates as he did so, his masked gaze intent and assessing. Penma'at had pressed his lips together in disapproval as the lector-priest stumbled once or twice in his phrasing.

Old Djeseret echoed the prayer silently, moving his withered lips; he could have recited it in the midst of a whirlwind. He was old and death hovered close to him. Hardly a time of life to take theft and sacrilege on his soul. What could it gain him now? He always had seemed more concerned with the Afterworld than with life, and Kamose had known him when he was a green youth in the temple gardens.

And yet someone in this chamber must be sweating with fear lest the theft be discovered. Kamose held the scarab longer while he stared at the six minor priests, all of whom he knew, and wondered if one of them had been corrupted so far—or even if someone in the Temple of Amun-Ra, while the emerald had been stored in its treasure room—

Enough. Kamose thrust the great jewel deftly into the Pharaoh's body, settling it next to the heart, and packed more myrrh-laden pads around it. Systematically he filled the thoracic hollow from the collar-bones down, until the torso presented a natural appearance again, and covered the incision in the lower belly with an engraved golden plate. This, too, Reni handed to him, speaking the appropriate incantation in a slurred and thickened tone.

I'll teach you better in time, Kamose thought grimly, *whether or not you are a thief. Not even whelps of the royal house conduct lax rites in my temple, or guzzle and swive during a mummification.*

The lesser priests now rubbed the corpse with a paste of spices, while new resin melted over a brazier. Using wide brushes, they coated the entire cadaver with it, sealing the golden plate in place thereby. If the thief was present, he must think that danger no longer hovered close above his head.

Let him think so, then—for now.

III.

Five days passed. False eyes of gemstone were seated in the Pharaoh's empty sockets. His jaws and face were bound up with fine linen bandages, each finger and toe wrapped separately, then capped with wrought gold. Kamose's minor priests wrapped his limbs and torso. The next day, a selection of precious talismans were placed on his body and then brushed over with molten resin. Tilting his head reverently back over the end of his bier, they poured more resin into his skull through the nasal passage. The following day, they bandaged the head and wrapped the entire body in further strips of fine linen. The prayers and rituals provided by Kamose, Penma'at, and old Djeseret never ceased.

Away from the *per-nefer,* investigation by Kamose's agents went on unceasingly also. Within it, he watched his subordinates with the eye of a cobra making ready to strike. By the fifth day, he felt that he knew the thief, and could even name his motive.

It wasn't Reni. That young roisterer had lost his swagger and indeed had difficulty, by then, in keeping his feet. Several nights with Mertseger were enough to humble the proudest, randiest he-goat. Kamose, amused, decided nevertheless that Reni's attrition must end while the lamia still managed to restrain her more deadly lusts.

"It will be unnecessary for you to keep any more assignations with the lector-priest," he told her.

"Ah," Mertseger said without regret. "He's virile, but—he will be no further use to me unless you permit me to slay him." She shrugged. "I think he will be of no use to anything female for some time now."

"You may not slay him."

"Have you found the thief, then, my lord?"

"Thieves. And I imagine they will come to find me on the morrow."

Kamose was smiling. Mertseger knew that smile; it meant that the Archpriest was aware of something that others were not, that he had a fatal surprise waiting for them. It was a smile steeped in poison direr than her own. Curving her lips expectantly, she asked, "Why, O Kamose?"

"To accuse me of stealing the emerald."

Mertseger's smooth brows drew together so that two tiny upright creases showed between them; in her; the equivalent of wailing, shrieking and tearing her garments.

"That's an absurd charge. Is there danger that they could succeed with it?"

So spoke her tongue. Her thought, rather; was, *Is there hope that they could succeed with it?*

"No danger at all," Kamose replied cheerfully. He understood her very well. "I have expected for days that the scarab will appear again, in circumstances contrived to make me appear guilty. It was stolen for just that purpose. A shoddy scheme, but it might have succeeded had I not become aware of the substitution." He laughed. "Don't ask me how they ever supposed I would not!"

"Yet the spurious gem now lies next to Pharaoh's heart. Where you placed it."

"Surely a difficult state of affairs to explain," Kamose agreed, "unless we recover the true emerald scarab tonight. How fortunate for me that we can. I'll garb as an ordinary stolist-priest, you as a priestess. We leave at once."

"For what destination?"

"The temple of Anubis."

The temple of Anubis within Pi-Rameses was little more than a chapel, though larger ones existed at other cities in the Delta. Still it boasted a gateway, courtyard and inner shrine. The single priest serving at night duty allowed Kamose and Mertseger in when he saw the parchment letter they carried, signed with his Archpriest's cartouche. If he discerned that the man bearing the letter *was* his Archpriest, he wisely refrained from announcing it. He hurried away to the courtyard.

"It is here?" Mertseger asked.

"Yes. I had the culprits followed closely enough to erase any question. Not that I was sure they were the culprits—then. Others were closely followed besides them."

Kamose bowed deeply before the atramentous, jackal-headed statue behind the altar. Its red tongue lolled between the jaws. Both hands held daggers, and a horned viper coiled around one forearm.

"Lord of Tombs, Announcer of Death, great seer and diviner; we come to undo sacrilege. We would set aright a perversion of the mortuary rituals by lewd and vile theft. Prosper our actions."

Mertseger bowed as well, fluid and supple of movement.

"Where is the emerald?"

"In a secret cache beneath the altar which clearly is secret no more."

Vipers were carved along the altar's sides. Kamose twisted the heads of several in apparently random order. Then he thrust against one end of the altar. It pivoted smoothly around. Beneath it lay a stone-lined cuboidal hole. It contained papyri in cylindrical cases and certain other objects, including a skull. Near the skull lay a pouch of gazelle-skin, tightly filled out by something rounded and hard.

"I believe we have it," Kamose said. "Had this been proved missing, and then found here in my temple—by the Vizier, let us say—how lamentable for me!"

He opened the pouch. A hard green glitter flashed at him. In a moment Kamose held a huge emerald scarab between his hands. Staring down at it—at and into it, with his magician's perceptions—he knew in a moment that it was real.

"Good, thus far. Now return we to the *per-nefer*. There is much to do yet!"

Twenty princely warriors guarded the *per-nefer,* posted there by Kamose himself. None was aware of the subterranean passage and hidden door which gave access to the embalming chamber through one painted wall. Soon, Archpriest and lamia stood beside the Pharaoh's corpse, sealed within layers of linen swathing and hard-set precious gum.

"Were you another man, I should say it had been an error to lodge the false gem within this mortal husk and then wrap it so securely," Mertseger said with transparently false respect. "Can you open the body and close it again?"

"I can open the very earth and then close it again, as you know, but that would be excessive and needless now. Watch the entrance very vigilantly, child of a serpent. Warn me if someone comes."

"Indeed," Mertseger said coolly, "I have no more wish to be trapped here than you."

Kamose laid the huge emerald blazing on Setekh-Nekht's linen-wrapped torso.

"The spurious gem is made of malachite and gilded lead," he explained. "To make it resemble the emerald, the thief had to place them side by side and cast a spell of similitude. A paltry matter; but it formed a sorcerous link between them—and of course they are the same size and shape precisely. To transpose them—*so*—without disturbing any matter in between, is an act but a little more finely skilled, slightly more subtle."

Kamose's somewhat oblique eyes looked into strange dimensions. His hands moved. They seemed to slide *past,* not through, the layers of bandage, the shells of hardened resin, the desert-dry flesh and rib cage. Then his right hand was empty, the left full.

"All is now as it should be."

"Not all, surely. The thieves are yet at large."

"They are about to walk into quicksand of their own volition. There is one more thing we must do to guide their steps. Come."

Sunrise came to the marshes, cities and harbors of the Delta, its vineyards and orchards. It found Kamose in his jackal mask and regalia, a picture of sombre, sepulchral dignity. Not even Mertseger knew what expression he wore behind the mask.

A procession came to the *per-nefer* while dawn was still red, before they could begin the day's embalming. A company of archers came with it as escort. A dozen scribes and priests of Thoth walked ahead. Most conspicuous and august, borne in a litter because of his arthritis, was the Vizier of Lower Egypt.

Kamose saw him, and the rotund, purse-mouthed man who rode in a second litter following him. This one clearly felt satisfaction so immense he could not keep it from showing in his face however he tried. He wore precisely the look of a glutton who had tasted something that delights the mouth as much as it gratifies the belly, and now looked forward to the full banquet.

"Beba," Kamose said, very softly.

"The Archpriest of Thoth?" Mertseger; who knew something of Beba, sounded incredulous—with reason, Kamose thought. "Is this plot his?"

"Beba would not have the wits or the daring. No, someone has duped him. He believes me guilty because it is his dearest wish."

The Vizier leaned upon a staff because one leg had become twisted by his ailment. Although the pain made him irascible, his judgement had not suffered thereby. He almost personified the great principles of order, harmony and justice which Egyptians called *Ma'at,* and his wisdom led him to doubt that Kamose valued these things cardinally.

Kamose pronounced a formal greeting. The Vizier advanced into the *per-nefer's* antechamber with a few attendants, and Beba waddled with them. Mertseger discreetly withdrew.

Although the Vizier returned Kamose's greeting, he did so in a bleakly formal manner; and lost no time thereafter.

"The matter is too grave for drawn-out courtesy," he said. "It concerns the Pharaoh's heart scarab. Has anything come to pass concerning it which ought not to happen?"

"No, excellent Vizier. It has not."

"A lie!" Beba said impatiently.

"But there has assuredly been an attempt at something which ought not to happen. Someone has essayed to steal the heart scarab by exchanging a worthless copy. My report of this sacrilege was sent by my ablest courier to your greatness at Hikuptah. It was dispatched—yes, two days gone."

"No!" Beba's chagrin pleased Kamose. "No! The worthless copy of which the—the Archpriest—speaks—was placed beside Pharaoh's heart. It rests there now!"

"If that were true," Kamose said austerely, "it would mean that you know a great deal about it. Yet that is not true. Nor do you flatter me.

Who supposes that such a thing could be done and I not know? All that passes in my Temple is known to me, august Beba. Some of my subordinates, like some of yours, I dare say, are crafty."

Beba glared up at his rival. "There are witnesses of high character who will swear the scheme to filch the emerald scarab was yours!"

"Then name them."

"The Third Prophet of your own temple, Djeseret, and a lesser priest, Ib!"

"Djeseret? Ah." Kamose's voice came muffled and unctuous through the jackal-mask's black muzzle. "Sad. He's reaching his dotage."

The Third Prophet, summoned, gave much support to his Archpriest's comment. He decried Kamose as a creature of utterest evil, one who blasphemed the gods and had contrived the late Pharaoh's death. Since the Vizier knew the precise circumstances of Setekh-Nekht's death, that accusation gained no credence. Djeseret then averred that Kamose had tried to steal the heart scarab to deny the Pharaoh joy in the Afterworld. Clearly he had believed for some time that his Archpriest was less reverentially pious than he ought to be, and someone had worked on that belief through the decline of Djeseret's superannuated mind. Worked upon it with skill. Kamose soon observed that Djeseret believed all he was saying.

"He stole the gem! He! It lies beneath the altar in the temple of Anubis!"

There was one thing Djeseret could not possibly believe was true. Not even in his dotage. He could not believe it because, as Kamose had concluded days before, he was the thief himself.

Kamose removed his mask at last, to show a face set in lines of vast patience.

"What lies concealed there," he said, "is a false copy I discovered before I penned my report to you, O excellent Vizier. The true emerald scarab is where it ought to be, within the sacred body of Setekh-Nekht. If Prince Rameses or yourself orders, I shall open the mummy and prove this, but I should view it as woeful desecration. Perhaps the most skilled augurs and diviners in Egypt—outside my own Temple—should test the matter. I leave it in your hands and those of truth."

That ended it, in effect. The Vizier looked as though he considered Kamose's response too glib and knew there was more in the business than appeared—but the scarab had not been stolen, and the funeral must proceed without scandal. He conscientiously took possession of the false scarab, followed Kamose's suggestions, and had two of his own trusted scribes supervise all further proceedings. Setekh-Nekht's mummy remained closed, and Kamose presided at his obsequies.

Beba, the Archpriest of Thoth, presented a picture of incarnate woe while these events unfurled.

EPILOGUE

"*Djeseret* stole the scarab?" Mertseger marvelled. "He?"

Kamose nodded. "To blame me. The dotard never thought of it as rascality. He persuaded himself—primed by someone else, I think—that I was spiritually unfit to be Archpriest of the Temple he had served lifelong. It's easy to make a righteous man commit acts of vile treachery if you only convince him they are his distasteful duty. The same person must have had Beba make the accusation, and so I infer that he ranks high in the priesthood of Thoth. I suspect he hoped to diminish me, if the plot succeeded, or Beba if it failed, and in either event to add to his own consequence."

"How that capon Beba slavered with joy to accuse you! Why did you let him off so lightly, my lord? You might have brought him down over this. Yet you assured the Vizier his motives were honest, and that Beba had been deceived."

"And how it mortified him to accept his status back from my condescending hand! I have no wish to bring him down. Having an incompetent at the head of my fiercest enemies is much to my advantage. My troubles will increase on the day an able man rises to lead that priesthood!"

"Such as the one who conceived this plot and used Djeseret and Beba as his cat's-paws? Do you know his name?"

"Not yet. One day I shall know, and deal with him. I am patient."

"You were lenient with Djeseret and Ib, also."

"Sending them to maintain a shrine in the western desert for the rest of their days is scarcely lenient. The Libyans may murder them. Certainly, if they ever take one step beyond the precincts of the shrine, I shall have them crushed like frogs between the stones." Kamose played with his pointed chin-beard. "Like our sagacious Vizier, I wish no scandal."

"And now you retreat to your mansion at Abdu for a time, with the Prince's leave."

"After he becomes Pharaoh, formally."

"May I accompany you?" The request came like poison mingled with honey.

Kamose rubbed his chin once more. Leaving her to her own malign devices would be madness. Mothers would wail for their infants again, and wives for their young husbands, throughout the Delta. Kamose had enhanced his fame greatly by ending Mertseger's reign of terror, and allowing it to begin anew would have the reverse effect.

"Abdu is a long, safe distance from Pi-Rameses. No doubt there are malefactors there, or in Thebes, who would be improved by your attentions, and I did promise you some diversion for your patience."

"Then I may come?"

Like unto a breathless little girl hoping for a gift, Kamose thought wryly. Knowing the risk, he said assessingly, "I believe you must, daughter of a serpent."

LAMIA

Mertseger the lamia had partly abandoned the shape of a mortal woman. The high midnight rooftop, with its garden of flower-beds in marble or basalt troughs and urn-planted aromatic bushes, gave her seclusion to cease her pretence. She knew herself safe. Her master's apartments in the palace were empty tonight, even of servants. The master, Kamose himself, was absent. Not even the prince, about to become Pharaoh, or his mother the widowed Great Queen, were likely to enter while Kamose was away.

Mertseger stretched, smoothly pliant. Shining scales broke through her skin on back, flanks and legs, their pattern as beautiful as their emergence was disconcerting. Her legs, converging, became a long constrictor's tail. She coiled it around a stone pot and squeezed hard for purchase, her brain alight with visions of ribs cracking in her embrace, of spines yielding, of the slow process by which she engulfed still-living victims—barely living, and wholly helpless, but living. It had been far too long since she had digested a meal more satisfactory than a goat. The red craving grew in her as she thought of the way things had been. Her eyes filled with a demoniacal glow.

She was Mertseger, the lamia! Once she had made her lair on a marshy islet in the swamps near Buto. All the Delta had feared her in a torment of fear. Virile young husbands had deserted their wives for her, to become first her lovers and then her provender. Mothers had wailed and shrieked for lost children—and neither crocodiles nor lagoon waters knew the secret of all such disappearances, by any means. Her terror and evil fame had grown so great that prayers were intoned in every temple against her. Exorcists and magicians had come seeking her on many occasions. Most had not found her. Some, accomplished and cunning, had done so, while others, merely attractive, Mertseger had chosen to find. All had vanished, and her depredations had continued.

Then—ah, then—Kamose had undertaken the task. Kamose, Archpriest of Anubis, most deeply learned and darkly practiced of all

Khem's magicians, old beyond the common, strong and vital beyond the youth of nature, had sought her. He had found her, besides, and not because she allowed it. Thereafter it was the lamia who disappeared, at least from the knowledge of common mortals, who supposed that Kamose had destroyed her, and praised his name gratefully. Which occasioned the magician a vast, sardonic amusement. In truth he had made her his slave. Mertseger had been frustratingly confined to human form and made to serve in his entourage as a priestess. Not that Mertseger had been wholly denied her appalling pleasures in his service. Sometimes he unleashed her against particularly obnoxious tomb-robbers, those who plundered temples, or traitors to Egypt. Besides that, he had made her his leman, a truly perilous thing, but he preferred her to any human woman, as he preferred his other mistress, the she-sphinx Nonmet. Nonmet, however, was far away in the south, watching over the tombs of kings or ranging the desert. Circumstances compelled Kamose to remain in the north, avenging a murdered Pharaoh, presiding over his obsequies, and guarding the life of his heir—all in his own unique, unholy fashion.

Mertseger hissed malevolently. Yes. Ah, yes. While engaged in these pursuits, Kamose had made a mistake. He had almost succumbed to the onslaught of a demon—one more powerful than she. Only almost, it was true, and he had repulsed the being, but since its attack he had been weakened, and there were signs that he would recover but slowly. He appeared to believe he had successfully concealed this. From Mertseger; from her! The lamia of Buto! She who was part of his retinue and shared his bed!

Kamose, after all, was a fool, a mortal human fool. In due time, she would make him pay. For the present, though, while the Pharaoh's funeral occupied him, Mertseger meant to award herself some delight. A victim made for her attentions had become available, here in the royal city of Pi-Rameses. In fact it was Kamose who had first shown him to her. Mertseger found that ironically gratifying.

She began willing herself into torpor. Shortly she lay face-down on the roof, her tail barely shifting. Her ghostly self—not the *ka,* for being other than human she had none—left her flesh and flowed down the stairway in the likeness of a huge mottled snake. She passed through the palace gardens and slid by the gate-house unseen. No one could see Mertseger when she left her flesh unless she willed it. Traversing the dark streets, she heard dirges and wailing for the Pharaoh, Setekh-Nekht, gone to his horizon ten sennights before. When his funeral was performed on the morrow, his heir, Prince Rameses, would become the new Living Horus, Rameses III. Utter ritual purity was required of all those taking part in the ceremony.

Mertseger hissed laughter. Purity! She herself would be there, in snowy linen, shaking a sistrum and dutifully wailing. For that matter, so would her proposed victim, though she meant to see that he attended in a rather shaken state.

Between two canals, near the city's southern lake, lay a great pillared cellar which had once been a store for oil and wine. Now it was a costly den. Its present owner had tiled the floor, hired craftsmen to plaster and paint the pillars, and furnished the whole. Its reputation stank like carrion pork in the nostrils of the virtuous. This never prevented its being filled to crowding on most nights of the year, even though the length and breadth thereof were ample.

Mertseger coiled and writhed exuberantly on the much-eroded courtyard stones. Anticipation made her joyful. Then she stood up in the form of a gowned, jeweled courtesan. Smiling, she sauntered unseen between the Libyan bullies who guarded the entrance.

The cellar's lamplit reaches stretched into dim distances before her. Without exception, it drew noble or rich habitues. Dancers writhed, music rippled, and servants lugged jars of river-cooled wine for the patrons. Mertseger found the one she desired at the heart of the cellar, in the vicinity of a large sunken pool whose water freshened the subterranean air, engaged in drink and song with revelers like himself. Oh, Mertseger knew him. His name was Reni, and he held the rank, the minor rank considering his princely birth, of lector-priest in the Temple of Anubis. As she watched him from the shadow of a pillar, her eyes glowed.

"More of the best!" Reni ordered, laughing. "They used to tell me in the temple never to drink without keeping tally of your cups. Why, good wine in any amount never hurt a man yet!"

The harlot with her arm around Reni's neck disputed him. "Oh, Sobek's can, beloved young man," she murmured, "if one should neglect paying for it! Well that you settled your debt with him tonight. He was growing impatient, as we could see."

The lector-priest glanced at Sobek, master of this den of turpitude, a large, apparently sluggish man whose drifting gaze missed nothing. "He said nothing objectionable to me. If he had, soldiers of my acquaintance could go through this cellar of his like flood-water through a village. And leave it in much the same state. Our amiable Sobek knows this, my sisters. He knows as well that I pay my debts."

The second harlot, known as the Gazelle, gazed at him from eyes made huge by kohl and malachite.

"You are rich tonight, my lord!"

"I never gamble," Reni said complacently, "except upon my own horses, when I am driving the chariot, or on my archery. And then I seldom lose. So, my sisters, will you have jewels, or lengths of the noblest colored linen? You may choose either."

They squealed with joy. Mertseger felt wickedly amused. This young cousin of the departed Pharaoh was to be part of his funeral procession on the morrow. He was also supposed to be a lector-priest. The event required a state of abstinence and complete ritual purity. Clearly that thought did not have first importance in his mind. Did he think himself immune to discipline from *Kamose* because of his kinship with the royal house?

Well, it mattered not at all what he thought. The time had come to disturb his complacency and bring him an intimation of his doom. Mertseger stepped out of the shadows and struck an attitude before Reni.

The two harlots felt the reprobate priest stiffen between them. He stared straight ahead—at what, they could not imagine, for they saw nothing. He said in a dry whisper, "The woman!"

Purple Lotus, the harlot who had her arm around Reni's neck, pouted, "What woman, young lord?"

The Gazelle looked where Reni was looking, and still saw nothing. His tone made her uneasy, as did the wild, haunted nature of his gaze. His response had been all that Mertseger wished. She smiled at him tauntingly. The form in which she appeared was one he knew. Had known in the flesh. Though diminutive in size, she had a queenly shape and poise, and her robe of translucent sea-colored linen argued strongly that she owned queenly wealth. But her attitude and smile were both as merciless as the tomb.

"Yea, what woman?" demanded one of his evening's cronies, a wealthy merchant's son eager to waste his parent's substance. "Are you drunk? No one is there!"

Reni became desperately eager to believe he was drunk in the next moment. While he stared with rounded eyes, Mertseger changed into a large, a very large, serpent. It swayed before him with the same fluent grace as the woman, higher than his head, and arched in menace. A loud hiss came from its mouth. No one but Reni seemed to hear it. Then the serpent was gone.

"Drunk? No! I'm under a curse," he said hoarsely. He had forgotten the girls he held. Both heard him. Purple Lotus only smiled and cast a significant glance at the wine-jar, but the Gazelle owned a more dramatic, superstitious turn of mind.

"Perhaps it came because you slighted the ritual purities while you embalmed the Pharaoh, lord," she suggested. "Maybe sacrifice at the temple would help—"

"A harlot advises me about clean living!" Reni thrust the Gazelle roughly away. "Listen, you witless trull, my blood's as divine as was Setekh-Nekht's. It should be. It's the same blood. Do you suppose his anger would fall on me as though I were some common man?"

The Gazelle had hurt her elbow and bruised her buttocks on the floor's many-colored tiles. She heard few of his words except the final ten. To those she replied, hot with spite. "You are less than a common man! Your piety is much less! Whence comes the curse on you, then, if not from your drinking and whoring while you prepared the Great One for his tomb?"

The angry question penetrated Reni's haze of wine and self-satisfaction, not deeply, but enough to disturb him, and then to arouse his intemperate ire. He lunged at the woman, who shrieked and fled. Set on thrashing her severely, he began to follow.

"Enough, Lord Reni." Sobek addressed him—Sobek, the vast wine-cellar's proprietor, who had been called after the crocodile god for a number of reasons. Notable among them was his habit of looking like a harmless, inert log until it was time to attack. "Enough. You are lucky as it is not to have been hurt tonight. It's well that you settled your debts with me when you arrived. They were over-large. Go in peace." Sobek's bullies were nearby, and ready to intervene.

Curling his lip eloquently, Reni stalked out. His servants, waiting in the street, were amazed that their master appeared so soon. Cockcrow or slightly before was his usual hour to emerge. Seething with displeasure, Reni ordered them to carry him homeward. He imagined a number of condign revenges he might take on Sobek.

That miserable pander, to speak as though Reni lowered the tone of his cesspit! Yes, but a woman is *haunting me.*

A lamia, it appeared. Dread touched even Reni's insensitive soul as he thought of it. He had supposed her a rich courtesan when he met her, jeweled and attended, on the night streets of Pi-Rameses. The wild pleasure she gave him had supported the belief. Sometimes her abilities had scarcely seemed human. Now it appeared that they were not.

Although scarcely timid, Reni shuddered. A lamia! But why should such a creature trouble *him*?

Mertseger might have informed him. Perhaps, she thought, returning to the palace, she would yet—on the night she lapped him in her serpent-coils. Still, before that happened, she meant to play with him further.

The unfortunate Reni had his own Archpriest to thank for his fate, really. Someone had purloined the greatest of the dead Pharaoh's burial amulets, a great jeweled scarab, a theft of fearsome sacrilege. Reni had been suspected for a time. Kamose had commanded the lamia to assume the form of a courtesan and discover if Reni were guilty, while forbidding her to harm him. He belonged to the royal house, after all, and despite the power and dread of Kamose's standing, even he must observe diplomacy with certain folk.

Mertseger felt no such inhibitions. For Kamose to dispatch her as a bona roba did somewhat offend her pride; for him to send her into the arms of a strong young man, and yet forbid her the deadly, natural culmination of such a union, did more than offend. The mighty magician had grown witless if he thought he could do so; sharpen her appetite, and then stay her passions, as though she were a servant girl he could send to bed without supper. Assuredly no.

Kamose had drawn her attention to the lector-priest and introduced her to his couch. The lector-priest should sate her cravings, then, no matter how high his connections, and no matter how his death might injure Kamose's credit. The lamia did not intend that Kamose should survive long enough to be much inconvenienced, in any case. She had served a mortal by compulsion for long enough. His recent conflict with a demon, and the lacerating weakness that resulted, were opportune for Mertseger. She would be free.

Soon, now, she would be free. And all Lower Egypt should wail and cry... Luxuriating in these thoughts, Mertseger returned to the palace, where her body lay in its half-ophidian shape in the rooftop garden, barely respiring. She entered it again and assumed a human shape, that of the priestess she pretended to be in the diurnal hours. Because it resembled not at all the shape of the courtesan she had been to Reni, he would not know her in the funeral cortege. Smiling, she relished that knowledge.

Observing Reni the next morning, she beheld distinct signs that he had drunk even more heavily after seeing her in Sobek's reprehensible den. He walked with great care. His hands were less than steady, though he hid it well from most of those around him. Neither did he fumble while lifting the Pharaoh's gilded coffin, with three other priests, onto the bier drawn by white oxen. The Pharaoh's sister and his widowed Great Queen wailed beside it, dressed as the divine mourners Isis and Nepthys. His son, Prince Rameses, walked behind them in the vestments of a priest, with the Arch-priest of Anubis at his side… the caustic, cynical Kamose, his lean face grave, a black garment made to resemble a stylized jackal-pelt cinctured over his sacerdotal linen, a heavy sable wig on his disfigured pate.

Mertseger, leading the procession of *muu* dancers, could have laughed for mocking joy. Kamose, walking so solemnly, an image of reverent virtue, for all the world—and before the gods—as though he lacked any inkling that the monster of the Delta, she whose depredations were a byword of horror, trod among the mourners and celebrants! Wherefore she trod even more decorously, schooling her face into lines of devout grief, and only now and then glanced ahead at Reni the lector-priest with glistening eyes. *Soon, O Reni, soon comes your end! And after you, Kamose! I warned him that* to *enslave one such as I is a perilous thing!*

The procession reached the dockside by the Lake of the Residence, where an ebon barge of royal splendor waited. The artisans of Kamose's own temple had fashioned it. Again, the lector-priest Reni helped carry the magnificent coffin aboard. This time he stumbled on the gangway and righted himself with great labor, straining, while the great carved and painted sarcophagus almost fell from his shoulders into the water. The other bearers also struggled mightily to prevent disaster. One later developed a rupture from his efforts.

Once successfully carried on deck, the Pharaoh's coffin was raised against the mast. Prince Rameses, with a ceremonial adze and great solemnity, performed the rite of Opening the Mouth, to restore his father's senses and grant him the power of speech in the Afterworld. Mertseger marveled. After her thousands of years, very little had power to astonish her, but the depths of mortal folly continued to do so. Who could suppose that such pitiful ceremonies would in any way mitigate death? They served only one sensible purpose that she could discern. Having performed those rites, and not before, Prince Rameses could legitimately take crook and flail in his hands, don the Double Crown, ascend the ancient throne of Egypt.

Perhaps one other sensible purpose. Just one. When buried in the royal valley with his treasures and furnishings, once a few years had passed, Setekh-Nekht could begin to supply the necessities of life to those men of enterprise and courage who would proceed to strip his silly crypt of all save the plaster and paint on its muraled walls.

This always occurred. Not even Kamose's dreadful magic could prevent it, nor the vigilance of guardian sphinxes. Mertseger, for her part, saw no reason to prevent it. Tomb-robbers were among the few classes of mortals to whom she gave any regard whatsoever. Their initiative deserved approval; so did their irreverence. Mertseger cast covert glances at her master. His bearing seemed even more somber and austere than usual; he spoke but now and then, to issue a command. The tilted Syrian eyes were sunken, and looked deeply weary. Those appalling vigils by which he had avenged the Pharaoh, and that encounter with a demon especially, might have taken a greater toll than even the lamia had heretofore perceived. She rejoiced. And carefully concealed that.

Kamose should not take too close notice of his minions, with such concerns to preoccupy him. The long voyage upstream to Thebes offered ample time to torment Reni, and once they arrived, and the Pharaoh's burial in the royal valley was complete—then Kamose would be absorbed in conclave and negotiations with the powerful priesthood of Amun. He could not avoid it. Politics made imperative demands. It had been rather long since he last visited Thebes. The perfect opportunity for a final visit to Reni, at a midnight hour…

Straining oarsmen, a score to a side, rowed the great barge across the shining lake dug by a thousand laborers, and into the canal which led to the easternmost of the Delta branches of the Nile. Turning southward, they passed quays and godowns, two-storied white houses of craftsmen, the mouths of other canals, and—towards the outskirts of the city—the still-imposing ruins of a columned palace of ancient times. Mertseger knew the place well, for Kamose favored it and sometimes held court there under sable canopies, regulating his temple's affairs. It appealed, she supposed, to his saturnine temperament and sense of the evanescence inherent in everything men made, besides being close to the River's cooling airs. She reflected with anticipation that it was by no means certain he would see it again.

The pleasant groves, orchards and vineyards of Pi-Rameses passed from sight; and stretches of papyrus and bulrush replaced them.

The Archpriest's lean face grew darker and bleaker of expression as the mortuary barge approached Bastet. A humor like some black radiance emanated from the man and forbade, without words, any to approach or address him. Most, indeed, became wary of even glancing in his direction. They knew rumors, at least, of the way Kamose had incurred the curse of Thoth in his youth, and of how the god's displeasure had claimed his wife and children in the city of the cat-goddess. He had hated the place with a diuturnal hatred ever since.

They harbored that night at Yun, the City of Ra, and proceeded on the morrow to the mighty town of Hikuptah, with its circling white wall. The priestess who was Mertseger paid further attention to Reni in that immemorial city, though she displayed no more transformations into a serpent, delicious though it was to frighten him. To deal him over-much inquietude might drive him to seek the help of his Archpriest, and save him. Instead, she provoked him in dreams, and he felt again the embraces of the courtesan he had known in the royal city, knew the supernal delights she had given.

Reni reached lubricious climax in his sleep like a green boy, and awoke with the proof of it spattering his belly. The experience puzzled him. Although a young man, he was somewhat old for that. True, the courtesan had been astounding in her ability to arouse and grant pleasure, like no other of his experience, but this did not make her supernatural. Lust was swiftly replacing the unease he had known in Sobek's den, when he had seen her appear like a vision and become a menacing serpent. After all, he had been drinking deeply… lamias were not common… Kamose himself had rid the Two Lands of the last one known… but it was strange that no one knew about that particular courtesan, or seemed to have heard of her, despite her accomplishment and evident wealth… and stranger yet that he had never been able to find her dwelling again.…

Mertseger was content. Precisely upon this power to arouse unreal, obsessive desire did she rely for victims. Mortal men yearned for the unreal and were never content with actual women. The sensuous carnality she could convey with such ease was, to her, the lure which culminated in feeding. And she fed fully as much on astonishment and pain and the horror of death as on red flesh.

Mortal men, being fools, did not comprehend that, even in their frequent telling of lamia legends. The descendants of that accursed, transfigured Libyan queen whose name they bore had lost their human womanhood ages before. Lust, though paramount in her prey (and the chief means by which she gained prey) was far from Mertseger's first concern. Pleasant as it had been to frighten Reni, Mertseger saw that the wiser course was to tickle his lust, to encourage it as a farmer brings along the grain-crop he means to harvest. The courtesan of Pi-Rameses must be much in his memory and senses, and deliciously, so that when he saw her again he would not be afraid, but come to her eagerly, with a swagger. For that Thebes, far upstream yet, should be the best place.

Until her purpose was achieved, of course, she would do best to walk wide of Kamose. During the voyage, he paid little attention to anything but the details of the Pharaoh's funeral. Incense burned constantly about the catafalque in the cabin aft, with priests of Anubis, Thoth, Amun-Ra, and Set keeping a vigil of honor. Outwardly sober and reverent, they cherished the rivalries of their temples in their hearts, and between the votaries of black Anubis and Thoth seethed not mere rivalry but hatred. Yet both knew Kamose would countenance no breach of decorum by either.

Beneath the deck of the wide barge lay Setekh-Nekht's tomb furnishings; a royal chariot, plated, gilded and dismantled for transit, beds, chairs, weapons, regalia, scrolls of his achievements, and jewelry in profuse array—a treasure escorted by two galleys filled with soldiers. Prince Rameses and his mother travelled in one of them, aware that the soldiers were scarcely needed. Kamose's sinister magic sufficed to protect the barge's contents.

Indeed, if in their jealousy the priests of Thoth had not contrived to remove Kamose from the task of guarding Setekh-Nekht, the Pharaoh would not have perished. The Archpriest continued to utter little but necessary orders.

Above Hikuptah, the River was often shallow and wound considerably among shifting mud-banks which tested the pilots' skill, seasoned though they were. Multitudes of small reed boats plied the water, as always, and pilgrimage craft were a common sight. Once a quintet of massive freight barges laden with building stone passed on their way downstream. The Nile had barely begun to rise. After the inundation, of course, little ships carrying surveyors and scribes would be everywhere, as the silt-covered fields were marked with their proper boundaries again, and after the harvest, emmer-laden barges would predominate, on their way to the great official granaries of temples, lords, and the Pharaoh. By then, Rameses would officially be Pharaoh, the third Rameses to wear the Double Crown, but he would wear it under a new name, his chosen royal name.

They passed the city of the jackal-god, Kamose's particular patron, to whom he addressed a prayer and intoned a blessing. With a wind behind them and the sail raised, they skimmed by deserted Akhetaten, the city of that Pharaoh of accursed memory whose name it was forbidden to speak.

Mertseger, as indifferent to him as to all kings and their claims to be divine, scarcely noticed. She sent the lector-priest lascivious dreams again, and brought him to ecstasies before they ended. He cried out rather compromisingly in his sleep. Rebukes came his way from the more straitlaced of his colleagues, though rather more of them offered amused gibes. Although puzzled, still, Reni did not seem displeased.

More miles of the river fell behind them. They came, finally, to the dark quayside of Abdu, the burial place of Osiris. Here lay great shrines and ancient necropoli, with the mortuary temples of Seti and his son Rameses the Great—both administered, much to his benefit, by Kamose himself.

Westward, by the hills at the desert's edge, lay Kamose's chief mansion and favored home, a terraced, pillared almost-palace of diorite and black granite. Yet it lay too far from the River for convenient use at this time. After Abdu, the River made a great eastward bend before the upstream journey led south again, and within the bend lay desert roads cutting straight across, while others, longer and more arduous yet, led to the great fertile western oases.

Kamose had a particular interest in the traffic of these desert roads; a veritable sheaf of secret reports and missives had awaited him in Abdu, brought there by a loping, grotesque messenger. He carried another thing besides writing, a green copper bowl, about a cubit and a half across, heavy and thick, with a cover as massive, clamped shut by a black bronze escarbuncle. This Kamose opened, to study its contents, before sealing it again. He ordered the messenger back to Kamose's mansion with all the documents and his replies thereto, but the bowl he kept, and took aboard the great barge, where he stowed it behind the array of *ushabti* figures meant for the Pharaoh's tomb.

None questioned him.

The barge and its attendant galleys came at last to Thebes, beyond the bend, city of Amun-Ra, once capital of Egypt. Even though Pi-Rameses enjoyed that distinction now, Thebes remained the seat of the Two Lands' most powerful priesthood and the greatest of all its cities, saving perhaps Hikuptah. Its wealth and the magnificence of its temples shook the mind. Even Kamose took care to remain on amiable terms with the priesthood of Amun-Ra. They had much to arrange in Thebes; the Pharaoh's interment and the coronation of his heir, all with high, glorious pomp.

Kamose saw his entourage lodged in the town and retired to the house he possessed in Thebes. Prince Rameses and his mother chose to stay with the Archpriest, an imposition he accepted, since he numbered the prince among the few young nobles whose society he could cultivate with equanimity and even, at times, pleasure. He derived greater pleasure yet from having the priesthood of Amun-Ra know how strongly he stood in favour with the new Pharaoh. And it was necessary, he reflected, highly necessary, to ensure that the prince lived and reigned longer than his unfortunate father.

"My time as Pharaoh is not to be placid," Prince Rameses said, showing no evidence of regret. "That we may discern even before I take the crown on my forehead, O Kamose. Those uncouth pirates, the Sea People, grow constantly bolder, and they were strong enough to overthrow the Hittites. The Libyans raid. The princes of Retenu, as always, are restive, not to be trusted, while the Kushites—"

He appeared to be searching for appropriate phrases. Kamose finished for him, dryly.

"—are the Kushites, Great One."

"Indeed yes. Where the Libyans are concerned, O Kamose, I believe nothing occurs in the western desert which you do not know. The west is the particular domain of your patron god. You know it well."

"For years I was a hermit therein. I had intended to ask your leave to retire to my mansion at Abdu for a time, that I may acquaint myself again with all the affairs of Libya—yea, and of Thebes."

Tiye-merenese, the widowed Great Queen, showed her displeasure. "We desire that you return to Pi-Rameses with us. My son will require your support."

"As Prince Rameses and as the Living Horus, he shall ever have my support, Great One," Kamose said smoothly. "Alas, my encounter with a demon while I countered the machinations of that Kushite wizard has cost me greatly. Even though loath to forfeit the sunlight of his presence and yours, I fear I should seclude myself a little if I am to be of worthwhile service again."

Tiye-merenese snapped, "How long is a little?"

"A year, if I may have leave. I promise that in that year the deplorable Libyans and vile Kushites shall both know I have returned to the south, and be reminded that they have masters."

The widowed queen studied him. The haggard state of the face beneath the soft felt skullcap did not seem to be assumed. Nor was his encounter with the demon any mere convenient tale, as she knew.

"A year is reasonable," Rameses agreed. "Try to delay no longer, worthy Kamose. You will be missed."

"You honor me."

"A year, then," Tiye-merenese said reluctantly.

Mertseger, walking the dark streets of Thebes, could not have been better pleased that she was absent from these dreary deliberations. Nor did it astonish her that Kamose had left her to her own devices on this night. He would scarcely desire that his demon mistress rest beneath the same roof as the Pharaoh and his mother! Nor, in his present unmanned state, would he wish her in too close propinquity to himself. Late, of course; much too late.

Mertseger's last victim had been a prince whose clandestine activities included banditry, sacking temples, and treason (that one with Kamose's well-planned sanction).

Tonight she would embrace a prince again. Afterwards, the magician himself should find his way, most agonizingly, into her serpent's belly. Then, then, then her predations begun anew, with none able to prevent her—she could surely find a way to lure the young Pharaoh himself. Egypt should fall into chaos. Mortals should assuage her unchecked appetites from the Delta to Kush, and shudder, and wail, and beg their unheeding gods for respite. And there should be none....

Even though Mertseger had never entered Thebes before, she had only to find the lector-priest Reni; and having seduced him in the Delta, had him as her lover for several nights, she discovered him again with ease through her demon's perceptions. Even lacking those, she would have sought him first among the dives of the east bank's waterfront, knowing his predilections. And there he proved to have gone. Standing well back, Mertseger watched him wrestle a bull-like boatman for the lewdly smiling Arab girl who—evidently—for the present was with the boatman. The latter, like all those who ferried for a living on the River, had every trick of filthy fighting absorbed in his bones' marrow. Reni, though, had been raised as a noble of the royal house, trained in wrestling by masters. He had seen service as an army scribe (of indifferent competence), then in a chariot squadron, and only enrolled as a lector-priest under Kamose after a scandal with his commander's wife. Active, belligerent and skilled, he surprised those who had wagered against him. After half-an-hour's eel-quick, eel-tough contention, he broke the boatman's arm. He splinted it, however, and bought the fellow a jug of darkest, most potent beer. He had stripped to a kilt and sweated profusely. The girl he had won moved her tongue over her lips. So did Mertseger, though for a contrasting reason.

Reni rose to claim his prize. Then, completely still, he looked past her as Mertseger stood forward. She wore the shape of the Pi-Rameses courtesan that he remembered, with pleated turquoise linen sheathing her small firm body, a winged headdress surrounding the exquisite face. Flanking her impassively, two huge servants armed with daggers and hardwood cudgels answered the question, without words, of how she had entered such a place unrobbed.

Reni's smile faded. His awareness of the boatman's wench seemed to fade with it, and as swiftly.

The courtesan approached him with light-footed grace. "You know me," she said.

"Yea, we were merry together in Pi-Rameses, and then you vanished with never an explanation. Explain now, my sister! Where did you go? What accounts for my dreaming of you so frequently?"

Reni considered himself no soft-heart, and had meant to demand these answers harshly of the woman, nor had he expected to find difficulty in doing so, for he had dealt cruelly with more than one woman before. Yet meeting her lustrous gaze seemed to bring a mist across his mind. A scent that mingled jasmine and lemon filled his nostrils, with a faint, underlying demonic fetor that aroused him wildly even though he barely sensed its existence. Nor had he intended to address her by that amorous, tender term, *my sister.* Yet the words had come from his mouth. The Arab girl intruded, anger in her face and nails like claws gripping the courtesan's arm.

It had pleased her to be won by a handsome, slumming noble, and did not please her to have his attention claimed by this other, clearly far richer, harlot. She proposed to say so, and more. Instead she whirled away, whimpering. For Mertseger's smooth arm had changed to a pustulent horror beneath her fingers, and the shapely head on her shoulders to a serpent's fanged gape.

Nobody else had noticed anything amiss, least of all Reni. Mertseger said persuasively, "O young lord, I had received sudden news of an inheritance, and had of necessity to journey here. Yet I could not forget you. I consulted a priestess skilled in love-enchantment. She cast a spell which she promised would bring you here, and see! It was worth the payment."

"A love-spell, eh?" Reni murmured, amused, yet content with the explanation, even relieved that it should be something so common and comprehensible. "You wasted the priestess's fee. I should have had to make this journey anyhow."

"So that you are here, I shall not ask why."

The ribald crowd saw them turn and leave together, her bodyguards following in a manner that warned against interference.

The Arab girl watched them depart. Hugging herself and shaking with dread, she reviewed the sudden monstrous transformation of the gowned woman, which no one else had observed. Oh! That handsome lector-priest would not be seen again! Raising her hands to her face, she realized only then that she still clutched Reni's jeweled collar and belt. He had wagered them as a stake in the wrestling match, which no longer appeared to interest him even though he was the victor. Swiftly, from long habits of squalid survival, the Arab girl tucked it out of sight until her mind should be calm enough to deal with the problem of selling it. She must profit by *something* from this sorry evening. If she pondered more, and shuddered to ponder, the likely fate of the lector-priest, she thought on it no more than briefly and shared her apprehensions with none.

Reni had forgotten her even more completely. Mertseger's explanation of his odd dreams and visions had satisfied him. With her insidious perfume in his nostrils and his arm about her compact waist, he hardly cared to inquire more deeply. A canopied litter of cedar and ivory waited for them. Its six brawny bearers might have been sibs to those who had accompanied her within. Reni, who as a lector-priest should have been versed in magic, had always used his rank to avoid both studies and practice in that area. Else he could have perceived at once whether the courtesan's servants were actual or illusory. Not giving so much as a transitory thought to the matter, he rolled behind the litter-curtains with Mertseger, fumes of wine clouding his brain almost as much as the lamia's enchantments. He entered her arms.

"I have a house in Thebes now," she said. "The inheritance whereof I spoke. Would you go there?"

"Indeed," Reni answered thickly. His mind whirled as with vertigo or drugs. He cared not. The litter moved as smoothly as a boat on calm water, and there seemed to be nothing but dusky-blue space in the world outside when the curtain stirred. It never occurred to him that they moved too smoothly for reality, much less that he might in truth be *walking* beside the woman through the darker, viler streets of Thebes while unaware of it. Even when they halted, and there was no sense of the litter being lowered, or the slightest jar when it touched the ground, Reni continued heedless. Finding himself in a walled garden of flowers and ponds, he never paused to ask himself where the woman's attendants had gone.

"You wrestled the ferryman excellently well, O prince," she murmured. "And I have reason to know how skilled you are at wrestling with a woman." Her dark eyes glowed.

Reni scented the strange fetor more strongly as he lowered her to the soft-herbed ground; and had he paid heed he might have felt, now and then, the soft tongue that caressed him bifurcate and quivering. He paid no heed. Eager for delight, he touched her, sliding the gossamer-fine pleated linen blindly aside. His fingers probed the joining of her limbs. She caught his wrist, raised it to her mouth, and drew his fingers between her lips one by one, until she reached the forefinger.

And with a hiss, bit it off.

Reni screamed like a speared gazelle. His eyes flew open; he looked at her, and screamed far louder. She crunched and chewed the finger while her eyes blazed like fire. Relentless coils lapped around his body. Her ophidian tail, grasping a tree for purchase, shook leaves down upon them.

He clawed at scales and relentlessly strong muscle with his one free arm. He might as productively have clawed at Khufu's pyramid. Above the contracting coils that bound him there still remained the shoulders, arms and pale breasts of a woman, but the head was wedge-shaped, armed with backward-slanting fangs—which quite lacked poison. Mertseger was made and endowed in no such kindly fashion.

Reni essayed another scream of horror. The feeblest gurgle emerged. His ribs began cracking.

Mertseger paused in the process of crushing him. With hands now gloved in black scales, she stroked his face.

Reni voiced a ghastly sound. His eyes bulged. No shred of doubt remained in his heart that this was death.

Then, behind her, a tall figure appeared, authoritative and sardonic even in dim outline. In the crook of one arm it carried—a rounded object of some sort. In its other hand flashed a *khepesh*, the famed sickle-sword of the Two Lands, a bronze scimitar, so familiar to Reni that he recognized it even in his extremity, in the dark.

Kamose swung it with precision. It sank into the serpentine body with a meaty noise. The lamia uttered a shriek, and the lashing of her cabled coils threw Reni aside. He lay swooning with pain, too far gone even to think, *O fool, why not behead her—it? Now are we both doomed!*

Kamose set down, with deliberation, the object he had carried in his left arm. He said coldly, "Daughter of serpents, you have not been wise."

Mertseger, sorely yet by no means mortally struck, appeared to hold that the folly was all her master's. And that he could now expect to be neither her master nor any other being's for long. All scaly constrictor now, she reared high to strike.

Then, swifter even than she, nerved and strengthened by dangerous potions, Kamose ripped the lid from the ancient bowl at his feet and snatched forth something white. It had fitted neatly within, so much so that it never rattled in the thousands of years since the bowl was sealed.

Mertseger recognized it. A deep whistling cry of pure fear came from her mouth. "Just so," Kamose confirmed, in a voice like metal. "Queen Lamia's hip-bones, the girdle of her womb, she who was the first mother of all your kind, O Mertseger! I obtained them long ago against such need as this, and weakened or not, I can work such sorcery holding them as you cannot withstand."

Mertseger's blunt head stuck like a mace at the Archpriest. He whirled aside, raised the white skeletal pelvis high, and roared a tremendous cantrip in a language older than Khem, forgotten before the first tribes along the River had worshipped either Set or the Falcon.

The bowl at his feet expanded, grew tall as he. No longer solid, but a fine copper lattice, it engulfed Mertseger in a moment. She sought to crawl out. Kamose tossed the bowl's cover high, spinning like a discus, and it too expanded to a thin fretted lattice.

Uniting with the bowl, it completed a spherical cage from which Mertseger tried frenziedly to escape.

Despite the seeming fragility of her prison, she met with failure.

Kamose raised the charnel pelvic girdle high in both hands, and uttered a word. Mertseger's prison shrank around her, glowing to red and then white as it constricted. The earth opened. The cage and its captive sank into a realm wherein Kamose glimpsed great passages, curtains of cobweb spun by monkey-sized spiders, the fantastic skeletons of primordial monsters, corrupting corpses and slinking, whey-eyed ghouls.

Then the riven ground closed over the sight of Mertseger, hissing and lashing about within the searing orb. The iliac ossicles Kamose held fell into fine dust which drifted about him.

"Seven years of *that,* esurient one, may convince you that when I declare it is I who choose your prey, it were best to listen."

He cast a scornful glance around him. Where the readily deceived Reni had beheld lotus-ponds and flowers, Kamose saw an empty lot where rank weeds grew, middens reeked, and vermin scuttled, at a juncture of several twisting alleys. Mertseger had brought her victim to the most insalubrious part of Thebes.

Reni lay gasping, some distance away, several ribs splintered and the stump of his finger oozing.

"You will live," Kamose said. "Consider this salutary. Osiris, Set, and my lord Anubis! Hathor, and Sekhmet the Lioness! Preserve me, all of you, I implore, from any more princely idlers playing at the role of priesthood!"

Yet Mertseger, he owned, had been no less foolish, and with far less excuse. She had known him, well. And knew him somewhat better now. Could she have imagined he would not watch her closely? Or take meticulous care to have the means available for curbing her scarlet hungers on the day when, inevitably, they would overwhelm both calculation and fear?

To escape from Rameses and his mother had been a simple matter of pleading indisposition and asking leave to retire. He might have arrived in time to spare Reni her savage attentions, had that been his wish.

He had not wished it. Reni's reprobate derelictions during the entire course of Pharaoh Setekh-Nekht's obsequies had been well known, also, to his Archpriest, and had called for a sharp lesson. This Kamose intended to make clear to the impious rogue as soon as he had partly recovered.

Whether royal or common, those who served in the Temple of Anubis served to a high standard, or they suffered.

Stalking from the scabrous plot of ground, Kamose clapped his hands to summon the physician and attendants he had fetched with him, against this need. *They*, agreeably for Reni, were no phantasms of a lamia's malign evocation.

WHAT ARE YOU WHEN THE MOON SHALL RISE?

I.

The gibbous Egyptian moon grew fuller. Kamose the Archpriest, pacing the colonnaded balconies of his house near Abdu, looked at the waxing white disk with utter hatred. Monthly, when it was complete, he formally cursed it with all the power of his magic and all the intensity of a never-ending rancor, so that it quivered and turned a sanguine crimson. It had always recovered, so far, during the hundred years of his enmity. Kamose lived in the desire that some month it would falter and perish.

This, to be sure, would not be the time.

"I am weakened," he said grimly. "Conflict with that demon brought me wounds that will not quickly heal. Nevertheless I will curse the moon as usual, and you will assist me in the malisons."

The young lector-priest who was accompanying him gulped. "I fear to do that, holy one. The—the power of Thoth—"

"—did not disturb you when you sought to steal his scrolls of enchantment," Kamose snapped. "You ignored warning after warning. Tell me not of Thoth's power, Amenufer. Except that I have driven a bond and taken service with a god of equal puissant wisdom, the priests of Thoth would long ago have brought upon me such a doom as would make seething vapor of a bronze statue. Glory to Anubis, Chief of the Hill of the Viper!"

The lector-priest seemed reluctant to affirm that utterance. Kamose looked at him forbiddingly. This foolish youth had, in his view, caused him trouble enough.

"You hesitate, O Amenufer? You owe me life—more than mere life. But for me, you would have incurred the anger of Thoth, as I did. You know now what comes of that! Also, you are no longer a priest of Thoth, if you forget, but a priest of Anubis. That's to say, one of my priests."

"Yes, holy one. Glory to Anubis, I agree. But will he not protect you? Must you curse the moon? Does it not offer provocation?"

"I protect myself. The best defense, as common wisdom says, is attack, and for the priests of Thoth the most favorable time to work ill against me is by strong moonlight. Accordingly, I rebuke and confound its source."

Amenufer offered no further argument. The pair made a complete contrast, in the day or by silver moonlight. Amenufer came of royal kindred. Handsome, slender, young, scholarly to a degree not quite healthy for his years, he knew very little that had not come from scrolls and papyri, and craved nothing so much as arcane knowledge. In fact he was much as Kamose had been at that age. But the Archpriest had changed over the decades, greatly. Lean, harsh, vehement and austere, he had the physique of a soldier or chariot driver rather than a priest, and indeed he had travelled with armies on campaign. Except for his well-kept hands he could hardly have been more unlike a scribe. And his reputation as the greatest and darkest of magicians resounded more loudly throughout the Two Lands than his integrity as a priest.

The conflict with a demon that he mentioned had indeed left him haggard, his faintly oblique eyes sunken, ringed with darkness. The young lector-priest had noticed. Despite his efforts to hide it, one could see that Kamose moved deliberately, with careful effort. If so much incapacity was manifest, how much had he successfully hidden? Amenufer wondered if the Archpriest really would recover from the demon's talon-stroke, as he had prognosticated he would do.

He sagely kept the doubt to himself, or thought that he was doing so. Kamose found the stripling's doubts, hopes, and fears somewhat easy to discern. Amenufer's hunger for arcane knowledge had caused trouble before, and in fact he had gained more than was wise or healthy, so that Kamose had felt bound to take him into the Temple of Anubis where he could watch the whelp closely. A cousin of the new Pharaoh, he had to be managed diplomatically—to a certain extent. Still, Kamose's long-established power and his favor with that same Pharaoh meant that he was not obliged to bear with Amenufer's perilous curiosity, or his impulsiveness, or lack of subordination, past certain limits. And Amenufer did possess enough sense to fear the Archpriest, when he remembered to be afraid.

"I have received gifts from the Temple of Thoth before, which showed strange properties at some phase of yonder ruined world," Kamose said reminiscently. "Once they introduced a servant into my household who had inherited the curse of shape-shifting from his parents. He became a killer leopard at the rising of the hunter's moon. He slew four of my guards and mauled a half-score others ere he died. He was meant to eviscerate me, of course, and came near it." Kamose had been forced to defend himself with a spear on that occasion, and in fact had been the one to deliver the death-blow. He saw no reason to mention that. He had outgrown such puerile boastfulness by at least a hundred years.

Amenufer said with a certain skepticism, "How did they dare, holy one?"

"Ah. This was long ago. I had not become the Archpriest of Anubis then, but some thought I was rising too swiftly. Besides, the priests of Thoth had their own reasons to disapprove of me, reasons you know. On a different occasion they sent me a marvelously wrought jeweled collar, which came putatively from the Viceroy of Kush. A little too marvelously wrought, with magic in its fashioning. When demilunar light fell upon its links, it tightened and strangled the wearer. I ensured in advance that it would be around someone else's neck. But a praiseworthy attempt."

Amenufer's tongue thickened in his mouth, and he found these remarks difficult to answer.

Kamose lifted his face to the source of that silver light flooding his estate, and the surrounding desert. Men made endless legends about it—and men were fools, as always. The sun-god was averred to have made Thoth his deputy and representative upon the coming of night, and to have allowed him to create the moon so that there should still be light after sunset. Thus his titles included "Lord of the White Disk" and "Measurer of Time."

All foolery. He had no more made the moon than Kamose had. The Archpriest knew that white orb for what it was, the blighted cinder of a world. Nevertheless, Thoth was its lord, as he was the divine patron of wizardry, mathematics, and writing. His priests could work their most potent magic by the full moon's light.

"A praiseworthy attempt at that stage of my career," he qualified. "It would be somewhat obvious now. But *something* is sure to occur in this month, when the priests of Thoth think me enfeebled."

The priests of Thoth did not merely think it. They knew it. Discreet for once, Amenufer forbore to declare that aloud. Besides, he disagreed with the first part of Kamose's assertion.

"I'm less sure, holy one. The Archpriest of Thoth, Beba—"

"—is pompous, righteous, dull, timid, and opposed to plotting, no doubt because he would do it very badly. Yes, O Amenufer. I know him. Yet someone bolder than he, at some rank in his temple's hierarchy, is plotting. Someone hatched the plan to discredit me by stealing the late Pharaoh's heart scarab. It surely was not Beba."

"Do you know his name, holy one?"

"I shall, in time, provided I survive the full moon. After all, what should I do, were I a priest of Thoth, emetic as the thought may be, and wished to make an end of Kamose? And knew that Kamose is now in retreat at his mansion near Abdu? An assassin's knife or garrote? Poison?"

"You joke with me," Amenufer protested. "All men know you are immune to poison, holy one."

"And have I not warned you before against believing what 'all men know'? But assume it is true. I am guarded by temple soldiers and by entities not mortal. We may discard those possibilities, if my adversary is not a complete fool. There remains magic. Come, Amenufer, you are a trained lector-priest, and lately belonged to the Temple of Thoth. What magic would you employ?"

"The sorceries of Thoth call for spoken or written spells. I should use the latter. Who spoke a hostile incantation in your retreat would be likely to find dire fangs at *his* throat before he had finished."

"How would you introduce a written curse or spell to my retreat, and keep me oblivious thereto?" Kamose asked gently. "Bear in mind that I expect such a thing."

"There must be many ways." Amenufer could think of several at once, yet he did not wish to seem too fertile in invention where spells to Kamose's disadvantage were concerned. "I, I have heard of sending a secret message tattooed on the scalp of a courier, after letting the hair grow to cover it. It might be done thus."

"It might; it has been." Kamose spoke dismissively. He had employed the trick himself in the reign of Usermare, Rameses the Great, while sending spies among the Hittites and the Syrian princes. In these days it was hackneyed and well-known. (If it sprang to Amenufer's callow, academic mind, it had to be extremely well-known.)

"Ill-wishers of mine," Kamose said, "have even inscribed curses on walls of this mansion which were to receive new murals, and then plastered over them, prior to the painting. They intended to creep out and scrape off the plaster at night, before moonrise, so that the White Disk at its height would touch the curse with its radiance."

The smooth comely face before him showed consternation. "But then, holy one—but then—some such malediction could be anywhere on your estates! The brow-band of a horse in the stables, the underside of a plug-hatch at the granaries, a roof-garden, a—"

"In short, anywhere. You babble."

Amenufer flushed angrily. Princely pride surged above the practiced subordination of the lector-priest. "No. I babble not at all. You have been absent from these estates for years; the granaries have been rebuilt and enlarged, and a new garden made adjacent to the main courtyard. Other renovations have been performed. A thousand places could contain some potent, hostile written spell. Can you search them all?"

"Such a written spell must be exposed to full moonlight before it becomes active. My minions are bound by the strictest curfew on nights of the full moon, O Amenufer; none stirs from his quarters between dusk and dawn, on pain of being stricken blind. This includes your princely self, if perchance you had thought otherwise, as from your manner of speaking just now I daresay you did."

Anger seethed more resentfully still in the young lector-priest. Yet he restrained it. Better and more harrowingly than most did he know the powers of that hard-muscled figure in the black linen kilt and skull-cap, and the unforgettable, hideous reasons he had to hold the ibis-headed lord of magic in such hatred. Amenufer knew what had happened to Kamose's wife and children, long ago. Also, to his horror, he had seen the Arch-priest's skull-cap removed. He shuddered even now at the recollection.

"I am accustomed to guarding myself against all manner of sorcerous attacks at the full moon," Kamose said. "I am still here. All that you said, and a thousand other things, are thought of. Be content and come within. You must read and practice the first stage of the malediction against the moon. Utter precision is required."

He understated. Failing utter precision, one would be left a mewling lunatic when the cursing turned against oneself. Although Amenufer feared the rituals, he perforce obeyed. But he turned his handsome, shaven head to survey the mansion's environs with a last dubious look. Built atop a grey and buff scarp at the desert's edge, its maze of colonnades, terraces, gates, courts and gardens formed a greater sprawl than most nomarchs' palaces. Conspicuous even in this dark splendor were the rich chapels and shrines to various gods; gentle Osiris, the mummy-wrapped Lord of Resurrection (in which Kamose believed not at all, nor desired to); Isis, the Great Enchantress; and fierce Set, master of desert and storm. Largest and richest of all rose the chapel of Kamose's own particular patron, Anubis, Lord of Tombs, the jackal-headed mortuary god, Announcer of Death, Opener of the Ways, Guardian of the Judgement Balance.

His image was everywhere. From the pyloned main gateway, a long avenue sloped downward, between a double row of couchant jackals, man's height, carved out of black diorite. The shield of every guard in the barracks carried the emblem. Craftsmen and painters in the workshops reproduced the likeness of Anubis incessantly. Beside the stone quays lining the canal dug from the Nile, aloof from the various barges and transport boats, even from the swift courier vessels, Kamose's personal galley was moored, long and dark. Its prow bore as a figurehead that same ubiquitous sable shape with the pricked ears and narrow cynoid muzzle.

Somewhere, anywhere, on this vast estate, this almost-kingdom, the priests of Thoth might have concealed a deadly spell. Anywhere. How could even Kamose, with his powers at low ebb, guard against their machinations? The funereal patron to whom he paid such constant honor had best be generous with the dark mantle of his protection, if he cared to keep the service of his Archpriest much longer.

II.

Kamose stood alone in his private chapel to Anubis, which also served him as a divination chamber. Fatigue seeped through him, settling into his bones like leaden corruption. The demon's claw-marks burned on his rib cage, a dull, hungry pain. He knew well that he looked haggard and ill. Amenufer, the young fool, probably feared he was dying.

Kamose knew better. He would survive this affliction and recover in a season, two at the most, provided his foes failed to destroy him in the meantime. They would surely try. He enjoyed the hatred of many.

Weakness draws hyenas, he thought bleakly.

Somewhere in this citadel or on his estates, a spell had been inscribed that was meant to destroy him. That was nearly certain. Stringent though his safeguards were, no precautions could be perfect.

Kamose gave thanks that he still possessed his immense sorcerous knowledge, and a skill in divination without equal—the latter being a special domain of his patron, Anubis.

Kamose bowed low before the image and altar. The statue of Anubis stared enigmatically forward. As always, the scarlet tongue lolled from his narrow black muzzle and a dagger glittered in each of his hands, while the traditional viper of royal doom coiled about one forearm. This puissant lord of tombs and necropolises equaled Thoth in power, and Kamose had rendered him long, impeccable service.

With expert dignity that concealed his desperation, he burned incense and asked the god's blessing. Bowing again, he turned about, looking towards the chapel door. Sunken in the floor was a bowl-shaped divination pool, rimmed with malachite and lined with blackened silver—a metal somewhat scarcer than gold in Egypt. It had been filled to the brim with water from a sacred temple lake. Incised at the bottom was a formal image of the god, striding forward.

"Lord of Tombs," Kamose intoned, "Announcer of Death, you who foresee destiny, give your servant knowledge of those who would undo him. Whom do you see? Whose shadow falls on the future? What is the instrument of their design against me? O Guardian of the Balance, Opener of the Ways, Master and Giver of the Secrets of Embalming, reveal it!"

The water grew limpid and transparent as air. Anubis's image moved, walking forward and passing from sight, to be succeeded by a procession of other divinities. Kamose had given offense to only a few of them; with most of the great ones he stood in favour, particularly Isis, mistress of magic, and Set the Defender, fierce lord of storms and the desert.

These and others appeared, moving through Kamose's intent field of vision, until at last—inevitably—Thoth, ibis-headed and crowned with a lunar disk, presented himself. The water of divination roiled, clouding over, as though the divine scribe was determined to obscure any enlightening sign. No doubt he was. Thoth knew unequivocally that Kamose was not his friend. The potent corrosive curses he leveled against the moon each month gave steady reminders of his hatred.

Kamose controlled that hatred. He coerced his spirit to clarity in the face of that most detested of all sights to him, ibis-headed Thoth, and gazed more intently into the water.

Kamose's patron returned, long jackal's muzzle grimly shut, confronting Thoth face to face in his representation of a formal image. For a moment the water cleared to the transparency of air. Above the heads of the two deities Kamose saw—briefly—a hieroglyph of a crouching lion, silver-white, with strange shadowy markings like those on the moon. Its visage appeared deformed, the profile malign and menacing.

The visions vanished, and the sacred water darkened. Mephitic bubbles rose to its surface. Anubis had given his votary a warning, and Thoth, apparently, had prevented complete or clear revelation. Kamose's lips thinned with bitterness, and he mentally reviewed a new phrase or two for adding to his curses against the moon.

The moon. And a lion white as the moon, bearing shadows like those of that blighted, devastated corpse of a world. Very likely a demon. Although Kamose believed—with reason—that he knew every demon in the Underworld, there were fiends of other realms and transmundane spheres with which he was not familiar. This might be one.

Anubis had warned him of it, despite Thoth's interference. Kamose trusted the Lord of Tombs. And Thoth's intervention confirmed, to a high degree, the involvement of his priesthood and temple—which in turn meant a written or inscribed spell to invoke the demon at the most potent time. Thoth, after all, was lord of both magic and writing. The most potent time would be the full moon. It always came back to that.

Kamose sat cogitating, while behind his grim face his brain chilled with an onset of fear. His enemies knew his weakened state, and they had prepared a doom for him. They had more realistic hopes of bringing it about now than at any time for decades. Well, he still had his wits, and greater arcane knowledge than all of them combined.

He quelled the fear. Fear was worthless; it had never in all of time achieved a thing. While the water of divination often did, it had surely not achieved much today. Kamose's facial muscles stood out starkly through his skin as he reviewed the alternative choices he knew. The most promising one—was the most desperate, also. More than two decades had passed since he last employed it. Did the present situation warrant such a measure?

He concluded that it did.

III.

Kamose sat in the great thronelike chair in his hall of audience. He wore nothing but black sandals, a pleated black kilt and the skull-cap which hid his hideously burned pate whenever he did not cover it with a ceremonial wig. Only his chief apprentice accompanied him. This man, a renegade priest from the Faiyum, wore a macabre goat-mask through which he breathed with effort, having stuffed it with sachets of protective herbs and spices. He would need them.

At the Archpriest's left, a small charcoal brazier glowed scarlet. He held a crystal casket in his right hand. The apprentice's masked gaze shifted in trepidation between the casket and the brazier—and he was a man of far stronger nerves than most.

"Watch me closely," Kamose commanded, "with your eyes and your wizard's senses. If my body moves or cries out, you will know that your aid is needed, and then—you must approach me and open that bottle you hold. Ensure that I breathe its vapors in, but for your life do not breathe them yourself, or doff that mask within this hall."

"I apprehend, holy one. Must you do this?"

"It appears so. Now be still."

Kamose opened the casket. It contained shimmering jetty dust—the pollen of a lethal flower which had grown in former ages of the world and been rare even then, which men had called the black lotus in vulgar parlance. Now it was extinct by any name. To Kamose's knowledge, greater than any other man's sorcerous knowledge, he possessed all of the dreadful dust which remained.

He measured five pinches over the glowing brazier, and leaned forward to breathe the smoke which arose in a thick, constant ribbon from the coals. The apprentice held his breath in fear, even at his distance, and within the protective mask. The effect of that atramentous dust in its first stages was a deathlike trance and such ghastly, burning nightmares as would leave most men insane. Some even averred that they were not mere nightmares, but glimpses of a monstrous reality beneath the bubble-thin skin of that which normal humans perceived and called existence. The apprentice did not know. He had long been completely aware, though, that his master was no normal human being.

Kamose's body arched in his black seat of power, slowly growing rigid. The lips lifted from his teeth in a grinning rictus. His heart hammered wildly, stumbled, then beat with leaden slowness. His breathing all but ceased. The smoke from the brazier drifted towards him, wreathing about his head in close eddies like some noxious coif. Like a live and predatory thing.

The apprentice watched with morbid fascination as the grisly nightmares his master experienced racked his body with slow, tetanic rigors. Once, he screamed appallingly out of his trance, and at the mere sound, the apprentice twitched in a spasm. He had read in ancient papyri that these nightmares increased a man's sorcerous powers and inured him to the fear inspired by demons—but he wondered if it was worth the price and if, should he ever dare them himself, his mind would survive.

The stage of nightmares passed. Kamose drifted on a great dark river. Here and there it bubbled, and the bursting turgesences vented sounds like wails of utter despair. Along the vague shore, spirits struggled, sometimes in formless conflict with each other, sometimes alone, always sloughing memory, essence, self in a sliding descent to nothingness.

The river itself flowed to the same destination. Even the monstrous fiery serpents which reared out of its waters, bringing ruin and swift annihilation to all they touched, were but manifestations of the river's force, doomed at last to the same end as their prey, for all their power and violence.

Running its course, the river spilled out into emptiness, a vast terrible void. It diverged in a multitude of aimless waterfalls, which in turn became a dreary mist, thinning to infinity. Willing it ferociously, Kamose retained form, assuming the shape of a scarlet vulture, a burning shape with wide ragged wings, drifting through nullity towards—cessation, oblivion.

He was not alone.

Something else existed, a monster of deeper darkness whose presence was instead an *absence,* its vast coils stretching through the void, the serpents that had infested the river being as threadworms beside it. This was the essence of annihilation and chaos, the end from which no new beginning comes, before which even time dissolves. Men gave it a name. Apep, the Destroying Serpent, they called it, and withdrew their thoughts from it in terror.

The immense blank head hurtled towards Kamose.

He did not flee. Nothing successfully flees from Apep. If Kamose truly confronted the Destroying Serpent, he was doomed, for all his potent magic. If, instead, it should be a vision of the black lotus, he might survive. With a scream of raging defiance, he flew straight into that gape an infinity wide, and vanished.

Vanished—from the void—and appeared again, drifting on wings of burning scarlet above his own estates near Abdu.

His ghostly eyes saw magic as distinctly as fleshly eyes see the spots of a leopard. Whatever was sorcerous in nature blazed with a scarlet fire akin to his own, from his personal galley moored at the canal quay, to the approach of a caravan of strange beasts with stranger drivers, plodding in a line far out in the western desert—and all inscribed or written spells, no matter how minute, no matter in what fashion concealed. The vulture's eyes saw everything.

He perceived the hieroglyph of a demon lion, close beside the main courtyard of his mansion.

That? So that is the way they introduced it!

Someone had been both devious and flaunting at once.

Kamose yearned to strike his vulture's beak into the culprit's liver and devour it by gradual degrees. He would, in time. Figuratively or literally, he would do it, after he had recovered his entire capacities.

Flying shapes whirled around him suddenly, flocking out of the waxing moon. They no more had flesh-and-blood substance than did he. They were spirits, lunar elementals in the shape of sacred ibises, the birds of Thoth, their slim curved bills sharp as lancets. Kamose's touch was fatal to them, and when the edges of their pale wings touched him, they shriveled as in a searing fire—but they also slashed his spirit, his *ba,* as if they had been honed sickles.

Kamose smote them with wings and talons. His great vulture's beak sheared heads from black necks, and though they were spirits, elementals, they perished nevertheless. Still, there were too many. Despite sending them down like blown leaves, Kamose weakened. Each stab of a down-curving ibis bill felt like a spear-blow. His former lordly glide turned to desperate flapping. He sank lower in the dark sky.

His estates, the canal, the river, rose around him. Something waited there, shackled to the earth—something that roared. Kamose knew much about desolation. He recognized the empty hopelessness in that roaring.

The sacred water had shown him a hieroglyph of a demon lion. Now he beheld the being itself. It bulked huge, thrice the size of a bull, moon-white and shade-grey. Its massive paws were swollen and deformed.

Nodules of leprosy marred its visage. A demon of disease, one of many that stalked the earth, like Namtar the plague fiend he had conjured once in far-off Babylon.

Kamose's enemies had gained control of this one. Lunging against its shackles, it roared again, showing teeth like pickaxes and a gullet like a cavern. These were emblems, a manifestation in visual shape of a monstrous reality, but the thing's urgent craving to swallow him was no emblem. It was fact, it was truth. The multitude of ibis-bills stabbed at him, driving him to the lion's maw.

Let them succeed, and Kamose knew he would become the lion-fiend forever, a foul shape of the night whose touch brought leprosy—and worse, far worse, a subject of the god he bore such complete hatred.

Frenzied, he turned on the flock of spirits, ripping and breaking them, scattering them for a few precious moments. In that time of respite, he screamed from his vulture's throat, "Bring me back!"

His fleshly body arched on his throne of power, and those same words burst from his human mouth as a command. The masked apprentice obeyed at once, dashing to his master's side, tearing the waxed stopper from the bottle he held. Its contents, phoenix blood on which basilisks had breathed, bubbled out in curious golden fumes.

Kamose's body sucked desperately at that amazingly potent distillation. As though carried on a desert storm, his *ba* appeared in the audience hall, visible to the apprentice's eyes—which, trained and inured though they were, flinched from the bright, terrible scarlet of its master's spirit shape. The great vulture settled over Kamose's human form and, merging with it, found safety from the dread, imminent peril which had threatened him.

Kamose's faintly oblique eyes focused on his apprentice. "You did well," he said thickly. "Leave now."

The apprentice left, on the instant. Even his mask might not have protected him from those vapors, had he dared linger. There were perhaps three other magicians in the world who could have breathed them into their lungs and survived.

Fatigue filtered through Kamose's flesh and bones like poison. The demon's talon-marks throbbed on his torso. Nevertheless, he smiled, and it was not a smile his enemies would have found reassuring.

"Clever," he whispered. Too weary to speak the words aloud, he thought, *if it had succeeded.*

Someone had expected that he would seek to discover the spell being employed against him. Someone had invoked the power of Thoth to baffle his attempt at divination. The same schemer had foreseen that Kamose would leave his body when other measures failed, and that same person had sought to merge Kamose's soul forever with a demon of hideous illness. Almost with success. Had Kamose been less skilled and prepared, there would have been no "almost."

Was this the end of it? Perhaps. But Kamose thought not. The actual spell, the hieroglyph of the white lion, still existed on his estate, waiting for the moon to enter its full phase—accursed orb of Thoth!

Now, though, he knew where it was. He would concede it had been introduced and concealed in a clever fashion. Indeed, someone had organizing talent. Kamose thought about it, his look wholly malign. Neither that nor any other characteristic the person possessed would save him, once Kamose's spies uncovered his name. And already it was clear that it could only be someone highly placed in the Temple of Thoth.

A matter for later. Kamose sat brooding on the fate he had just escaped, while the vapors of phoenix blood dissipated from his hall. His enemies had invoked a doom, the lion of leprosy, which he now inferred had its lair on the moon—hated world of barren desolation! Nor had he seen the last of the demon yet.

Until it appeared, he would content himself with his periodic cursing of its abominable lair. Alas, alas that he was weakened, and his maledictions would carry less corrosive efficacy on this occasion. Not on that account would the passion behind them abate, however; not on that account would he omit them.

Never.

IV.

The rising moon was a perfect milky circle. Kamose, gaunt and sunken-eyed, raised his face towards it with a glare that to his witnesses seemed insane. His massive, powerful chief apprentice, no longer masked, frowned across his heavy face. The steward of the household swallowed, hands moving restlessly as though he yearned to cover his ears. Kamose's newest acolytes, Amenufer and Reni, young men both and cousins of the new Pharaoh, glanced at each other with a mutual wish to be elsewhere—and their temperaments differed so greatly that it was rare for them to be in such perfect accord. A small group of scribes further down the portico set down their master's words with shaking hands, in a crimson ink blended of viper's poison, myrrh, and blood.

"Ancient my enemy, moon of desolation, fall from the sky and depart! Ancient my enemy, moon of baneful sorceries, fall from the sky and shatter! The knives of the gods dismember thee. The storms and whirlwinds of Set's Majesty destroy thee wholly. The fire of implacable Sekhmet the Lioness consume thee. Horus the Falcon avenge me upon thee and make thy name to perish out of time. Be thou feeble in the sky before Ra. Be thou devoured in thy passage through the Underworld by the great Destroying Serpent. The Lord of Terror who prepares the slaughter-block and dost feed upon the inward parts, he shall fasten thee in fetters, he shall cause thee to fall helpless into the Lake of Fire…"

The words spat and erupted from Kamose's writhing lips. He invoked demons whose very names were unknown to most sorcerers. He prescribed dooms and torments beside which slow dissolution in acid would have seemed a delight. The air curdled around him. The rising moon trembled as though seen through heat haze; a sullen, hectic crimson tainted its whiteness.

Kamose, chanting his imprecations, hoped wildly that this would be the time—the month when that abominated world shattered like a plate and left the sky forever. Hatred, black yearning made him almost believe it, though he had attempted the same thing so many times before in his full strength, without success.

Rubescence faded from the moon's surface. It continued to rise. Livid with disappointment, the Archpriest waited in the shadows of his balcony, a walled courtyard before him, his newest garden beyond it. The leaves themselves ceased rustling, as though in dreadful anticipation. Moonlight streamed down.

A tonitrous roar boomed over Kamose's immense estate. He had expected it. Reni and Amenufer saw his skullcapped head turn steadily to the left, looking towards the garden. Then, aghast, they saw a huge white shape leap atop the wall, a lion, but monstrously greater than any lion of a sane or normal world. The garden wall crumbled under its weight, tipping it into the moonlit courtyard.

Yellow eyes in a deformed visage fixed a hellish stare on Kamose. It trod purposefully forward on disease-swollen feet. The two lector-priests, who had endured the merest incurious flicker of the demon's gaze, recoiled shaking, but other than that, found they had been stricken immobile. They stood filmed in chill sweat.

The creature roared again.

It made another deliberate step towards the long balcony.

With a single leap, now, the demon would be able to reach it and fall upon Kamose. Very clearly, that was its purpose. Reni and Amenufer had the same terrified thought in their minds; what would Kamose do? He was acknowledged the greatest magician of Egypt, upper and lower combined. What would he do?

He did nothing at all.

The lion of leprosy crouched for its leap.

Smoothly, then, with hardly a grate of stone, the entire courtyard tilted on massive pivots, the side which faced Kamose and his minions tilting upwards, to expose a cuboid of deep blackness beneath. Sliding backwards, away from them, the demon fell into the pit. The courtyard paving fell back into place, with the ease of precise counterweighting and the irresistibility of hundred-ton granite slabs. A muffled, terrifying roar came from beneath the paving.

Amenufer cried out, and Reni voiced a smoking military oath. Even the chief apprentice goggled like a yokel; he had been ignorant of the device. His master had lived three times his years, and the courtyard had been constructed before he was born.

"Come," Kamose said calmly, but sweat of relief dewed his own countenance as he left the balcony.

They followed him in haste down hidden stairways and passages. A reek of boiling tallow filled the air as they neared Kamose's objective, an annular corridor where great heated crucibles stood in niches, evidently having just been emptied through conduits into the stone-lined pit below the courtyard. The foreman in charge of this function bowed low as his Archpriest approached.

"It is done, holy one. The monster does not seem much affected, though, and the deluge we gave it would scald an elephant to death!"

"I did not expect it."

Amenufer babbled. "Perhaps—perhaps it can even break out of this prison, after the way it shattered the garden wall!"

"Perhaps." Kamose answered, "provided it could gain a secure footing. Difficult, when it is ankle-deep in boiling tallow. When a demon takes material form, it becomes subject to many restrictions of matter."

"But with time, holy one—" Reni began.

Another of the demon's roars vibrated through the rock corridor walls. It sounded desperate. Not triumphant, menacing, or ireful—but desperate. Kamose showed bleak satisfaction.

"Time," he repeated, "is what I have gained while it slips and scrambles. In darkness, my children—in utterest darkness. There is sorcery and power in moonlight. This demon is a creature of the moon. Without access to moonlight, it falters, it weakens, and soon will be moribund." He smiled. "Simple solutions are often most efficacious. Mighty spells—should be saved for when they are truly needed."

"How did you know, holy one?" Reni asked, with greater awe than he had shown his Archpriest on any former occasion. His princely rank made him bumptious, and even a fearful encounter with a lamia (from which Kamose extricated him) had not wholly cured that. "That yonder monster would come through the courtyard?"

"A lesson for later. Now, witness, and be sure the monster ceases to exist. Before long, let us hope, since its outcry makes such indifferent music for mortal ears."

The striving horror roared again. Already its noise grew discernibly weaker. Kamose waited with arms impassively folded.

EPILOGUE

Reni and Amenufer were related to the royal clan, after all. Kamose found it politic to treat them with courtesy, even though one might be a headstrong, bombastic reveler and the other a scholarly lackwit. Therefore he gave them the honor of supping with him in private. His chief apprentice joined them, also, a man worth a hundred of either princeling in Kamose's view. However, he did little of the talking. Both younger men were afire with triumph and relief. No doubt their own parts in the story would become more central when they recounted it to their boon companions in future.

"Did you divine the threat in the sacred water, holy one?" Reni asked. "That the demon of leprosy would appear, and come through the courtyard in that shape of a monstrous lion?"

"I did not. A hostile influence marred the divination, O Reni. I perceived nothing, then, but the hieroglyph of a crouching white lion—a clue, indeed, but a somewhat ambiguous one. It became necessary to quit my fleshly body and seek further illumination in the spirit shape of my *ba*."

"A perilous measure," Amenufer said, showing off his occult knowledge before Reni, whose interests ran far more strongly to women, gambling and the hunt. "In spirit form one is vulnerable to evil magics that would have little effect on a magician in his corporeal house."

"I am glad to have you tell me," Reni said. Lector-priests were trained in magic, and despite his neglect of those studies, he knew that much.

"It proved most perilous this time," Kamose agreed. "My enemies desired and awaited such a step, and they sought to trap my spirit, bind it forever within the form of the demon of leprosy—vile eternal torment which gives a sure indication of their regard for me." His eyes glittered. "I shall ascertain the name of their leader and give him suitable proof of *my* regard, at some appropriate time."

"But they failed, holy one," Reni said, after an uneasy pause. "I presume you did learn where the spell to manifest the demon was concealed? Somewhere in that garden beyond the main courtyard?"

"Presumption," Kamose answered dryly. "The spell was the garden itself, which is new. It was constructed during the past two years, by my orders, yet in my absence." He spread a sheet of papyrus on a low table adjacent to their supper. "Here is a plan of it."

They stared uncomprehendingly for a few moments. The intellectual Amenufer grasped what he was seeing first. In competitive haste, he gabbled his revelation out.

"Yes! The whole garden is a hieroglyph—of a crouching lion! The gate and porter's lodge, here, form the mouth and muzzle, while these planted shrubs above it are the mane! The fishpond, here, is an eye. This approximate oblong of the main walled garden forms the body, and so it continues. These flower beds form the auxiliary glyphs. They hid it by making it too large to see!"

"True." Kamose said curtly. He drank strong dark wine that had not been drawn from earthly vines or trees. "They, whoever *they* may be, would be gratified that you admire their ingenuity. Still, they were unsuccessful, and there will be trails to follow in the discovery of who planned and designed this garden, who oversaw its construction."

"I do not understand how you had so cunning and huge a trap prepared for the demon, holy one." Reni puzzled over the question. "Did you perhaps make it by magic in one night, after you discovered the secret of the garden?"

"You, supposedly a priest, ask me that! I did not." Kamose's debilitated condition at present made any such thing impossible, though he had no intention of sharing that information. Certainly, at his best, he could have created such a mechanism in a single night, summoning demons and genii to perform his will, but hardly in secret; even young dolts like Amenufer and Reni would have noticed. "I constructed the courtyard trap long ago," he explained, "and not for demons. I foresaw the possibility of some large band of armed invaders swarming into it, daring to assail me in my own mansion. Libyans, perhaps." He added in the tone of a careless pleasantry, "It is not the only surprising device to be found on these estates."

While they considered that, clearly finding it a disconcerting notion, Kamose himself poured them a further drink. They took it as a matter of course, the mere due befitting their princely rank.

They were mistaken; the draught was nepenthe, which would cause them to forget the events of the night, though they did perhaps owe it to their standing that the liquor had not been fatal in its effects.

Kamose believed in keeping his secrets.

THE COMPANY OF THE GODS

Both by vulgar repute and in the minds of those who were fit to judge, Kamose ranked as the greatest magician of Egypt. No vizier or viceroy was feared as the Archpriest of Anubis. Or as little known by other human beings—some of whom, in any case, deemed him human no longer. This compound of fame, dread and mystery meant that more lies were told about him, and solemnly believed, than even about Pharaoh. The legends swarmed like locusts.

One purported to explain his allegiance to the jackal-headed mortuary god.

When a foolish, studious young priest (the legend averred) Kamose had sought and found the secrets of all magic contained in the Forty-Two Scrolls of Thoth. He copied them in sorcerer's ink, washed the ink from the papyrus and drank it mixed with an unearthly wine. Having done so, he acquired the knowledge permanently; not even the god could remove it.

Thoth was affronted, and sent a fearful retribution, so that Kamose lost his wife and children to death. He was also compelled to return the forty-two scrolls one by one, wearing fire on his head.

Thereafter he was insane for years, dwelling in the desert as a hermit, with jackals and vultures for company, and a cowl over the hideous burns on his pate. When he recovered his reason he left Egypt to travel the nations of the world, assimilating and practicing the magic he had learned.

Kamose returned to Egypt at last, a sardonic, powerful and supreme magician. After a certain momentous adventure in Damascus, he had also become quasi-immortal, and perhaps quasi-human withal—but Kamose by then had ceased to value his humanity over-much.

He still carried the displeasure and curse of Thoth, Lord of the White Disk, the One who Measures Time. Not even Kamose could ward himself against that; to live in Egypt again, he needed the shielding power of a god as great as the one he held in loathing.

*   *   *

There were others who desired the bond and service of a magician so lordly.

Crossing Sinai with a band of nomads, Kamose stood at dusk one night on the outskirts of the camp, the black goat's-hair tents behind him and the braying of asses in the cooling air. As usual, he wore a skull-cap over his seared scalp; it was a sight that even the tough-minded nomads did not care to behold. Or Kamose to display.

A small fierce sandstorm whirled out of nowhere. Lightning forked from the starry, pristine sky. Amid thunder, the storm ceased and the lacerating sand dropped to earth again. Nothing but the finest dust still remained airborne. Through that fulvous haze a shape trod towards Kamose.

It was manlike and powerful, wearing a warrior's kilt, yet the head was neither human—nor a mask. Bestial, it had a curious snout, long ears clipped square at the tip, and a mane of hair like a roan wild ass's. The scarred hands held a huge harpoonlike spear. Even Kamose felt his stomach clench as he met the ferocious look of the being's eyes.

He bowed—but not low. "Welcome, O Majesty of Set."

"I welcome you, O Kamose! You return to Egypt. The hostility of Thoth awaits you there. Vow yourself to my service, become my priest, and I undertake to protect you. Not even the ibis-headed wise one cares to affront me. That is *because* he is wise."

Kamose considered the offer—or the summons. Set could perform as he promised. Although many held him in low esteem because he was warlike and violent, still, he took his station in the prow of Ra's boat each evening as the ancient, senile sun-god made his journey through the Underworld prior to rebirth in the morning. Set with his terrible harpoon fought off the onslaughts of his ancient enemy, Apep the Destroying Serpent, to protect the helpless Ra through the night voyage. Hardly any god but he was mighty enough. For that reason, men called him Set the Defender.

Among other names.

Kamose reached his decision.

"I will not. Awe do I feel for you, mighty Set. But you are the patron of foreigners, and I have lived enough in foreign parts; the desert's lord, and I have lived enough in the sere desert. You are the master of storms and upheaval, while I seek an ordered life again. I will not serve you."

Set roared in wrath.

"O fraud! You are partly of alien blood yourself! Now for this insult I will place enmity between you and all tribes of foreign seed. For your life's days there shall be no friendly or trustworthy dealings between Egypt and other lands. When foreigners come against Khem in war, or when savage tribes invade, it shall ever fall upon you to turn them back, whether by sorcery, or espionage, or the assassin's deadly wine, since you boast a disdain for open war."

"Nothing in that," Kamose said, "differs at all from past centuries."

The sandstorm struck again, fiercely scouring skin from flesh, and lightning scattered the nomads' beasts. When the storm passed, Set had gone.

Kamose employed his magic and physician's skill to heal the injured among his hosts. He divined a water-source even they did not know, and broke it open so that they might drink deeply. This placated their anger. They muttered among themselves, but conveyed him to the Egyptian copper and turquoise mines of Sinai, where they bartered flesh and cloth and departed. They were glad to see the last of him.

Walking among the rocky crags and valleys of the mining outpost, Kamose saw a being shaped like a woman come to him at sunrise. Her shape was a wonder of symmetrical grace, her even-featured visage one of harmony and poise. A single tall ostrich feather trembled in her headdress.

"I am Ma'at," she said. "You refused the service of Set because he is violent and you seek order. I am order, justice and truth; I am that by which Egypt lives. Vow yourself to my service and priesthood, O Kamose, and you shall become the greatest, wisest judge the Two Lands have known. The ordered life you seek shall be yours, and honor besides."

"No, great one," Kamose said. "You are all that you say. But you are weak. Wherever war and turmoil arise, whenever greed for power overwhelms men—which is a frequent happening—then you are ignored. You fall into a deep, obscure pit; and only when some strong hand restores order by force are you even glimpsed again. Shall you protect me against the malevolence of Thoth? Shall he defer to you, observe justice and truth—he, who destroyed my wife and children for what I had done? I will not enter your service, nor be one of your priesthood."

The level eyes of Ma'at flashed. "You have chosen ill. I am justice, and you have rejected me. You have said that war and turmoil and greed are all greater than I. When these things come to trouble you in the future, look to your sorcery and cunning for help. Do not appeal to me! Expect no aid from justice or rightful order!"

"Lady of Truth," Kamose said sardonically, "I have known better than that for many years."

He continued on his way to Egypt and reached its eastern gate, the frontier fortress of Zaru. Once he had identified himself, and performed a service for the commander there, he was welcome. Still he lay restless in his chamber at night, fearful—even he—of Thoth's enmity now that he had returned to Egypt, and wondering which deity to take as his patron.

A presence appeared to Kamose at midnight. It possessed manlike form, wore the tall *atef* crown flanked by plumes, and held Egypt's emblems of divine kingship, the crook and flail. Its skin was green as a spring crop. The snowy linen wrappings of a mummy swathed it, and bound the legs together.

"I behold you," Kamose said, "Lord of the Quiet Heart."

Although he spoke imperturbably, his own heart pounded. Despite all, he remained mostly human; and this was Osiris.

"You know why I have come. I seek your service in devout probity for your life's days. Perform this, and I offer you life beyond the tomb in the Fields of Duat, life pleasant and blissful while your name endures. Life, moreover, with your family that perished, whom I and I alone can restore to you hereafter."

Kamose's heart hammered harder. His mouth dried completely and a deep yearning filled him. He parted his lips to croak yes.

But it had been too long since he was a believer. Too much harsh knowledge had come his way since he was a priestling and young married man. His mouth curled. Rebellion blazed in his deep-set eyes.

"Never think to deceive me! You promise what you cannot give! Those who worship you are cowards afraid of the dark. They will believe anything rather than believe their existence can cease, that death is ineluctable and final. *You* were treacherously killed and could not prevent it. What are you now? A feeble wraith, a ghost in funerary shrouding. You have nothing to offer me or anyone. Begone, shadow."

The figure wasted even fewer words than Kamose. It said only, "You will never enter the fields of the blessed, though your name resound to the ages and there be offerings made at your tomb for ten thousand years," and dissolved upon the air.

Eyes ablaze with a bitter pride, Kamose said to the empty room, "I knew that before you declared it."

He embarked upon a ship for the capital. That stage of his journey lay along one of the River's several branches in the Delta, between the Nineteenth Nome and the Fourteenth. A lovely, fertile region, swarming with fish and birds, its gardens lush, the granaries bursting, it would have gladdened a heart less filled with heavy concerns. Kamose needed a protector of divine and formidable power. Suppose the next to approach should be Thoth, bringing Kamose's doom?

At midday he sat brooding on the deck while the rowers bent and strained in a sweating double row. Then he heard water dripping on the deck behind him. A liquid voice said, "I greet you, Kamose, returned from exile."

Wearily, by now, the magician turned his aquiline head. The Nile god confronted him. Water streamed from skin blue as the River. The body was manlike, with a braided beard, but with bare pendulous breasts, suitable to the power that nourished Egypt. In the crook of each arm the figure carried a brimming vase. Water-plants crowned its head.

"My obeisance to you," came the answer, limitedly sincere, "Lord Hapi, you who flow through the Underworld, the sky, and through Egypt."

"Master of magicians, you know why I appear."

"Yes. I have received others."

"I, who provide food for gods and men, can ward you from the anger of Thoth—or the anger of Ra, if you had incurred it. Without my bounty they would both starve beside their worshippers. Become my servant and your cattle will wax fat, your fields flourish, your granaries be full."

"Less than Set, less than Ma'at, and less than Osiris, will I serve you," Kamose told him scornfully. "What are your promises worth? Your inundation bursts beyond all limits to whelm villages and towns. That, or your waters rise but slightly, so that harvests are meager and famine scourges Egypt. I have seen the granaries of your own temples empty, your own priests groaning with hunger, their sacrifices and loud prayers equally vain. This errand has wasted your time and mine. With fortune, I will see you no more."

"You will see me when my waters cover your vineyards and smash your vessels," Hapi answered, in a voice like rising flood-waters. "Plant your fields on the highest ground, and establish your harbors on canals far from my banks."

The figure departed. Kamose smiled bleakly and said, "I plan nothing less."

He arrived at the capital, Pi-Rameses, with its great royal palace built by the Lake of the Residence, its temples and the riverside mansions of the mighty. Kamose disembarked from the ship, a tall sinewy figure, with little in the way of baggage and nothing in the way of companions. He walked the thoroughfares of the city, looking at its temples, but he entered none; and once when he passed a shrine to Thoth, he spat on the ground before it. A childish gesture, and one which might have placed him in danger, but his hatred overwhelmed him. He hurried on.

He needed a divine patron and protector.

The sun god, Ra? No. Ra's power waned upon the earth when he entered his boat to travel through the Underworld in the hours of night, while the power of Thoth became greatest while the moon shone. He would be strong when Ra was weak.

Horus the sky-falcon was primarily a royal god. Kamose owned not one drop of royal blood. Ram-headed Amun, then, the paramount god of Egypt? The so-called "Lord of the Thrones of the World"? Kamose smiled cynically. Amun's rise, and his altered name of Amun-Ra, had been a matter of mortal politics after the princes of Thebes cast out the foreign rulers, the trebly-cursed Hyksos. Before that he had been an obscure local god represented by the symbol of a goose. Despite his ostensible greatness, no matter what wealth and power accrued to his temple, Kamose did not feel inclined to gamble on Amun against the antiquity, wisdom, and sorcerous power of Thoth.

While he sat considering, under a sycamore tree beside a well, a new shape crossed the courtyard towards him. This one resembled a woman, mature and ripely fertile, in a gown which bared her dark-nippled breasts. She wore the golden mask of a cow. One hand held a sistrum, while a girdle of golden sycamore leaves circled her waist.

"O Kamose, welcome to Egypt again."

"I salute you," he said with no evident joy, "great Lady Hathor."

"You know why I have come, and what is mine to give."

"Yes." Kamose's voice sounded like the stone lid of a sarcophagus grinding shut. "And I know who you *are*. Goddess of music, goddess of joy, she who protects pregnant women, watches over children.

"My wife was pregnant when the malice of Thoth destroyed her. Where were you? My children died of a like cause in the City of Bast, may it be overthrown and wholly forgot! Where were you? I would as soon enroll in the priesthood of that deceiving whore the cat-goddess as in yours. Say no more to me, Lady Hathor. I learned in the past what your protection is worth."

The mother-goddess turned rigid with incredulous anger.

"Woe to you, Kamose! You reject all that lies in my gift when you reject and revile me! Never think to marry again or have other children!"

She faded on the hot shimmering air.

Kamose laughed, as a crocodile weeps. "I've no such intention."

That night he did not sleep at all. In the hours before dawn, he walked on the rooftop above his chamber and gazed at the turning stars. With a greatly perturbed mind he considered his choices. Lacking some great deity's protection, he could not remain in Egypt so long as Thoth was hostile. And he would never make peace with that one. Yet he had given offense to several others.

Kamose knew he might depart again. Alas, his spirit sickened at the thought of doing so. It was rightly said that whoever had once drunk of Nile water would yearn to be by the Nile forever. Even for such as Kamose it was true.

"Magician."

The somber voice had a quality other than human. Kamose turned, sighing. He was weary of being approached by gods who sought his allegiance and had nothing to offer him.

On the far side of the roof stood a form taller than he. It wore a kilt, jeweled belt and collar. Below the glittering collar it was man-shaped; above, it had the head of a black jackal. Torches in the hands of two veiled attendants cast light on the narrow muzzle and high pricked ears. The attendants had the wild unbound hair and torn robes of mourners.

"Lord Anubis," the magician said, and felt his heart stir for the first time in some response of affinity. This, among his other titles, was the

Announcer of Death, and Kamose had walked unconcerned among the shadows of death for many years now. This, withal, was the guardian of tombs; and while Kamose had committed crimes of magnitude, violating tombs did not appear in the catalogue. He did not believe he had done that even when he plundered the Scrolls of Thoth, for in that case, the spectral inmate of the tomb where they were hidden had come to him and offered them, in exchange for a service. No. Among the gods, he had at least not outraged this one, nor had this one given him offense.

"You have shown yourself difficult to please, and careless whom you offend. What say you to me, then?"

"Say, Opener of the Ways?" Kamose spoke slowly. "I say that you are surely as ancient and wise as my enemy Thoth. As learned in magic. More skillful, if anything, in divination. You alone, not Ma'at or any other god, are just, for you, who are Death, treat all alike. Your vengeance falls on those who desecrate tombs of commoners and Pharaohs. Neither would any but a complete fool question your power.

"Therefore, I will swear myself to your temple and join your priesthood."

The jackal's voice said, "I will accept your service."

Kamose accordingly became a priest of Anubis and rose in the temple's hierarchy. That career, which began in the reign of Usermare, Rameses the Great, continued and prospered through the regnal years of Merenptah, Seti the Second, and Setekh-Nekht, whose death by Nubian sorcery he avenged in a way men shudder to relate. As Rameses the Third began his reign, Kamose was celebrated as Egypt's greatest magician, and had long been the funerary god's Archpriest. He stood high in the new Pharaoh's favor. Thoth's enmity, also, had not harmed him under the somber aegis of the Lord of Graves. It was thus agreed by most that his choice had been wise.

So they told the legend in the Two Lands of Khem.

THE ARCHPRIEST'S POTION

I.

Si-hotep had walked a number of dark and dangerous paths for the Archpriest Kamose. He had served him, though only occasionally and when called upon, for eight years. Now the summons had come again. This time it was unusual, in two respects. He had half expected it, could guess closely at the reason—and the work seemed easy for a man of his talents.

Usually the Archpriest's tasks were enough to make a hero sweat, and came as an utter surprise.

"It's true, then?" Si-hotep murmured. "Someone *did* try to steal our late god-king's heart scarab while he was being embalmed?"

"Not try." Wesu, the jeweler's scribe, shook his bald and shiny head. He was a thin man with scraggy wattles on his neck, squatting at a low table in a dusty back room amid a glitter of minerals and semi-precious stones. He looked at Si-hotep from sad pouched eyes. "The thing was done. They replaced the true emerald scarab with *this.*"

This, Si-hotep assumed, was the inlaid box Wesu clutched protectively in the crook of his arm.

"You had better open it," the thief said patiently, "unless I'm expected to find the reprehensible one who made the thing without ever gazing upon it."

Wesu silently opened the casket. Within rested a green stone gem in the shape of a beetle, its base clasped in shining metal. Lifting it out, he set it on the acacia-wood table. Si-hotep examined it briefly, turning it over to scan the blessing cut on the flat underside in classic hieroglyphs and rubbing the metal setting.

"Malachite and gilded lead. The workmanship is fine, though. Few could match that."

"And there are no errors in the inscription," Wesu added. "Whether the craftsman is fully literate or not, he knows enough to copy a blessing or text with precision. He's had training—a good deal of training."

Si-hotep lifted an eyebrow, but allowed Wesu his attempt at superiority. The thief had trained as a scribe and artist in a temple school himself as a boy—had been the swiftest learner there, but kicked over the traces at being expected to match his pace to the slower boys, and far worse than that, ask no irreverent questions. He could judge the copied inscription's accuracy well enough.

"The holy one believes it was done less to steal a great gem than to disgrace him."

"It's likely," Si-hotep agreed. "Who could sell a gem so huge? An emerald at that? But having it vanish, when it was supposed to be buried within the Pharaoh's body—that would indeed make the Archpriest look inept. Or worse."

"He presided over the embalming. However, he also discerned the substitution and found the true heart scarab in time to replace it. Someone had hidden it in his own temple."

"Discerned the substitution," Si-hotep echoed. His mouth quirked. "Can you not say he saw through the trick, like anybody else? Where is your master Ganesh? I ought to be talking to him, not his scribe."

"My master is in Syria, organizing a caravan and buying gems," Wesu said curtly. "I speak for him at such times. And the holy one commands that you find who plotted this theft. He is certain it was some high-ranking priest in the Temple of Thoth."

"So?" Si-hotep's sharp-boned face grew thoughtful. "Well, they have been his enemies for long. It's how he became the greatest magician in Egypt, they say—by stealing the Scrolls of Thoth, long ago. Not *their* Archpriest, though, I take it? Not pompous fat Beba?"

"Kamose, the holy one, says never. He hasn't the wits or daring. Beba became Archpriest of Thoth because he was the one candidate bland enough to content everybody. It's some ambitious underling, surely."

"And he's covered his tracks well, if Kamose doesn't know his name by now. But that is of no concern to me. I'll find this artisan for him."

"One place you need not waste time seeking him is in the Temple of Thoth."

"Teach your grandmother to suck eggs," Si-hotep retorted. "Of course not. Were the counterfeit scarab made there, even Beba might have noticed."

Wesu grimaced. He had never liked the thief's confidence or aplomb, less because of his wickedness than because he seemed to enjoy life, while

Wesu himself was a disappointed failure drudging his days away. He also disliked the last thing he must do in this conference, but the Archpriest Kamose had commanded it, and what he commanded, one did not ignore.

"Our master sends this," he said, reaching for a tiny crystal bottle which shone among the litter on the writing-table. "His express order is that you use it only if the need is dire."

"And how is it used?" the thief asked. He did not reach for it.

"You drink the contents—if you must. It gives one the power to walk through walls. For an hour, more or less, depending on how large you are."

Si-hotep whistled softly. "If that potion were made in quantity, there would be no skilled thieves left before long!"

"It cannot be made in quantity. Griffin's blood is one of the constituents, I'm told. The bottle holds three doses."

"Three? The holy one is generous." Si-hotep turned the bottle in his fingers. There were tiny hieroglyphs cut in one side, next to gradation marks. Without hesitation, he pried out the stopper and poured one precise dose into his wine.

"Are you mad?" Wesu cried, aghast. "Did you hear me? You know what it is to disobey the holy one! His express order is that you drink it only—"

"If need is dire. I heard you. Believe me truly, scribe, I am not about to swallow this. You are."

In a sudden, inexorable movement, the thief held the cup to Wesu's mouth and a small bronze dagger to his scrawny neck.

"I suspect poison," he said. "Drink. Or I open your wind-pipe."

The knife-point dug painfully towards the cartilaginous airway he had mentioned, and a thin red thread ran down. Wesu opened his mouth to protest. Si-hotep poured the wine between his lips. Before the scribe could vent one cough, Si-hotep dropped his dagger, clamped Wesu's head and jaw immovably with one arm, and pinched his nostrils shut with the other hand. Wesu struggled madly, but he was small, of sedentary habits. Although not a large man himself, Si-hotep seemed to be made of bowstrings and braided leather. He held the scribe with ease. Wesu's choking and spluttering, confined within his head, seemed about to burst his ears, but in the end, the wine had nowhere to go but down his throat. He slumped across the table with streaming eyes. Si-hotep forced the remainder of the cup upon him. Wesu, cowed, imbibed it all.

Si-hotep watched him with a grimmer face than usual. Forcing what might be some hideous bane down a man's throat was no light matter, even to him, ready as a rule for most crimes and any mischief. But—rather Wesu than himself.

Wesu cursed in vile phrases. "You hyena-sired whelp of a whore! Why did you do that?"

"Because the holy one," Si-hotep said, using the phrase with edged irony, "is beset by priestly and political enmities, and those are bad for an honest thief. No matter how useful I have been to him now and then, if I should be caught this time, he might prefer that I stayed eternally silent. Or—he might send a potion that does no more than clear water, just to make me bolder. I mean to know. Be cheerful, little man. Think what you'll be able to do with the power to walk through walls for an entire hour!"

Wesu's lifetime of frustrated fantasies glared in his eyes as he considered that. Then fear replaced it.

"It may be poison as you say!"

"That never troubled you when you thought it would be in my stomach."

"The Archpriest of Anubis will punish you as you've never dreamed in nightmares!"

"I doubt," Si-hotep said, "that he will think you worth it. How long until you gain this wondrous ability to walk through walls? Has it begun yet?"

Wesu blinked, then screwed up his short-sighted eyes. "I feel strange. The room looks strange."

"How?" Si-hotep asked sharply.

"The light—it has changed! It's pale grey now. It comes from everywhere and makes no shadows. The walls, the door. They shift... they slide... it is as though... I see past them."

This puzzled Si-hotep. "Do you mean, through them?"

"No! Past them! I see past this room to the courtyard outside. A brindle dog is there, lifting its leg against the wall. The same sort of shadowless light is there that comes not from the worshipped sun." Wesu flinched and covered his eyes. "It has an evil look."

It sounded unwholesome, and Si-hotep felt more pleased than ever to have tested the potion on someone else. Yet none of this told him what he most wished to know. He seized the scribe's chin in his fingers.

"Tell me this. Can you *walk* through that wall in the same way that you see through it?"

"I can. I can do more—see!"

Wesu closed the empty casket before him with a shaking hand, and fastened its catches. Then, clutching the green stone scarab, he lunged his hand at the box.

Si-hotep watched intently. Despite owning quick hands and a quick mind—despite knowing all there was to know about legerdemain and surreptitious theft from the person—he did not quite perceive what happened. He saw Wesu's skinny hand vanish into, or past, as he had said, or even *behind* the closed box in some baffling trick of perspective. When it returned to his field of vision, it no longer held the scarab.

Narrow-eyed, deeply suspicious of craft, the thief thumbed open the catches. He tilted back the casket lid. The malachite back of the carven beetle gleamed within. Si-hotep wordlessly lifted it out. If a duplicate, it was exact to the tiniest detail, even a minute disproportion of one of the hieroglyphs on the underside. Also, the casket was too shallow, its sides and base too thin, for any trickery with hidden compartments.

That, of course, did not prove there had been no sleight-of-hand. Si-hotep had seen priestly magicians do far more impressive things which he nevertheless *knew* were trickery. Wesu was no priestly magician, though, and from the frightened way his eyes were shifting, his actions had been no trickery. Si-hotep doubted he could act that convincingly, either.

"Walk through that wall," he said again. He knew of no way to counterfeit that. If Wesu performed the act, his potion must have the properties claimed for it.

The little scribe did not seem to be listening. Rather, his eyes bulged with horror as he scanned Si-hotep's face. He pointed a shaking finger.

"I see beneath your skin! Eyeballs in red sockets, Si-hotep! Flayed muscle and pulsing veins! I see, I see, I see!"

"What? You are mad or drugged, little man! My skin is still with me!"

"I see past it. And your ribs!" Wesu's eyes glittered with revulsion—and, it seemed, a sudden feeling of power. "If I wished I could reach past them and tear out your lungs!"

Si-hotep, startled, backed away a couple of paces, showing his small deadly knife. It was possible, to be sure. If that potion allowed a man to reach into a closed casket without opening or breaking it, then, just as truly, he might reach into a man's chest—but Wesu lacked the quickness, especially after giving warning. Let him try and Si-hotep would fillet his arm.

"It's unsafe to say such things to me, my friend," he murmured. "I am still waiting for you to walk through a wall."

Wesu sneered, turned around, and did precisely that. Si-hotep's mouth fell open. Had anybody else been in the dusty little room with him he would have controlled the impulse; it had been a long time since he betrayed amazement or dismay. Then he realized that Wesu might be looking in through the solid wall—or *past it*, as he insisted on saying. Past a solidly enclosed room? Past a solidly enclosed chest cavity, for that matter? Past them in what possible direction? It made no sense!

He adjusted his features to an expression of sardonic self-possession nevertheless. Those were matters for considering later. Plainly, the potion did come from the Archpriest of Anubis, and plainly it did everything claimed for it. Maybe even somewhat more.

Si-hotep reasoned that the Archpriest would never have sent it unless he conceived his agent might require it desperately. It was important to him that Si-hotep's quest should succeed. Therefore, if he took this precaution, he must expect the thief to encounter supernatural trouble somewhere along the way.

A sobering notion.

In the meantime, though, Wesu had gained the power to enter any sealed vault, any treasure chamber in this huge rich city. Si-hotep's professional instincts came to the fore. To waste the opportunity this brought would be coward's folly. Watching the blank wall, he saw the scribe appear again, coming through (past? around?) the solid barrier in a subtle and baffling shift of perspective that human vision could not encompass.

Wonderful!

Si-hotep welcomed the scribe enthusiastically, and then called on his most fluent and affable powers of persuasion.

II.

Planning and perpetrating a robbery of sufficient scope to do justice to such amazing opportunity, all within an hour, would have been beyond even Si-hotep, except that he had considered and reconnoitered many potential jobs in the city. Layout, contents, methods of entry and departure, he had studied it all, and he remembered the relevant information. Some he had discarded as not being feasible.

Naturally, Wesu's sudden ability to walk through walls changed all past definitions of feasible.

"Khentau's treasure vault?" the little scribe babbled. "That thieving official? I have heard of it, and of the ways his house is secured, but it will not thwart us now!"

"You may have heard," Si-hotep said, stepping through the dark streets of Hikuptah, "but I *know*. His mansion is closest of those I have studied with a view to raiding. Important, you will agree. We have but an hour."

Wesu snapped his ink-stained fingers exuberantly. "Long enough, O Si-hotep!"

"Gods of Khem! I am glad you approach the business in such high spirits," the thief said, amused. "Just keep your head and do as I tell you."

The little scribe's state reminded him, in fact, of a man become merry-drunk. His fantastic new power had gone to his head and given him the daring for a nefarious adventure. Si-hotep doubted he had been able to find the nerve for an adventure of any sort in all his timid life before.

So, then. It was past due. And this night was the night.

"That dim grey light you told me of. Do you still see it?"

"I do indeed! Ever since drinking the potion! It comes from everywhere. Even in shadows and dark alleys, it is the same."

"Then I hope it will also be the same for you within the vault. You will not have to trouble with a lamp. What is it like when you walk through a wall? I have asked this before and had no good answer."

"Curious," answered the scribe, pensively though not very illuminatingly. "It's as though two different vistas open before me—one, whatever lies directly on the wall's other side, and if I look a little differently, even narrow my eyes or turn my head, some other, having nothing to do with it. That first time, in the back room of the jewelry workshop, it was a thicker grove of trees than I ever saw before, and of an unknown kind, green-gold in a strange cool daylight! I did not like it. I would not have stepped in that direction unless a lion were behind me."

"Strange, indeed!" Si-hotep agreed. Having lived all his life in Egypt, he could scarcely imagine cool daylight, and rather thought Wesu must be embroidering. "Just be sure, when you walk through the treasure vault wall, if another way also opens before you, pay no heed—not if it leads into the women's quarters of the royal palace. Fix your eyes and mind on the loot."

"I'll deviate not a finger's width," Wesu promised. He chuckled. "I'm a poor man."

"Not after this night."

"Half shares, remember!"

"I have seldom worked with a partner," Si-hotep said, "but when I did, I never cheated one unless he began the game. Half shares, yes. I advise you to remember it also. Maybe you could tear out my lungs without breaking my skin, as you said, but you will never have the opportunity, and if you did—the Archpriest still wishes me to do him a service. He would have something dire and final to say to you if you deprived him."

Wesu shivered. "Half shares."

Neither man felt worried to excess by what the Archpriest might do about their thieving. Si-hotep had looted freely from officials, traders and even temples. The Archpriest of Anubis had never objected, either in person—Si-hotep had not met him, nor did he desire to—or through his underlings.

It went without saying that Si-hotep had never robbed any temple or shrine of Anubis, the jackal-headed lord of tombs and the mortuary process. Kamose would most assuredly have objected to that. Although tomb-robbing had been a constant curse in Egypt since before the pyramids, it had declined sharply when Kamose rose to head the Temple of Anubis; only madmen engaged in the practice now. The somber archpriest appeared quite indifferent to the robbing of other temples—particularly Thoth's. As for robbing Khentau, he might well think that a virtuous action.

A wide area of patterned brick paving fronted the official's mansion. It possessed an outer wall too high for anything but the house's roof to be seen beyond it, and too strong for anything but an elephant to break. The builder had set no opening therein but a heavy gate, while the porter's lodge beyond it was more like a guardroom, which the porter never left during the hours of darkness, and for good reason. So Si-hotep informed his companion in a murmur.

"But why?"

"Because there is a great white baboon of evil disposition turned loose in the front garden, and a watch-leopard at the rear. All the human guards are within the house."

"Then how am I to reach it?" Wesu almost yelped. "Even though I may walk through walls, I cannot fly, or fight deadly beasts."

"I will deal with the beasts," Si-hotep answered. (He would not have expected Wesu to deal with a house cat.) "You need do nothing but wait until I signal you. There will be a mighty commotion, but that will only mean that my plan is working as it should. Do not run when you hear it."

"Commotion?" Wesu said uneasily.

Si-hotep took the scribe by his scrawny throat.

"Think of the loot; half shares. Think of this too. If you do run, I will catch you, and cut your throat when I find you."

He led Wesu towards the rear of Khentau's mansion wall and pushed him into hiding.

"Stay."

He had gone before the last sound of his whisper faded on the air. Wesu looked and listened in vain for any traces of him. It was as though Si-hotep had dissolved in the dark.

Lean, compact and relentlessly self-trained, he stood by the outer wall of the mansion. He carried no tools except a coil of supple cord woven out of women's hair and oryx sinew, with a tough wooden hook at one end and a noose at the other. Despite its thinness, it could almost have moored a trading ship. Si-hotep tossed it to the top of the wall, climbed without dislodging it again, and lay flat for a moment, scanning the gardens below. In front, towards the porter's lodge, were flower-beds, shrubs and an ornamental fishpond; to the rear, fruit trees, lettuce patches, and such. The mansion itself, and other formidably high walls at either side, separated the two areas.

Si-hotep squirmed along the top of an inner wall, glancing towards the back of the house. A man five paces distant could hardly have heard him, but he knew the leopard would. Yes, here it came. Loping in disciplined silence, it reached the foot of the wall, glaring up at him with eyes like yellow flames. It crouched to spring.

A slinky running noose dropped over its head and tightened.

Si-hotep stood, bracing himself atop the wall, and heaved the leopard off its feet. It writhed wildly, a hard-muscled, twisting burden that nearly yanked him down, but the thief pulled it higher and then swung it like a plumb-bob, back and forth, higher with each straining arc.

A man would swiftly have been strangled and dead, broken-necked, from such treatment. Even the leopard suffered, and may have been close to fainting, though it continued to struggle. Writhing at the end of the cord, it rose above the top of the wall, and Si-hotep, turning, swung it over into the front garden like a man throwing the hammer, just as it caught the cord with a taloned paw and slashed it through. It hurtled yards and crashed into a bed of blue centaureas. From this it rebounded, spitting, in a lethal humor.

Barking angrily, the baboon loped over to investigate.

Baboon and leopard are natural foes.

The resulting fight was all Si-hotep could have desired. While the beasts' handlers and several guards rushed from the house to begin the thankless, risky task of separating them, Si-hotep returned along the top of the wall, coiling up his shortened cord. A swift "Hist!" brought Wesu running, and drawing a breath, he used the ability the archpriest's potion gave him to step through the wall of the rear garden—or *past,* as he insisted on calling it. Si-hotep lowered himself to join the little man.

"No beasts at the rear of the house now," he murmured. "Let us enter while all's confused."

Confused it was, as he had designed it to be. Guards and handlers alike supposed the leopard, scenting the baboon, had somehow leaped or scaled the wall to attack it, though just how it might have done so baffled conjecture. While they were occupied and distracted, Si-hotep gained the mansion's roof and helped Wesu after him, then entered the house through one of the ventilation hatches. He became uncomfortably aware in the course of that exercise of having wrenched a back muscle in dealing with the leopard. Still, the most taxing feat of the evening was done, and he had been both adroit and swift in performing it. Well up to his usual standard, in fact.

"The treasure vault lies at the very center of this house," he murmured in Wesu's ear. "Khentau had the mansion built merely to contain it, I think; his hoarded wealth is everything to him."

"Yea," Wesu answered. "He has never even married."

"A fortunate thing for some woman."

They moved surreptitiously to the corridor behind the treasure vault. The vault itself was a great strong square room, its brick walls five cubits thick with no internal hollows, the floor made of diorite slabs in three layers.

When Si-hotep first obtained the specifications from the architect, he had not been impressed; he had encountered other treasure chambers with strong floors and walls, and their weakness often lay in the ceiling. Sometimes, these were ludicrously easy to penetrate.

Not this one. It possessed a roof as strong as the walls, supported by a double row of pillars and titanic beams of Byblos timber, proof against any thief who did not have half a lifetime to spare. It completely lacked air shafts or windows, what was more; no means of surreptitious entrance at all.

Its doors were the only way in or out. Heavy diorite slabs moved upon mechanisms that slid and rumbled loudly. Even knowing how they worked, no-one could have opened them without rousing the entire house. What a happy circumstance, Si-hotep thought, that it was no longer needful to open them to gain access.

"Enter," Si-hotep whispered, "and select the booty. Do not forget… once you obtain it, you will need me to get you safely away."

Wesu licked his lips, in a way that looked to the thief more like apprehension than greed. Then he squared his shoulders and stared at the thick blank wall. His eyes widened for a moment, and he flinched, seeming to find it necessary to gather himself again before he dared move forward. Si-hotep felt a strong wish to ask what he saw, besides the other side of the wall, but that would not have been businesslike.

"Something is there," Wesu said, and his voice quivered.

"What?" Si-hotep demanded. "We don't have all night."

"I do not know! I see a shadow that moves and glides, but it is huge, immense, and it changes form!"

"To be sure," Si-hotep agreed, puzzled. "Shadows do."

"Not in this way."

Si-hotep had no concept of what his accomplice meant, and did not care, with time slipping away and the guards so soon to return.

"Do you wish to spend the night quaking at shadows, or to be rich? In there with you. I will wait here. I'll never budge from this corridor, be sure, O Wesu!"

The little man nodded, and stepped forward—or sideways, in some indescribable direction, for that was how it seemed to Si-hotep, watching him closely. He could not comprehend the nature of it however keenly he observed, and whatever defied Si-hotep's understanding, irked him. Also, something in Wesu's remarks about an immense shadow caused him unease, made him recall stories that had frightened him as a child, of demons that haunted the night.

Nevertheless, demons were not likely to do worse to him than Khentau's Libyan guards, if they discovered him. Si-hotep climbed to the roof-beams and crouched there below the ceiling. Being a jeweler's scribe and expert fence of stolen gems, little Wesu should have no trouble choosing a sackful of items whose weight was low and value enormous.

The guards returned, then, talking in their savage language—of their recent task, no doubt, and asking each other how the leopard could have leaped over the wall when it had never done anything of the kind before! Si-hotep flexed the lean muscles of his back, wincing at the pain but breathing very lightly and gradually. Sometimes men heard tiny sounds without knowing they heard them, and became aware of someone's presence in that way. That never happened to Si-hotep. And no matter how clumsily Wesu moved, he was unlikely to be heard through five cubits of brick, particularly if he spoke the truth about seeing a dim grey light everywhere, under the influence of the archpriest's potion.

Si-hotep counted silently to himself. When he judged it time that Wesu should emerge from the treasure vault, he had planned a way to distract the guards. Then they would escape through the front garden. The baboon, if still alive, was surely too badly mauled to resume its duties tonight. Probably they had shut the leopard in its cage as well, deeming it too excited and bloodthirsty to be useful again at present.

Si-hotep smiled to himself, thinking how much simpler that would make it to escape, and of what Khentau would say when he found his treasure vault robbed.

Then Wesu's scream echoed in the corridor.

Muffled and distant, it still held such terror as to chill Si-hotep where he crouched among the rafters. Moreover, it went on, drawn out to appalling length, and when it ceased at last, the thief wondered if Wesu was dead or merely lacked the breath to scream further.

It was not repeated. Si-hotep had extraordinarily sharp ears, but even the Libyan guards had heard that shriek, and while they disagreed a good deal among themselves as to whence it emanated, some did insist it had come from within the treasure vault. They hadn't a notion of how it was opened, of course, and at length agreed to wake their master.

Si-hotep, for once, reached no swift decision.

The cry had come from a man incapacitated by pain or horror. Wesu, if still conscious, would commit no adroit theft; most likely would not emerge from the vault standing on his feet. What had happened, though? Some fatal trap which he in his inexperience had blundered into? Maybe. Possibly. But somehow it was the little scribe's edgy talk of a shadow immense beyond the normal, a shadow whose shape *altered,* which intruded into Si-hotep's memory.

Gods! It came down to one thing in the end. Or two. For this venture, willingly or no, Wesu was Si-hotep's partner. Even though loyalty was a vague and elastic principle with Si-hotep, still he recognized it, and tossing it upon the midden in the face of the unknown would affect his self-love. So would scurrying off without the loot he came for, when he had managed everything well and bravely thus far.

He drew the tiny crystal bottle from behind his belt. It glittered in the light of the corridor lamps. Si-hotep ran his thumbnail down the side to the second of the gradation marks. Then he removed the stopper and drank one precise dose.

III.

Sliding down his gullet easily, it seemed to have no particular taste or any immediate effect. After a moment, his skin prickled, and his vision moved strangely in and out of focus. A curious flaming intensity sang along all his nerves. He felt light-headed, and clutched the roof-beams more firmly, lest he topple down.

The light-headedness passed. He stared down at the lamps and their light seemed to fade, replaced by a uniform greyish luminescence. Dim though it was, everything seemed clearer when seen by its light.

Two Libyans passed below Si-hotep's perch, talking about the leopard and baboon, no doubt. As he watched them coming, a strange sliding perspective changed his vision, and he seemed to see them from impossible new angles... two different ones at once, though he could not have described how. Precisely as Wesu had declared, he seemed to see *past* their skins and ribs, a grotesque, unnerving matter. What passed beneath him appeared to be a pair of hideous flayed ghouls with rolling eyeballs and raw red muscles exposed to the air. Glimpses of pulsing lungs, coiled intestines and other internal organs further edified Si-hotep as they passed from sight around a corner, still talking.

It had been some time since the deftest thief in Hikuptah had shuddered. He discovered the sensation again in that moment. He also became determined to enter the treasure vault before any more of Khentau's guards appeared, to grant him the privilege of viewing their innards.

It occurred to him, though, that Wesu had perhaps not boasted idly when he had said he could remove Si-hotep's lungs by merely reaching for them. Supposing a man's hands could follow his vision in this strange new direction...

He abandoned that line of thought. He was a thief, and a fine one, not an assassin. He gazed at the wall of the treasure vault.

It opened, or else turned as though on some smooth, silken pivot, showing what lay beyond—except that in truth it did neither, but only *seemed* to. The wall remained where it was, as thickly solid as always, but Si-hotep saw a way that led past it, a way denied to mortal senses except under the influence of the archpriest's potion. He only had to move a finger's width, or less, in that weird direction, to pass the solid obstacle of the wall completely, for in that direction, it did not exist.

Another thing that Wesu has said now proved true. Looking, Si-hotep beheld two vistas, not one; the inside of Khentau's treasure chamber, with its chests and stone shelves temptingly laden, and a second, far stranger one. A grey and buff desert rolled away below spires of fretted sandstone, the sky above crusted with more stars than Si-hotep had ever seen, blazing down in indifferent glory. There was hardly a speck of the sky to be glimpsed between them. Si-hotep could not imagine what might happen if he leaped in that direction, and he felt no wish to discover. He focused with determination on the treasure vault, swung in on his cord, and landed lightly in the middle of the floor.

Someone whimpered nearby.

It was Wesu, huddled on his knees with his arms wrapped around his head and a urine puddle of his own terror stinking under him. There was no-one and nothing in sight to account for his state. Si-hotep's first reaction was one of supercilious distaste. He had known that Wesu was scarcely a hero, but had not thought him this abject!

Then he remembered the ghoulish appearance of the Libyan guards to his altered vision, and that bizarre desert under those alien stars. He wondered what the scribe had seen, and whether it was anywhere close, in this world or in that eerie other direction the potion allowed a man to see.

He decided this was fruitless speculation, and that in any case he preferred not to discover the answers. He went to work. Gems, gold collars, and armlets whose fine workmanship increased the value tenfold went into the leather satchel dropped by Wesu. The thief worked with cool-headed speed. Although it would take time to bring the master of the house, persuade him of the need to open his treasure chamber, and then to work the mechanism which parted the diorite portals, still that would occur, and presumably before morning came.

Wesu's whimpering set Si-hotep's teeth on edge. What had he seen? Or... *what had seen him?*

He shut his mind to those notions and went on looting methodically, till he had crammed the satchel with the smallest, most precious, and most easily sold items. Swiftly, he fastened it shut and made sure the buckles were secure. Glancing again at Wesu, he saw no signs of recovery, and knew he would have to carry the shuddering man out of danger.

Bah! Weakling! I ought to leave him. If he weighed more or knew less, I would. But—he is light, and I do not have to lug him far.

Si-hotep turned to the massive diorite doors and let his gaze lose focus, slide past them to the corridor outside. Less time must have passed than he thought, for Khentau had not arrived yet, but four guards and his major-domo waited, the latter a lean fellow just out of bed, blinking like an owl.

The rear wall, then.

The corridor that way lay empty. Si-hotep seized the satchel of plunder, slung Wesu over his shoulder and turned to depart. He would be glad when this theft was done.

His vision shifted as though in a turning kaleidoscope, and he looked once again into a different place than the corridor beyond the massive brick wall. This view was awesome, terrific; a landscape of igneous stone riven by eruptions and lava flows, sometimes red, sometimes a hot yellow, scabbing on the surface with a fragile crust. Great clouds of dust and cinders filled the sky. Constant lightning, sheets, cataracts of it, gave the only light apart from the glowing lava. Of water and life there was none.

Si-hotep squinted, seeking that trick of perspective that would show him the corridor again, his heart pounding. The hideous landscape faded. He looked again into a prosaic hall adorned with wall paintings of indifferent quality, and could have kissed each cubit thereof. Now, for certain, time to go!

Shadow swept across the corridor wall and half of the treasure vault. Its characteristics were abnormal in the highest degree, beginning with its color, a glossy black-purple, dense with an appearance of solidity. Si-hotep heaved a jar of precious oil into it and found that this invasive darkness was certainly not solid. The jar hurtled through it and thudded among bales of fabric on the far side. No, the adumbration was by no means solid, any more than some common shadow cast on any wall or floor—but unlike these it had thickness as well as length and breadth. And it brought frigid, blighting cold into the treasure vault. The thief saw his breath smoking before his eyes, felt his face and fingers turn numb. Backing away from the wall in some haste, he shut his eyes and turned his head aside lest his eyeballs freeze.

Bending a little under the weight of his plunder and the sodden Wesu, Si-hotep risked another glance at the shadow. It swept immensely through the rear half of the chamber, and just as Wesu had said, it altered strangely as it moved. Thick ripples passed over its surface. It erupted in bubbling spherical clusters. For a moment it narrowed dramatically, until it was merely as thick as the body of a hippopotamus. Si-hotep shuddered, for the thought had struck him; if this was indeed a shadow, then what sort of entity could be casting it? What had a three-dimensional shadow?

He received an inkling.

The shadow vanished, and something with substance swept through—or over, or around—the wall to Si-hotep's right. It looked for an instant like a huge expanse of bumpy squamous hide. There followed masses of wet fleshy ropes big as papyrus reeds, pliant, scarlet-hued. There followed rigid matter, grey, pitted and porous, with a ghastly red jelly seething in the cavities. Next, growing out of it, appeared something quite indescribable, except that it seemed turgid to bursting with a bluish-white fluid through which myriads of black specks surged, all in the same direction.

The astounded thief began to suppose that he was seeing various aspects, or segments, of some single being, the same one which had thrown that fantastic shadow. And that, whatever it was, it made gods appear powerless and demons appear benevolent. That to touch it meant death. That to be noticed by it meant worse than death. Shaking, he cringed back into a corner, letting Wesu drop, and screamed inside his mind for the thing to disappear.

Behind him, the treasure vault doors slid open with a rumble of massive diorite. The Libyan guards rushed in, and beyond them in the lamplight stood Khentau. They should all have fallen on their faces trembling, at the sight of the entity—or its shifting cross-section—but not having taken the archpriest's potion, they never became aware of its presence.

Si-hotep, for an ephemeral moment, envied them. Then, seizing all his courage, he turned his back on the nightmare to his right. He slung the satchel over one shoulder and met the Libyans with his bare hands. They laughed—at first. They stopped laughing when Si-hotep, agile as a mongoose, dodged their spears and reached into their bodies. He gripped the first guard's lungs; the man fell, fighting painfully for breath. He sank fingers into the next one's entrails and squeezed lightly. The result was instant, agonizing colic that caused the man to stop in his tracks, making gasping fish mouths.

The third lunged with his spear. Si-hotep caught the shaft and heaved it aside. He kicked, and his foot slid past the Libyan's armor and stomach muscles, to merely tap a wine-swollen liver. This one also dropped with a croak of pain.

In quick succession and with equal ease, he disabled three more, doing nothing fatal to any of them. Although the thief could be ruthless on equal terms, using this unnatural power to kill would have seemed too much like crushing insects. Men were not insects, not even raping, marauding, never-to-be-civilized Libyans. Still, seeing them fall like leaves all around him would have amused Si-hotep greatly, except that he had not forgotten what was behind him. He flung Wesu over his shoulder with the satchel, and ran.

Burdened so, he would have been caught easily except that he could escape past any solid wall, and left the pursuit seeking him, baffled, in all the wrong places. Si-hotep escaped through the front of the house and moved through the garden towards the outer wall.

He found no guards there. It should have warned him. It certainly would have, were his wits not disordered by what he had seen. He remained sufficiently himself to glance behind him now and then, however. That saved his life when he glimpsed a feline shadow and heard a snarl.

They had not caged the leopard after all.

Si-hotep was already dropping the flaccid scribe as the leopard rushed upon him. He swayed aside, to grapple it in a desperate hold with an arm around its neck and his legs locked under its belly. Normally it would have twisted free and killed him in a moment. These circumstances were far from normal. Si-hotep plunged his hand into that strange adjacent space now made accessible to him, past spotted hide, muscle, and bone.

His hand brushed spongy tissue before closing on something tough that pulsed and pounded at a high rate. He gripped, twisted, ripped. It took all the strength of his sinewy hand and arm to tear the thing from its membranous nest.

The leopard screamed. It writhed briefly, with torrents of blood bursting through its chest cavity, before it lay twitching. Si-hotep dropped the heart and seized his satchel of loot again in his ensanguined hand. With little enthusiasm, he lifted Wesu across his shoulders also.

Staring past the wall of Khentau's garden with sweat-blurred vision, Si-hotep again saw the suburb on the other side of the wall, and something else as well, away at a curious right angle. This time the additional scene was strange past comprehension, and warped by mad tricks of perspective into the bargain. Out there, at a vast distance or else ominously close, glided the thing Si-hotep had seen from the treasure vault—only not, this time, in passing cross-section. He beheld it all—or as much of the entity as human vision could see.

The sight would bring him sweating out of dreams for months to come. He was to be grateful, always, for inability to fully perceive or wholly remember. And yet fascination filled him with a mad urge to leap into the realm he beheld. It lured even while he guessed shrewdly that he would be annihilated in some fashion beyond conceiving if he did.

With a hoarse yell of refusal he scuttled for the known environs of Hikuptah, and went into hiding.

Later, trembling in a disused courtyard, he looked at the figure of Wesu as he chewed his lips and drooled. Si-hotep wondered if the man would recover, and how close he had come to being so disordered himself. Too close, he suspected. He experienced a strong urge to hurl his night's plunder into the street and leave it there—but no, it had been too hardly won, and he was still a professional.

As a professional, he asked himself sourly what the Archpriest of Anubis would say if he learned how Si-hotep had used his potion. Maybe nothing. Triple curses on the man, Si-hotep was still bound to track down the maker of the false scarab for him! Success in that mission would probably induce Kamose to forget this raid on Khentau's treasure room. He would remember and punish, on the other hand, if there should be failure. Si-hotep cursed again. It was unfair; he had never asked for the potion. Surely, when Kamose sent it, he must have known the thief would be suspicious enough to try out its powers. Why else give him a bottle containing three doses? It seemed inconsistent with a warning never to use the potion but in direst emergency.

After this night, Si-hotep was not likely to.

CORPSE'S WRATH

The thief had not been followed to Kiya's house. He made sure of that. Not for a thief's usual reasons, either, since he did not visit Kiya's house to plunder it. In fact he supported her.

Skirting the market-place near his destination, he glanced at the white disk of the moon, sacred to Thoth. Bats flitted across it. Somewhere a jackal howled. Si-hotep paid no heed to omens normally, but the occasions on which he was called, through agents, to perform some task for the Archpriest of Anubis were never normal. He liked neither the flight of bats nor the jackal's cry.

Gliding into the alley behind Kiya's little house, he listened intently for a few moments. He heard nothing but a dog lifting its leg against the alley wall and, over by the market-place, a drunken potter stumbling home, singing a song to which he had forgotten half the words. Well and good. Si-hotep had taken even more than his usual meticulous care not to be followed. He was—*almost* satisfied. He approached Kiya's dwelling.

His preferred way of entering was by climbing a convenient palm and so gaining the roof. Tonight, though, he varied it by slipping through a shadowed window. He never made enemies if he could avoid it; so far as he knew, none of the victims he robbed had even heard his name, and still less Kiya's. It could happen, though; the gods themselves were not perfect. If nefarious men had entered her house to wait for him, he meant to surprise them and not vice versa.

He heard the wheezing snores of Kiya's servant, deep in a peaceful sleep in her ground floor chamber. That reassured him, though not completely. He moved quietly through the upper rooms of the little house, then crept up the few narrow steps to the roof. He found it bare and innocent in the moonlight. Only then did he return to the room where Kiya slept—the most comfortably appointed she had ever slept in, much less owned, all of it provided by the thief and maintained by his lawless activities. He cleared his throat.

Kiya slept very lightly. That was all it took. She rolled over, her tangled hair flying, and said sharply, "Who's there?"

"Si-hotep. I hope the knife I gave you is now in your pretty hand."

"Y-yes. Si-hotep? Then what colour is the dress you gave me twelve days ago?"

"It wasn't a dress. It was scented oil. The dresses, three, were before that, and I am glad to find you cautious. Should I describe them?"

"No! Ah, Si-hotep!"

She scampered to his arms, a lithe former beggar-girl who had gained some much-needed flesh since meeting the thief, but she kept hold of the knife in case she had made a mistake. Si-hotep, long used to moving nimbly in the dark, took that wrist in a sinewy hand for safety. After a long kiss that settled his identity, he removed the knife and put it aside. Then he led Kiya back to the bed. He realised as he made heated merry love to her that he had missed her keenly, and not for the first time, the knowledge brought him qualms of disquiet. But he forgot it as she held him close and said love-words.

Kiya lit the lamp afterwards. Its light slid over her brown skin and the thief's. Running his hand down the smooth channel of her back, he said with regret, "I must be gone well before dawn. There's a job in progress, Kiya, and until it's done and the loot disposed of, I cannot come near you. No, don't worry about me. It's an ordinary business, and should not call for more than ordinary care."

That was almost true. The "loot", though, so to speak, was a man, a dangerous brute of a man who did not wish to be found, but whom the thief had to find. He regarded it as work far beneath his talents. A time-consuming bore, too. Still, the darkest, most feared magician in the Two Lands of Khem had ordered that the man be found. Alive. Si-hotep gathered he had been involved in some plot to steal the late Pharaoh's jewelled heart scarab. A fool's plot that Si-hotep would not have touched with a pole.

Kiya surprised him. She said severely, "That is not what I hear. It isn't gold or jewels this time, is it, but a man who works with them—a temple craftsman who has done wrong and gone into hiding? A bad man. What do you want with him?"

"I never want anything at all with fellows like that," Si-hotep told her. "Market place chatter."

"Sometimes it's right! Walk wide of this one. His name is Perkhet—" She watched his face as she spoke the name. Si-hotep didn't react. "—and they say he beat his wife to death."

The market place chatter for once was correct. Si-hotep said with a shrug, "Bad, right enough. A matter for the watchmen and the judges, though, not for me. It's jewels I'm after tonight, Kiya. Wish me luck and wait in patience till you see me."

He departed, then, before she could cling or express further worry. A sack of faience, spices and dyes remained in a corner to show Si-hotep had been there. It would support the girl for some time, and none of it had been stolen, if a busybody neighbour should accuse her. Si-hotep was a careful professional—no, a master of lone hand thievery.

And nevertheless Kiya worried.

II.

"He's the third! And I tell you Geb's angry ghost had them all!"

The man giving his fearful opinion in the waterfront beer-house was a Nile boatman—that was to say, one of an obstreperous breed of roughs and brawlers. They crowded into dives like this one fresh from days of man-killing labour on the River, and an hour later the walls shook with their fighting. Si-hotep had been haunting such places in search of his man for days. Although a temple craftsman, a jeweller, he had been born a boatman's son. Under the necessity of hiding he might well have returned to his origins.

"Ghost!" The response, from a brawny lout with pop-eyes and chewed stumps for ears, could hardly have been more scornful. "Do ghosts hang men up by the heels and slit their bellies? Someone did not like them, that's all—someone whose cargo they stole, I am guessing."

"Slit their bellies and cut out their eyes!" the first boatman enlarged with gloomy relish. "Likely enough that's what happened to Geb. It was past due. But he's stubborn and vengeful enough to return."

Si-hotep had heard that subject talked about, sometimes in subdued tones, in other dives besides this one. Three men unpleasantly killed on the Hikuptah docksides since the last full moon made a strong encouragement to be cautious. The more so when some attributed the deaths to a ghost or demon. Si-hotep wondered glumly if a supernatural agent had been sent to find and silence the man he wanted. If the late three gruesome deaths were its work.

He thought not. The men, highly-placed ones no doubt, who had tried to discredit the Archpriest of Anubis, were clever and subtle as well as skilled in sorcery. If the dread Archpriest had not learned their identities yet, but was reduced to trying to trace them through their lowliest tools, then by Hathor they must be! They would not send a demon so clumsy it had to kill three men at random before slaying the right one. No, this nasty business belike had nothing to do with Si-hotep's.

The frog-eyed boatman continued to scoff. "Geb's boat capsized and he fed a crocodile! It was past due, as you said. Never saw a boat worse kept. Bah! A man should at least broach his second jar before he talks of ghosts."

"To me you say so?" The other man rose with his voice turning to a bellow. "To me? I've killed three crocodiles and made ten men ghosts! I'd drink you senseless on my worst night! A bull hippopotamus was my father and a lioness my mother! I—"

He was broad, chunky and tough, but Frog-eyes reached out a casual hand and twisted his nose. The believer in ghosts struck his hands apart and hit him. Servants carrying jars of beer and a naked dancer in the middle of the floor scampered aside. The fighters struggled, bit, stamped and generally sought to maim, swaying and grunting.

Frog-eyes clamped a wrestling hold on his opponent's arm and sought to break it. The other, bending slowly forward to the floor in an effort to save his limb, seemed only to be delaying the fracture. Then he brought up from that very floor a fearful heel-of-the-hand blow. It swept around in a half circle and snapped Frog-eyes' jaw when it landed. The sound filled the air of the grog-house.

Except that he was a Nile boatman, said by the effete to be a barely human breed, Frog-eyes would have been unconscious. He remained on his feet, and more; he kicked the other man in the middle with a force fit to rupture his liver. Hurtling back, he collided with a newcomer. That impact made even Si-hotep wince a little. The newcomer did not fall down, though, or even stagger.

He was big. Big, hard and brutal enough to stand out even in this company. Naked except for a loinclout, muscled like a nest of entwined pythons, he turned his shaven head from one combatant to the other.

"Your fight is over," he growled. "Sit down and be quiet or get out. Else I'll drown you both in a cesspit."

Eyeing him, Si-hotep thought he looked like the only man in the place who could carry out such a promise. Either Frog-eyes was mad with pain or didn't give a curse. Broken jaw and all, he flung himself at the stranger, roaring wordlessly.

The stranger hit him. Once. Then he seized him by the neck and thigh, raised him off the ground, and dashed him down so that his back met the stranger's rising knee. The move could have snapped his spine if knee had met backbone squarely, but it struck to one side and crushed a kidney. He writhed, rolled, and was hauled to the door by the beer-house's chucker-out, who had done nothing to earn his keep until then. The other brawler crept after him into the darkness, evidently set on murder.

Si-hotep looked the newcomer up and down. He appeared hard as cedar, and suitably battered from fighting over the years—yes—but his skin lacked the outdoor look of the other boatmen, and in general he seemed better treated by life than they. It was just an impression, formed by smoky lamp-light. Still he thought it enough to make the fellow worth investigating.

He stared at Si-hotep in no friendly wise.

"What do you think you are looking at, fish?"

"I don't quite know," Si-hotep answered frankly. "Whatever it is, it blocks my view of the dancer. Sit and drink with me if you like. If not, I ask that you step aside."

The stranger's gaze turned red. Si-hotep made ready to grasp his knife. To stop this one he would have to strike at three or four vital spots in succession while staying out of his grip. Killing him was not permissible, though, if he should be the man Si-hotep sought; the Archpriest had no kindly response to failure.

The brute changed his mind about mayhem and showed a grin. "You will stand me beer? I've never refused it yet, but tell me why, mannikin, tell me why."

"I'm seeking a bodyguard," Si-hotep answered, most affably, but letting some worry show. "By your looks you would do. I would pay well, but I can tell you now, you would earn it. There'd be some danger; it calls for a man who can stomach desperate deeds."

"Someone craves your blood?" the brute suggested. He hunkered down beside Si-hotep, scarred brawn in a loinclout.

"Several do."

Which they did, but only as the unidentified thief who had robbed them, not with any knowledge of who he might be.

"Name two in particular, and tell me why."

"I owe gambling debts to the one who matters. But another knows he is not the father of his wife's baby. Their names would mean nothing to you; they dwell in Thebes. Therefore I left the city for a while, but friend, I must return. If you've no taste for travel to Thebes, well, then, drink your good beer and we will part company."

"I might like to see Thebes," grunted the other.

Looking him over, the thief felt his first impression confirmed. His excitement was rising. His new acquaintance might be brawny, tough as harness leather and battered by fighting, but he was not just a Nile boatman. His sunburn did not go deep enough. Si-hotep watched his hands as he gripped his beaker of beer, and quelled an urge to shout in triumph. Yes! He'd thrown three sixes at last! The stranger's hands were not those of a man who constantly rowed and hauled on ropes. He'd stained them deeply with pitch, but the only thick calluses they bore were on the fingers, where a jeweller grew them. A large good-luck pendant of the Nile god hung around his neck, too, just over the breast-bone. Perfect to cover the spot where jewelers braced a bow-drill for endless hours. All men of that profession soon had a smooth callous in that place, round and hard.

Si-hotep felt a surge of triumph. Here was his quarry. He had drunk and gamed in waterfront dives for twelve days, searching for a jeweler in hiding, a man who came from a family of boatmen and might well return to the scenes of his early life in an effort to disappear. Now, perhaps, he had him. A man who had probably fashioned a false copy of the emerald scarab meant to be buried with the late Pharaoh, as part of a plot against the Archpriest of Anubis. More fool he.

"You have a name?" he asked.

"Webenu the boat-builder. And you?"

Webenu, indeed. It was Perkhet. The thief would have laid gold to stale bread. Meaning this was a man who had been a swaggering, drunken terror to the community of artisans in which he had lived, and capped his misdeeds by battering his wife to death—a crime not greatly condemned in some uncouth lands, but in Khem abhorred.

"Ra-hen," the thief said. "I am a cargo scribe on the *Blue Perch*. You will have seen the ship. It returns to Thebes in three days. Can you come along?"

"Maybe." Perkhet looked him over with undiminished suspicion. "But not on your say-so! Get the master of this ship to vouch for you and I may think about it. Here's a warning—if you are anything but what you pretend, I'll serve you as you just saw me serve a stronger man than you, and the last thing you hear will be your own spine breaking. Understand?"

"You're not ambiguous," the thief conceded.

He had found his man. This was Perkhet, not Webenu, and not a boat-builder. All that remained was to trick him aboard the *Blue Perch* where the crew could subdue him and carry him upstream to Kamose the Archpriest's dark mansion. Si-hotep preferred not to wonder what would happen to him there—very much preferred it.

He was only certain that Perkhet would tell the Archpriest's minions all they desired to know.

III.

Many beakers later, Si-hotep decided his new drinking companion was satisfied of his bona fides. Enough to approach the *Blue Perch* with him, anyhow. The vessel really did hail from Thebes and he really had come to Hikuptah aboard her, as a cargo scribe using the name Ra-hen, though not of course all the way from Thebes itself. The Archpriest Kamose's agents could arrange anything.

"Those two fools whose fight you stopped, brother," he said, his arm around the other man's shoulder in drunken affection. "They argued about a ghost, a ghost, a ghost—that kills men—hangs them by the heels and eviscerates them. Is there truth to that?"

Perkhet hawked and spat, careless of whom he hit. "You must be as great a fool as they, to ask. Two fellows have died that way. Found with swollen footprints made in their blood. Eyes ripped out as well." He chuckled ghoulishly. "Someone disliked them. But a ghost? I doubt it."

Si-hotep felt less sure. He had encountered a ghost once. He knew the thing was possible.

"But supposing a man had been killed like that himself, and his corpse sunk in the river, lost to decent obsequies? His lich or spectre might come back. And without eyes it might seek blindly, slay at random—an ill prospect."

He exaggerated a shiver. He had not entirely faked it, however. Perkhet, drinking deeply, remained cheerfully scornful.

"You'd better go back to Thebes, little man. You're too easily scared for the Hikuptah docks."

Si-hotep had not often been called timid. He could not recall that those who had done so were outstanding for wit, either. He took Perkhet's aspersion as a tribute to his acting.

"I'd sooner chance my luck in Thebes, so long as you are beside me. But I must have an answer by tomorrow night. If you are not interested, I must find another, or—"

"Or jump ship, eh? Stay here? If you wish me to be interested, you had better make me believe you can pay. Men with heavy gambling debts are bad risks that way."

Si-hotep shifted his gaze in dissembled worry. "My parents are rich. Ask the *Blue Perch*'s captain. Were all else to fail I would get your price from them."

"It makes no odds to me where you get it. Listen, though! If you cheat me it will be you who is found hung by the heels, eyeless and gutted—here or in Thebes. I care not. Now in Amun's name, show me this cursed ship."

"At once?"

"Know you a better time?"

Si-hotep did not. They finished their beer and left, Perkhet ostentatiously taking an ugly hardwood cudgel which he boasted he "never needed against fewer than four". They moved together along the Hikuptah waterfront, where the lapping Nile bore up a thousand ships and boats. Si-hotep smelled fish and grain, varied kinds of foreign timber—cedar, fir, ebony—hides, oil and spices. Ships from all over the Delta and beyond rubbed creaking sides with vessels from far up the Nile.

Perkhet said little. They were passing a flat-decked barge which had off-loaded its granite cargo and now rode empty, when he unleashed his surprise. Without the slightest warning, he swung his massive arm across Si-hotep's chest to knock him off the dockside. He fell on the barge's flat deck, twisting like a cat. Despite that, half the breath was knocked out of him and he hit his elbow agonisingly hard. Then Perkhet sprang after him, dropping through the air to land on the thief with dazing impact and immobilise him in a wrestler's hold.

Si-hotep did not immediately react with fear. His first mortified thought was, "Taken. By this oaf. Me! And so easily."

Then came a stab of fear. Perkhet's hands could slay him with one violent twist. Si-hotep had his knife, of course, strapped to his thigh under his linen kilt, but he dared not kill Perkhet when Kamose the Archpriest wanted him alive. Better a quick if ugly death, here on this rocking barge, than the anger of Kamose.

Si-hotep concealed both the knife and his own considerable wrestling skill. He struggled dramatically against the grip of arms like hippopotamus bones sunk in layered ship's rope, and voiced a terrified gurgle. If Perkhet meant to question him before killing, Si-hotep might still retrieve the advantage. If not—Kiya had better find some dull decent craftsman and marry him, for she would not be seeing Si-hotep again.

"Fool!" Perkhet snarled. "You think I will go aboard a ship I haven't chosen with some stranger who drops from the sky? I have questions, and you will answer quickly. If you pause—if I think you've lied, even think it—your neck breaks. Understand?"

Si-hotep uttered an abject croak.

"Who are you? What's your lay?"

He was questioning, not killing, and that had promise. He even relaxed his grip by a generous finger-joint's length. Si-hotep feigned a choking fit and then gasped:

"I'm what I say! Cargo scribe—temple of Amun-Ra—Thebes. In trouble. Need protection."

"In trouble you surely are! And there's no protection. Not from me. Do you know who I am?"

Si-hotep had no more doubt now.

"I care not! If you do not want the pay I offer—let me go! I'll forget you. Find another."

"You will forget the sun and this world if I turn your neck a hand's width more! Listen to me, jackal! I have trouble, too. Folk are looking for me, and you may be their creature. Eh? If that's so, your one chance to live is to speak truth. Who sent you?"

"No! Don't know Hikuptah. I'm from Thebes."

With a growl, Perkhet ran him to the side of the barge and forced his head into the water, holding him down. The thief had a chance to twist free. He resisted the temptation. He could hold his breath nearly as long as a frog. At various times he had lain in prolonged hiding in fishponds, tan-pits and worse. In the end Perkhet hauled him up. The thief coughed and retched in a great display of helpless misery.

"Now the truth! Or I drown you!"

"No!" Si-hotep croaked. "Listen! G-gaming. I've lost much. That's true. The creditor would have me—rob the temple. I dare not. Need someone—to frighten him. And his two bullies. It's truth. Truth!"

It rang true even to him. He'd rehearsed it enough. Now, he hoped, this fellow would believe and take the job, thinking he had intimidated his new employer into malleability.

Si-hotep never found out. Instead, he heard a sudden swirl and gurgle of water on the far side of the transport barge. A manlike shape clambered aboard. Water streamed from its shoulders and legs as it shambled forward. Wet dark prints of swollen feet showed on the deck behind it.

It moved as silently as Si-hotep could have done. Crossing the deck diagonally, it emerged from shadow into the moonlight. Si-hotep's marrow chilled and his throat closed in horror. For the moment he could do nothing but point his arm and stare mutely. Perkhet sneered, taking it for an ancient trick. He raised his fist.

A thick wet hand closed over it.

IV.

Perkhet's brutal face changed even before he turned around. He looked at what gripped him, and sank to the deck-boards in a faint. An immediate dead faint. His bones seemed to melt as he slipped down.

The figure stooping over him showed slick and slaty-skinned in the moonlight. It stank of putrefaction though it showed few signs of rotting. The black holes of eyeless sockets showed between the forehead and cheeks. Entrails bulged in loops out of a gutted belly, hanging down. River water dripped and streamed from it, pooling on the barge's deck.

Si-hotep thrust against the deck with both heels, moving desperately away. Loathing assailed him. Madness threatened his mind, and in some irrelevant part of it he cursed the Archpriest Kamose. At his bidding, the thief had found Perkhet—and now this thing had found Perkhet also.

He yearned to leap over the side and swim. But he dared not. The Archpriest was hardly known for indulgence towards failure.

Before Si-hotep's appalled eyes, the dead thing bent over Perkhet. It moved quickly and surely; more bad news. It dropped a hand to the jeweller's chest and sank swollen fingers mercilessly into his chest muscle. The other hand flashed to his face. A dead thumb gouged, Perkhet screamed like a speared donkey, and writhed on the deck with blood rilling down his cheek. He screamed on. The dead hand came forward again, to grope at Perkhet's face. It sought the other eye.

Si-hotep lunged, his knife out and glittering. As the wet grey thumb began to press on Perkhet's second eyeball, the thief cut the tendon that moved it. Then he seized the forearm and slashed the inside of the wrist for good measure. Those tendons separated also. A surgeon could not have been quicker or defter.

The walking corpse flung out its injured hand and forearm, to knock Si-hotep rolling along the barge's deck. The power in that swing made him feel as though he had been kicked by a rhinoceros. Breathing was effortful torment. Ribs might be broken. His legs felt like wet twine as he rose.

He still held his knife.

Perkhet's howls had not lessened, in volume or frequency. He had writhed away from the thing that attacked him, and lost skin thereby; more blood dripped down his massive chest. The grisly lich advanced on him. Si-hotep, moving faster now, lumbered up behind it.

Lumbering was not a gait to which he had been reduced before. He did not like it. Nor did he like the notion of coming to grips with this thing again. It had the scarred brawn of a Nile boatman—not as large as the howling Perkhet, but seemingly even stronger in death, and proof against pain.

Not invulnerable, however. That was established.

It had no eyes, yet it turned its head as Si-hotep came on. Could it hear? Had it heard his footsteps, or the throb of his heart? Yes. Why not? If it moved despite being dead, it could have hearing.

Perkhet tried to escape into the water, dragging himself to the side of the transport barge. The lich's head promptly turned towards him. It sprang in pursuit, found his ankle and began dragging him back. None of Perkhet's previous screams had equalled his production now.

Si-hotep leaped on the dead thing's back, passing an arm about its throat, and stabbed one ear, then the other, with his awl-sharp knife, giving a neat vicious twist each time. Ear-drum and inner ear alike were destroyed. The lich, with equal precision, broke Perkhet's ankle before it released him. Then it caught the sinewy living arm across its dead throat and flipped Si-hotep over its shoulder. The thief, an agile wrestler and acrobat, landed without injury, but the dead thing retained its awful grip on his arm. It could tear his shoulder-joint apart in another moment.

Si-hotep cut the tendons of that wrist too. Although the strength went out of the terrible dead grip, the fingers did not open. And its slick cold obscene touch revolted him past reason.

The thief kicked hard at its riven belly. His foot squelched among the grey-black entrails, and again his flesh crawled. Legs braced on the lich's trunk, he dragged his arm free. He twisted aside just as a necrotic foot stamped down. It would have crushed his chest if it had struck.

Si-hotep rose, still shaken. The grey-skinned thing groped the air with its hands, flailed them like clubs, blew air from its dead lungs in a hollow wail that was the first sound Si-hotep had heard from it. It appeared baffled. Blind from the beginning, it was now deaf also, and its hands lacked gripping power. Good. The thief should be able to gather Perkhet, who would give little trouble now, and depart.

He felt more than eager to do that. The jeweller had crawled into the bow of the barge and now crouched there, glaring from his one eye. Si-hotep approached him.

The dead thing rushed after the thief with sudden terrifying accuracy. Its swollen feet boomed on the planks. Si-hotep, glancing over his shoulder with a pang of terror, understood. It could not see; it could not hear. However, it could *feel* the vibration his light footsteps caused in the planks, as a snake feels such vibrations through the ground and knows when to slither aside.

Then it could probably scent him.

It remained blind and deaf, though. Si-hotep dodged its onslaught easily. In his growing confidence he even took a fleeting few heartbeats to wonder about its purpose. And who it was. Or once had been.

A boatman, clearly. Some waterfront thug with a life of crime behind him. An enemy or a group of them had killed him nastily. Now, lacking a tomb, it had returned from some crocodile's larder for revenge. Whether it had been a boatman named Geb, or someone else, and whether it could find its murderers or was striking at random, were questions of minor concern.

The thief ducked beneath a swing of one dreadful arm. Bracing himself for the sickening touch of its flesh, he lunged at one leg and cut the big tendon behind the ankle. The lich tried to fall on him like a tree. All his celerity barely got him out of its way. He flung himself on the other calf to cripple that one, but the thing anticipated him and slammed its knee into his breast-bone.

Si-hotep went down. A dead hand seized him. Its grip began closing. Astonished, Si-hotep kept his head, and realised this was the hand on which he had cut only the tendons inside the wrist. Its fingers could still close.

They did, and broke his arm.

Si-hotep groaned in agony as the dead fingers continued to close, but he had felt pain before. He dropped the knife from his strengthless hand. Before it fell half a cubit he had caught it in the other. He made two desperate, deft slashes, and the lich's fingers lost their power. With a third precise cut he filleted the brawny arm from shoulder to wrist. Then, setting his teeth, he tore his broken arm free of the dead thing's weakened grip.

He nearly fainted. Sweat dripped from his face. It head-butted his forehead as he swayed before it. Si-hotep sprawled at the edge of the deck with his world turning dark. He heard a splash as Perkhet managed at last to fling himself into the water, and rolled after him in a semi-conscious tenacity of intent. He dared not lose the man now, and the deck of the barge was no place to be.

With luck the horror would crawl up and down it for half the night seeking the pair of them.

V.

The water's silken coolth brought back Si-hotep's senses, and some of his cunning. One arm trailed useless; he oared through the dockside water with the other, kicking lightly with both feet. Perkhet floundered and splashed more noisily, with hoarse screams that he was drowning.

Si-hotep forbore to swim to his aid. He would doubtless grab the thief and drown him too. Better to wait until he lost consciousness, if he did, and bear him up then. Once again, fleetingly, he cursed the Archpriest Kamose, all his works, schemes and intentions, and the evil luck that had ever made him aware of the thief's existence. Then he turned his full attention to staying afloat, staying close to Perkhet, and doing both unobtrusively.

Somewhere behind him, a heavy splash sounded. Noises of floundering, struggling motion followed. His blood thickened as though at the onset of death.

The undead corpse was in the river with them.

Si-hotep continued his one-armed swimming, side by side with Perkhet. He made himself think. Here in the water, the thing would feel vibration from their swimming as well as it had sensed their footsteps on the barge deck. Maybe much better. Hamstrung, with maimed hands, it could do no more than dog-paddle, but tireless as it seemed, it could pursue them until they wearied, and unlike them it had no broken bones.

It still had teeth. Si-hotep envisioned those dead limbs flung around him, that dead weight dragging him down, those dead jaws grinding and grinding into his flesh until they found something vital. Terror assailed him. He fought it.

They could belike stay ahead of their grisly pursuer for now. Perkhet's powerful arms pulled him through the water at a good pace despite his broken ankle, but they must leave the Nile before they wearied. The thief's broken arm trailed uselessly and hurt like hot skewers.

To Perkhet he called, "Hear me, thou! We must get out of the harbour—and seek my ship. Unless you have other friends who can assist. That thing follows us still!"

"What is it?" Perkhet nearly screamed. "Why does it want you?"

"I think it wants you!"

Perkhet did not dispute him.

"I crippled it!" Si-hotep continued. "On land or a ship it can barely move. We must get out of the water, I tell you. Must! And then—stay together."

"Together? You dirty jackal, I've lost an eye because of you! I'll tear you limb from limb if I can lay hands on you!"

"Together—we can prevail over it! I have both eyes, both feet! You have both arms. It broke one of mine. Decide."

"Yes," Perkhet croaked.

Si-hotep did not believe him, but the assurance would do for the time being.

"Then swim around the stern of that ship there," he said. "To the left."

Perkhet splashed obediently in the designated direction. They were confined, now, in a narrow water-lane between two vessels. The jeweller's one eye rolled wildly as he realised what a trap it made, but he kept going, impelled by that fear. Si-hotep looked out for a dangling rope.

He discovered none. But he was discovered, by a cargo-guard who looked over the ship's side to learn what the splashing might be. The man and his mates were watchful in the night hours for thieves. Si-hotep could have told them they had found one now, of unmatched quality. He chose not to.

"Help us!" he called. "Help us! We have been beaten and thrown in the harbour! I have a broken arm—my companion lacks an eye! Save us!"

"Watch the dockside!" someone said sharply. "It's a trick. Their friends are ready to lift all our goods!"

"No trick!" Si-hotep vowed. "I'm a cargo scribe on the *Blue Perch*, up from Thebes. The captain will reward you. Only haul us up, before we drown!"

Si-hotep shook water out of his ears and listened with dread for a clumsy splashing.

The cargo-guard rapped out some shrewd questions anent the *Blue Perch*, her load and her dealings. Si-hotep answered them, glad he had thoroughly prepared for his role. Any further waiting, though, and either he or Perkhet would begin screaming.

"That's right enough," the guard conceded at last. "They must be from the *Blue Perch*. Haul them up."

Si-hotep took advantage first, or tried to, but Perkhet shouldered him aside and went up the offered rope hand over hand, nearly stamping on Si-hotep's head in his desperation to gain safety. The thief clung with his good hand, any sympathy or fellow-feeling for Perkhet draining out of him. Ghastly visions of *something* paddling through the night with empty eye-sockets and entrails drifting beneath it like weed under an old boat, assailed his fancy.

Then it came. The slow deliberate splashing he dreaded. His mind threatened to split and topple like stone in a quarry. He said hoarsely,

"Haul me up now, for the love of all gods! I've a broken arm and I hear a crocodile!"

The men above him laughed, but they dropped a looped rope. Si-hotep caught it with his good hand and struggled to slip head, shoulders and one arm through it. An indistinct shape moved clumsily through the water in the dark narrow lane between the two vessels' sides. A wet blind head moved as though searching. The thief kept rigidly still in the water and yelled, "Pull me up!"

"By Hapi!" someone declared above him. "There is a crocodile!"

Si-hotep did not enlighten him. He fumbled for his knife and discovered that he had lost it while swimming one-armed. His blood chilling, he called out urgently, "A crocodile! Pull me up swiftly; the temple of Amun-Ra will reward you greatly!"

The men above began hauling on the rope. Si-hotep, emerging from the water, slipped half-way through the loop and fell back. Something bumped blindly against him, and cast clammy arms around his thighs, to his consternation and loathing. He clung to the rope with his good hand. He began to rise, and the insensate clasp on his legs began to slip, but the thing weighed heavy as a sack of offal. Besides, it clung with dogged persistence. If Si-hotep lost his grip and fell into the water with it, he would not come out again.

He dragged one leg free and stamped on a dead shoulder that felt like stone. It flung its damaged arms about his thighs again and struggled to raise its grip to his waist. Si-hotep frantically slammed his knee against the heavy jaw and neck with all the force he could gather, to no avail. And his hand was steadily slipping from the rope.

"Look out!" bellowed some would-be helpful fool above him.

A snout and two yellow eyes appeared in the narrow gap of water. The cargo guards' torches caught the hungry gleam of those eyes. The snout advanced smoothly, a great hinged jaw opened to show teeth like rows of daggers, and the jaws closed on the thing that embraced Si-hotep. It was torn away from him. Charnel-smelling arms flailed wildly, beating the scaly snout. Then the crocodile rolled, went down, and Si-hotep saw no more.

Nearly fainting for all his insouciant nerve, he was whisked to the deck above and rolled choking beside Perkhet. There were only two thoughts, not over-coherent, in his mind. One was that no other man could ever have been so glad of a crocodile's close proximity. The other was that a certain Archpriest could find someone else to conduct his manhunts in future.

VI.

Si-hotep was back in the dark water. Dead arms clung around his thighs in a clumsy, groping embrace, and a weight like a granite block dragged at him while he held to a rope with his good arm, his grip gradually slipping. Loudly as he shouted to the men above to pull him up, there came no answer.

Death was clinging to him, eager to draw him down to the slimy harbour mud. Each breath he took was one more lost out of a meagre number left. He used knees and feet with skill on the malign, insensate thing that gripped him, but to no effect. And despite his desperate grip, Si-hotep's hand slid down the rope until the water covered his head.

He sank. Flailing in frenzy, his broken arm struck the bottom of the ship, and the pain obliterated even panic. He struggled in the black water, and slowly comprehended that he was struggling on a light bed in Kiya's house, that she was beside him, holding him with gentle strength to keep the broken arm still, and that he had been dreaming.

"Keep still," the girl said firmly. "You will hurt that arm. You had a nightmare."

"I did," he agreed. "About the jackals who beat me and tossed me in the Nile, about sinking in dark water." That was all he had told her. "It's good to wake and find I am not there, but here."

"With a broken arm that I have to tend!" Kiya scolded. "You should not—no honest man should—go near the waterfront."

"I am not an honest man."

Si-hotep's arm hurt, the horror of the dream lingered, and he felt intolerant. Still, he controlled his impulses. No need to quarrel with the girl.

"I was employed to find someone," he went on. "For success, high payment. I have succeeded, and now I'll be paid. True, I didn't reckon a broken arm into the account when I said yes, but so it turned out." He made himself grin. "Luckily, I have you to look after me."

"Huh!" the girl said. "A broken arm is the only thing that could keep you here long. I know."

It was good that she knew. Si-hotep did not deny it. He held her in the curve of his good arm. She was warm, alive and humanly harmless, an antidote to dark recollections. But on the other side of him the broken arm throbbed in its splints. His skin remembered the hideous touch of the lich. A chance occurrence—he felt certain neither Kamose nor his enemies had sent the thing—but it showed how dark events and presences went with any business of the Archpriest's.

He hoped the man would require nothing more of him for a long time. Rumour said he had gone into seclusion in his mansion at Abdu, even that he had suffered a sore hurt from a demon he had invoked. Maybe he would not recover. The thief had delivered Perkhet into his hands, and he preferred not to imagine how the Archpriest's servants might be inducing Perkhet to divulge all he knew.

What if some such horror touched the girl next time?

Si-hotep smiled sardonically to himself in the darkness. Let him not pretend to noble virtue. Kiya was a tie to normal living. She threatened his cheerful lack of scruples. He was Si-hotep, the thief, the best thief in the Two Lands of Khem, daring, deft and best of all—unknown. Except to the cursed Archpriest, and he was a special case. Anonymity meant survival.

It was time to leave Kiya, in part for her sake, and more for his. Wherefore Si-hotep held her more snugly with his good arm, and pillowed her head more comfortably on his shoulder. The perfume he had stolen for her crept into his brain through his nostrils.

When my arm heals, he thought. *When my arm heals I will go.*

RETURN OF GANESH

A wail of utterest despair and grief swelled through the halls of Kamose the Archpriest's mansion. His functionaries, those who were human, shivered to hear it, all but his major-domo, the blandly cynical eunuch Rahen. That person had developed a taste for horror to replace the ordinary human passions of which he was bereft.

Rahen knew what was going on. The Archpriest, himself, was questioning a captive—a rare instance. The prisoner's knowledge must be urgent to obtain. Rahen had seen the man when he arrived, a massive, burly brute with one eye recently gouged from its socket. He must have been ill-advised enough to resist being taken.

The desolate cry died away, though it left echoes. Another voice, that of Rahen's master, took its place, apparently posing questions. Harsh and demanding, it reverberated even through the heavy walls of brick, though the words and the sense were muffled to unintelligibility. Rahen on the whole felt glad, incorrigible spy though he was. The timbre of Kamose's voice sounded alien. It scraped at Rahen's eardrums and caused his flabby muscles to contract along his bones.

He had known this to occur before. The Archpriest was extracting the last shreds of relevant knowledge that sorry creature possessed, all without touching him physically; so much the eunuch could surmise. But given a choice the captive no doubt would have taken physical torture and found it less ruinous.

Another sound filtered through the thick walls then, more feebly than the Archpriest's voice. It cheeped, whimpered, sobbed. A normal person would have felt his skin crawl to think that those noises came from the throat of one who was—or had been—a strong, brutal man. Rahen licked his lips.

This interrogation had continued since the previous afternoon. Rahen's master had ordered him to be close at hand from sunrise onward. He did not imagine he would have long to wait now, to see the result.

Complete silence, now, from the sealed chamber. Rahen pictured the Archpriest breaking the seals on the inner side of the portals, one by one, intoning countercharges and dismissals to the demon depicted on each. Stresses quivered in the air; grey shadows cast by unseen beings, or by nothing, departed. The bronze-bound cedar doors boomed wide.

"Rahen!"

Ponderous in his white linen robe, jowls quivering above his jewelled collar, the eunuch still responded swiftly. The Archpriest of Anubis waited, as lean, harsh and energetic as Rahen was sleekly self-indulgent. He wore only black sandals, kilt and skull-cap. The recent lacerations of a demon's claws showed lividly on his rib cage. They were healing; reluctantly, but still healing.

Behind him, crouched against a pillar, something mumbled and drooled. It made the eunuch think of a man a hundred and twenty years old, virility and continence both long vanished, and a mind also, muscles wasted, bones brittle, dried up like a dead locust. Yet there were still strong young teeth in the slack mouth.

It had one filmed sightless eye. The other socket lay empty. By that Rahen knew the being. By that only, for yesterday this object had been a mighty man, sullen, glowering, muscled like intertwined pythons, showing no fear even though he knew his situation. The Archpriest had extracted more than information from him, without laying a finger on the fellow physically. Yet he had wept and blubbered before the end.

Rahen bowed low.

"Destroy this," Kamose said. "Give it seemly embalming and a tomb, though, with its name inscribed. The name is Perkhet."

"At your behest, Holy One," Rahen fawned.

Kamose was meticulous in all matters that concerned death, embalming and the grave. He had to be. His patron Anubis, the jackal-headed lord of tombs, stood between him and the enmity of the Temple of Thoth—of the god Thoth himself, whose scrolls of magic Kamose had long ago stolen. Satisfying Anubis was imperative. His archpriest might be cynically indulgent towards, even appreciative of, thieves who robbed the living, the rich, the powerful, and temples other than his own. With tomb robbers he was relentless.

So Perkhet went to his tomb, and a better one was made for him, there in the necropolis of Abdu, than he deserved. By then Kamose had travelled downstream in a nondescript vessel that no-one noticed in the vast traffic of the Nile. He went without fanfare or companions, save the boatmen and a raffish mongrel dog, in a poor scribe's disguise. This was one of many false identities he used. When he went ashore he maintained himself as a poor scribe would, writing letters and petitions for those who required them, in exchange for food and beer from a farmer, or a pair of shoes from a cobbler. In this fashion he made his way to a customs outpost in the eastern Delta.

There he considered all he had learned from Perkhet. Despite his poor and brutish origins as the son of a boatman, Perkhet had become a jeweler of conspicuous talent in a temple workshop. Sadly, his violent, intemperate nature had led him to disaster. After beating his wife to death (a crime lightly regarded in savage nations but taken seriously in Egypt) he had lost his position. His freedom with it. Then someone had promised him a change of fortune if he would make a copy of the late Pharaoh's heart scarab. An exchange had been contrived, part of a scheme to disgrace Kamose.

The scheme had failed. Now Kamose sought the men responsible. They were somewhere in the hierarchy of the Temple of Thoth, doubtless, though their tracks had been well covered.

From Perkhet he had obtained a name. It belonged to the go-between who had recruited Perkhet to the complex plot. The Archpriest now thought it best to direct the next stage of the search himself. He had a spurious identity in Hikuptah, also, a most appropriate and useful one; that of Ganesh, a foreign jeweler and discreet fence who often travelled to Syria and elsewhere buying gems. Familiar with Hikuptah's rich society and its underworld, having wealth and resources, Ganesh—yes, Ganesh was the man for this task.

It was time he returned from abroad.

II.

Kamose, transfigured into Ganesh the jeweler, sat in his inner chamber behind the workshop where his artisans laboured. Padding and fringed Syrian robes made him bulky instead of leopard-lean. A wig and large false beard of curling hair hid most of his face. Other pads fattened his cheeks. Even his hands were altered. Gloves cunningly made from the skin of an ape rendered them thick and hairy.

Dust lay everywhere in the room. It eddied in the air. Trays of gems, bottles, jars and statuettes made of semi-precious stone were arranged with anomalous (considering the dust) neatness on serried racks. Receipts and inventories lay before Ganesh with a scribe's equipment nearby.

At present he was not working on them. On a small adjacent table stood a jug of rich beer, two clay beakers, a plate of bread and a dish of shining dates. Yet Ganesh was the only occupant of the chamber.

A driller and polisher with hunched shoulders entered. Like Ganesh, he was Syrian, unlike Ganesh, a slave, captured in battle. He limped from old wounds.

"The messenger is here, master."

"Show him in, Kert."

The man who entered carried a reed satchel. Of middle height, he stepped jauntily. He had sharp cheekbones, quick eyes, and a mobile mouth with an impudent cast. He and Ganesh had dealt together for years. The man supposed he knew him. Not knowing who Ganesh really was, of course, he did not know him at all.

"Be thrice welcome, Si-hotep, most resourceful of... finders."

Si-hotep was a thief. If careless or boastful, he would have been a byword in the mighty city of the White Walls for his skill, and soon after that, captured. Being discreet instead, he remained unknown. Ganesh knew about him, but that was inevitable, since Ganesh fenced his plunder.

"Your return from Syria gladdens my heart, most hirsute of jewelers." Glancing more closely at the visible part of the Syrian's face, in particular his sunken, dark-rimmed eyes, the thief asked, "Are you unwell?"

"A fever and flux that came to me with that cursed donkey caravan," Ganesh grunted. "Nothing of import, now that I am again where I can appeal to Egyptian physicians, and it is nothing to do with business. El the Merciful! Did you have to frighten my scribe into a shaking idiot while I was absent?"

"Oh. Wesu. My regrets and apologies, good Ganesh." Si-hotep helped himself to the beer. "But never would I drink a potion supplied by—the one we know of—unless I tested it first. If Wesu recovers his wits he shall have his share of the loot. Do you wish to see it?"

"Not for half a year, as you well know! The rapacious Khentau whom you robbed is still searching the city for the culprit. Or any clue to him. All Hikuptah throbs with wonder that his treasure room could be looted."

"It well may," the thief agreed. "Even I couldn't have done it without the Archpriest's potion."

"Ah, the potion. Yes. The bottle you were given held three effective doses, I'm told. You forced one on Wesu and later took one yourself. That leaves one."

"I have it still. And nothing but desperation will make me swallow it, O Ganesh, though it gives a man the power to walk through granite walls."

Ganesh shrugged his heavy shoulders. "It was never intended but for emergencies. You discovered the man he desired you to find, and handed him over as required. The one we know of is content."

"That's pleasant to know," the thief said scathingly. "I almost went as mad as Wesu when I drank the potion, and then came close to being torn limb from limb by a wrathful lich! The man who made the false scarab lost an eye—and more than that, I take it, when the Archpriest laid hands on him."

"Nay, be careful, youngster," Ganesh rumbled. "Neither names nor titles where *that one* is concerned."

"I'm out of patience," Si-hotep retorted, irked by the word youngster. "I'm weary of whispers and circumlocution when we refer to him, and weary of the tasks he sets me—which used to be occasional, but seem to grow more frequent lately. If the jackal's servant has a new one in mind, find someone else to perform it. My arm is still healing. My professional arm, O Ganesh! I'm reduced to living on blackmail for now—moderate and discreet, but far beneath me, nevertheless. I'm a thief. Him we do not name—red hemorrhoids afflict him!—he may be pleased, and ought to be. I am not."

The jeweler gave a fat chuckle. "Calm yourself, my thief. Because of you, we have learned who recruited Perkhet. It was Khentau."

"*Khentau*?" The thief forgot his resentment and laughed aloud. "The same one? Rare coincidence! Although come to think of it, that corrupt official is a likely man for the go-between. He's not like Perkhet, to vanish without causing comment, but I daresay he'll be handled."

Ganesh was silent.

The silence drew out.

Si-hotep recognised its quality quickly, and said with a lifted eyebrow, "Not by me!"

"Ah." Ganesh shifted his bulk in his chair and took a swallow of the rich beer. "It happens that—the one we know of—has sent me a communication, a letter, to do with Khentau. He wishes you to visit the man again."

"I decline."

"Come, nimble thief, you know better! It's all right. The holy one knows of your hurt. Neither walking through walls nor your fine skills of burglary will be called upon. You need merely play the part of an exorcist and deceive Khentau a little."

Si-hotep received the information with total mistrust. "Khentau is superstitious, and always calling upon physicians for some fancied ailment or other. I know his weaknesses. But why should he resort to exorcists?"

"He to whom we refer with discretion will see to it that Khentau feels an urgent need for one. Never fear but that you will be able to meet his need, O Si-hotep. In exchange—you must demand the name of the man behind Khentau, who was the man behind Perkhet."

Khentau will divulge it, the disguised Kamose thought. *My sendings will haunt him till he begs to do so. Not that the name itself will lead very far. This schemer is cunning. Still it will be one more step.*

Khentau, I will make that the extent of your punishment. Awarding you a worse fate might give it away to the schemer that I am hunting him out. Besides, you are not worthy of more thorough treatment.

You will never know how lightly you are escaping.

III.

Khentau should never have acquired a bad conscience, for he was a man who worried. Unfortunately greed mastered him. Greed had driven him to steal, in his official capacity, for years. Then it had brought him to arrange for Perkhet to commit the great crime of counterfeiting the Pharaoh's heart scarab. The offered price had been one he could not resist, despite the danger.

He regretted it now.

In the private chapel of his mansion, he prostrated himself before a statue of Osiris, with its tranquil green face and shrouded body, and desperately denied his faults.

"Oh lord of the pleasant afterworld! Let not my heart speak against me in the hall of truth! I have not done evil to mankind. I have not oppressed the members of my family. I have had no knowledge of worthless men. I have done no murder.

"I have not made the first consideration of each day that excessive labour should be performed for me. I have not brought forward my name for exaltation to honours. I have not defrauded—"

As he babbled the conventional litany, Khentau's heart spoke against him indeed. It grew heavier with each point he made, each crime he denied. In his capacity as Head of Irrigation and Controller of the Granaries he had, in fact, committed most of them. Only of murder, and the oppression of his own family, did he feel truly free. Nevertheless, he consoled himself with the common belief that offerings could placate the gods, and spells deceive them. He protested harder.

"—not robbed the temples of their oblations. I have not diminished from the bushel. I have not turned back the water at a time when it should flow. I—"

Fear weighed his heart for all his words. The gods perhaps could be deceived or bribed. The dread Archpriest of Anubis was another matter. Khentau thought of him, shivered, and went to bed wretched.

Recent events in his house had been ominous. His treasure room, which he had believed untouchable, had nevertheless suffered entry and rifling. No one could say how the thief had come or gone. Also, Khentau's prized watch-leopard had died with no mark on its pelt but nature's dark rosettes. An agent of the Archpriest? A sign that retribution was near? It was all too possible.

Khentau slammed his fist on the wooden neck-rest of his bed, and hurt himself.

Never married, he kept eight young female servants and slaves, but he summoned none of them that evening. Sleeping badly, resorting often to the wine-jug beside his bed, he had fragmentary evil dreams. And then, finally, one that was all of a piece.

He dreamed of Perkhet, that hulking brutal fellow whose mallets of hands were so incongruously skilled at fine jewel-work. It was Khentau who had suborned him to make a copy of the late Pharaoh's heart scarab. In Khentau's dream the brute loomed over him, leering.

"You soft prize pig," he mocked. "I'm caught, you know. See what happened to me. Look."

Khentau looked. Black shadows thickened around Perkhet, and among them a monstrously tall shape in priest's robes began to interrogate him with dreadful words. Perkhet cowered and screamed. He writhed in agony though no-one touched him. Horror-nauseated, Khentau saw him *shrink* with each contortion—shrivel—wither as with extreme age. The process drew out interminably, and when it ended at last, the massive brawler had become like an ancient monkey. One eye-socket gaped empty. The remaining eye looked filmed and blind. The thing cackled in Khentau's direction.

"This befell me because of you," it said like rustling sere grass. "Because of the scarab I made. Your turn is coming, soft prize pig. Wait for it."

Khentau shook in icy fear, and then awoke—with intense relief. He assured himself it had been a dream, only a guilty dream, with no real meaning. He reached for the jug, swigged and gulped. A dream!

You are not dreaming now.

The susurrating voice was the identical one of Khentau's nightmare. Before him crouched the same gloating, wizened figure. It spoke the truth. He was not dreaming now.

His scream awoke the whole house.

When servants came rushing with lights and staves, the ghost had vanished. Khentau retained enough presence of mind to see that they would doubt his reason, if they disbelieved him, and very likely flee his house, if they believed. He muttered an excuse about a nightmare. Shaking, he made no further attempt at sleep, but spent the rest of the night in his treasure chamber, going over its contents with his scribe and an axe-bearing guard.

Next day he laboured at his official duties. He worked excessively hard in an effort to forget, but dreaded each inch the shadows of afternoon lengthened. That night he retired to bed with two of his maidservants. Both, perhaps, were surprised by his energy, not knowing what fuelled it. After his desires were satisfied he ordered them to remain in his bed, afraid of solitude. He was still breathing deeply when he rolled over to slumber.

He awoke.

Faint greenish-yellow light flickered along his chamber's walls. And those walls had changed. They bore scenes of judgement—the well-known theme of a heart weighed in the balance while the jackal-headed funerary lord, Anubis, tested the scale and Thoth stood aside to record the outcome. The hideous Gobbler waited to devour a soul that proved guilty, but in this painting it was not the conventional (and puerile) compound of hippopotamus, crocodile and hyena, rather a triple-jawed fiend unlike anything known in Egypt. Its purulent eyes seemed to glare with hunger at Khentau. The painting had that awful quality peculiar to nightmares.

Khentau felt nauseated, but that was only the beginning. Something with a clinging, scratchy grip touched his shrinking foot. Looking down he saw a beetle, an emerald green beetle large as a man's two fists, crawling over his instep. Half a dozen others glittered and crept on the bed-end. He would have yelled, but his throat shrank shut. The flesh drawing away from his bones with revulsion, he hurled himself out of bed, and regretted it at once.

A green carapace crunched under his scrawny bare foot. Wings fluttered; spiny legs twitched, broken. The entire floor of his chamber crawled with shining green dung-beetles. He flung himself back into bed and huddled there. That, and the violent movement that had gone before, awakened one of his bed-mates. He was not sure he wished her to awaken. As it was, he could hope he was mad, but if she saw the same thing…

The first thing she did see was a sight that Khentau had missed. The spectre of Perkhet crouched near the door, nodding and grinning with a toothless leer. He, or it, held a lamp that shed the greenish light. One of the great beetles clung to his scalp.

The girl's eyes bulged. Unlike her master, she had no difficulty at all in screaming, and continued more loudly until she roused the house—for the second night in succession. Porters, the butler, Khentau's Libyan guards, all came running. Again they found nothing out of the ordinary in their master's chamber. The painted walls were normal, the spectre of Perkhet had vanished, and no sign of any beetles remained.

Except scratches from the barbed feet of one, bleeding on Khentau's calf.

IV.

"The lamentable Khentau's servants begin to desert him," Ganesh laughed. "Fear afflicts the pig-boar! He consults diviners and exorcists! It is time for you to visit him in the guise of such a one. You ought to find him—receptive."

Si-hotep agreed. It did amuse him to think of meeting face to face, in the guise of a benefactor, the very man whose treasure-room he had looted. It was not the sort of chance that often came a thief's way. Besides, he really would be a benefactor to the poor peccant scoundrel, since he would bring an end to the haunting. Accordingly, when Khentau's major-domo ushered him into the official's presence, Si-hotep's heart sang with the pleasure of mischief.

He confronted an anxious man. Being haunted had cost Khentau his pompous assurance. The thief introduced himself by a false name, claiming to be a magician of remarkable power, specialising in divination and exorcism, enjoying the favour of Thoth; and Khentau listened, his skepticism diluted by desperate hope. He noted the "magician's" youth and tawdry finery, of course, but he did not have Si-hotep ejected. Ganesh had been right; he was receptive.

For his part, Si-hotep observed certain things about Khentau. He wore a profusion of charms against evil—the traditional Eye of Horus, *djed* pillar, and more obscure periapts. Others, mostly images of beneficent gods, filled the room to the point of clutter, and incense burned before a little shrine to Osiris in an alcove central to one wall. Someone sat on a stool in a shadowed corner, and Si-hotep lifted a questioning eyebrow.

"Lord, it were better that we were private."

The person in the corner rose and stalked forward. Shaven, aged and wrinkled, he wore an expression at once intensely serious—and hostile. Si-hotep at once guessed him to be a magician. He had heard that one named Mereruka was a member of Khentau's household. After failing to protect his master against Si-hotep's recent robbery, though, and then proving helpless to halt the hauntings that had plagued Khentau since, he had probably found his influence in decline.

"The lord Khentau has received a score of charlatans lately," the presumed magician said. "He does not need the presumption of another! You, stranger, have the signs of one strongly about you. If that is the case it will soon be discovered. You would be wise to go.'

"The learned Mereruka, I take it," Si-hotep smiled. "What have you accomplished to ease this illustrious lord's mind?"

"What do you know of my mind?" Khentau barked; but the bark cracked at the end into something more like a squeak. "Mereruka, leave us. If this is another faker you may be sure I will know how to treat him."

Mereruka, with a sour smile, departed. It was obvious that he relished the thought of Si-hotep's being sent on his way with a beating, and expected just that outcome. The thief drew himself up and radiated assurance.

"I have divined your trouble, lord, and you need not explain it. You are afflicted because of a wrong you have done, by the spectre of a man you suborned to perform it, and beyond that it were better to be discreet." Khentau paled and grew sweaty. "But the spectre is withered, shrunken and aged, when the man you knew was in the prime of his strength, and it has one eye, though the man you knew possessed both. Besides this, swarms of scarab beetles attend his ghost when it appears. Not so?"

Khentau grew sweatier yet, and his mouth quivered. Then he controlled himself and snapped, "How do you know this? I am no man with whom you may trifle!"

"I do not trifle, lord," Si-hotep said reprovingly. "Neither does this phantom. All others have failed to end his attentions. I can do so. Also, I ask nothing, not even a meal, until I have shown you success."

"In that at least you are unlike the others. Say further."

"You must make an offering at the mortuary temple of the Pharaoh Setekh-Nekht, justified."* Si-hotep named the amount. While more than substantial, it was not beyond Khentau's means, even after Si-hotep's raid on his treasure. Khentau did not protest. He was distraught indeed. "The haunting will not end until this is done."

"I'll travel to the temple at once," Khentau promised. "But when I have made the offering—this horror will end?"

Horror, Si-hotep thought sardonically. *You haven't seen horror, you poor shifty goose. And my fear is that nor have I, yet.*

He answered, "Yes. So that you may be sure of my truth I will accompany you. Once the offering has been made, this ghost will depart. However—"

"There is always a however,' Khentau said sourly.

"This one is minor, lord. To make sure the ghost does not return, you must then do one thing more."

"And what is that?"

---

* the late Setekh-Nekht.

"Nothing great or difficult. I will name it when the time comes. When the ghost has left you in peace for a few nights and you know I am true of voice."

"So be it."

Khentau's voice cracked slightly. Striking a bronze gong to bring his major-domo, he gave instructions to prepare for travel. The Valley of Kings lay far upstream, but travel on the blessed Nile was easy, particularly for wealthy men.

Si-hotep accompanied him as arranged, and might even have found the voyage pleasant if Khentau had not brought Mereruka with him. The wrinkled magician now saw Si-hotep as a rival to be reckoned with, not as a mere charlatan, and this altered perception had deepened his feelings from scorn to detestation. Also, Khentau's worn nerves impelled him to incessant whining. Perkhet's recurring apparition, for that matter, rasped Si-hotep's own brazen nerves with remorse. Telling himself that the man's doom had been merited did not descend smoothly into his stomach. He would be glad to see this assignment end.

Apart from unfamiliar feelings of remorse, and Mereruka's resentment, Si-hotep did not like Khentau's bodyguard, who consisted mainly of long slabs of fibrous muscle and a brooding scowl. He never commented on the nightly comings of the spectre. Just once on the journey did Si-hotep hear him laugh. That occurred when two fishermen in a reed boat were attacked by a hippopotamus and their craft ripped asunder. They barely escaped from the ill-tempered monster. Khentau did take them aboard, to do him justice. His conscience had become tender since the ghost began haunting him.

They arrived at Thebes. The thief had been there on four other occasions, but had never cared for it as he did for the city of his birth, Hikuptah. They were not there long. Khentau crossed at once to the western shore and made the required offering at Setekh-Nekht's temple. It was a pompous ceremony of incense, priestly vestments and rodomontade, and it bored Si-hotep greatly. But it met the conditions of Khentau's atonement, and Si-hotep had all confidence that now the visitations would cease. Kamose the Archpriest was no maladroit by repute, and he had sent the spectre to begin with—or, more likely, one of his minions had.

"It is done," Khentau said, looking lugubrious; he had just parted with a donation large enough to grieve any man, let alone one distinguished by his degree of avarice. He sent Si-hotep a resentful glance. "You had better be correct in your prognostication that the haunting is over, fellow."

"I said, lord, that you must do one thing more."

"You did." Khentau's countenance grew more vinegary yet.

"That unhappy spectre, while a living man, it would seem was suborned to copy the Pharaoh's heart scarab." Si-hotep spoke with unctuous tact. "By divination I learned that behind whatever man bribed him was another man, hiding his identity in darkness. Reveal that man's name to me, lord, and these disconcerting visits will no longer be. I give you my assurance of it."

"Reveal the man's name?" Khentau bridled. "How should I know? And what is his name to you?"

"Nothing," Si-hotep said, lying cheerfully. "If I divined erroneously, you do not know the name—but I have never divined erroneously." This was true only because he had never performed a divination in his life. "The spectre will plague you without end if you divulge the name not."

Khentau was silent for a time. Copious sweat betrayed his agitation. At last he spat forth a name. Si-hotep's powers of dissimulation were tested to keep him from gaping. This, indeed, was a surprise.

He mastered his astonishment and murmured, "Then all should be well, lord."

Within his mind he called Khentau a grasping extortionate monkey.

Despite the truth of the insult, Khentau was left in peace that night, and the nights following.

V.

Si-hotep felt far happier. The spectre had departed. Khentau had ceased his frightened whining. The rowers were happier also, since the little ship, returning down-stream, ran with the current and their work had become light.

Even Wab the bodyguard showed signs of affability now and again. He actually sought Si-hotep's company; not that the thief considered it reassuring, for in a fellow like Wab ulterior motives were too likely. He probably acted under orders from Khentau, who gained confidence by the day and grew correspondingly haughty.

"I'll be glad to see Hikuptah again," Wab said.

Short, abrupt sentences were his idea of conversation. Si-hotep supposed he was unused to talking much in any case.

"Oh, yes," he agreed. "There are many fools in a great city—but wine-shops and pretty girls by the score to make up for it."

"Girls!" Wab guffawed and began bragging about his prowess as a lover. He crowded Si-hotep while doing so, and even threw an arm around his shoulders. Si-hotep did not care for that. Perhaps Wab felt expansive now that the ship was no longer haunted, and perhaps that was all, but they were close to the gunwale and crocodiles abounded in the river.

The ship sped faster as the Nile began to rise. Thebes lay far behind, and they came to Abdu, the great place of pilgrimage with its temple to Osiris. Inland among the bluffs at the edge of the western desert, served by a canal, lay the estates and sombre mansion of Kamose. The terrible Archpriest was said to be at home now, withdrawn into seclusion for a while by leave of the young Pharaoh. Khentau paused there for just one night to take on supplies. Si-hotep might have used the opportunity to slip away. He decided to stay, no matter how untrustworthy his host's intentions. Khentau was less dangerous than Kamose.

Mereruka remained in the vessel's small cabin amidships. Whatever he did there was not for Si-hotep's benefit, as the thief soon concluded. He loitered by the cabin door, stretching his ears, and was not amazed when Wab promptly appeared at his side. Later, in the afternoon heat, he relaxed with his back against the cabin's side. Again Wab appeared almost at once, looming above him.

Khentau has given this ape his instructions.

"There's other shade on the boat, scribe,' he said, courteously for him. "This is my master's cabin."

"I will not intrude on his privacy," Si-hotep answered. "He does not have a woman with him."

"Nevertheless, get up." Wab kicked at the soles of Si-hotep's feet for emphasis.

Si-hotep did not fight, in spite of his surge of anger. Wab clearly hoped for that; he was poised and ready. The thief accompanied him to the bow and shared more beer with him in spite of the burly thug's scarcely hidden contempt.

He'd regret that scorn before long.

Drugging him proved so easy it was scarcely fair. Si-hotep never employed banal devices like hollow rings; they were the province of amateurs and jealous wives. A simple phial with a snug stopper, and his own adroit legerdemain, had always been enough. Si-hotep slipped the phial from its stitched resting place behind his belt and held it close against the neck of a beer-jug while he poured. His thumb and forefinger eased out the stopper, and the phial's contents spilled into Wab's cup along with the beer. The bodyguard saw nothing. Si-hotep, drinking to fair weather with a flourish, returned the phial to its hiding place with his other hand.

The soporific acted slowly. Wab, suspecting nothing, merely became steadily more sleepy. Purring snores vibrated in his nose by sundown. The rowers, too, rested on their benches, while a light breeze blew northward and the brawny steersman kept the vessel steady. All rather idyllic, to a naive observer.

Like a shadow, Si-hotep approached the cabin and climbed onto its roof. Not a board creaked. The thief lowered himself to his belly near a fissure between two boards where light gleamed yellow, and attempted to look through without much profit. He employed his knife to lever splinters away with exquisite patience. Working by tiny increments to avoid noise, he made the crack slightly wider. Si-hotep had mastered skills such as that even before his interest in girls became urgent.

He applied his eye again and beheld Khentau seated on a stool, looking fixedly at something. Mereruka? No doubt.

A boring delay followed, with Khentau barely stirring and never speaking at all. Nevertheless, he could not be so intent on anything that lacked importance. Si-hotep waited. The discomfort of the hard boards was as nothing to a man who had once hidden in a cesspool all night, breathing through a reed, in order to get his hands on a sack of gold bangles from Kush.

Finally, Mereruka stepped into his field of view. The old magician held something in one hand—and since it was foreshortened from above, Si-hotep did not identify it at first, though he felt immediate, ugly suspicion. Then Mereruka held the object at arm's length for his master's inspection—a wax manikin, lean and symmetrical in form as Si-hotep, besides being similar in hue. Such things were often silly pretence, of course, made by village girls crossed in love to curse their rivals, and quite ineffectual. Not this time. This wax image had been formed by a wizard of genuine ability.

His other hand held a long bronze pin. Slowly he thrust it into the wax doll's elbow-joint.

Si-hotep had suffered severe pain before, and this time he had a presage of what was coming. Barely in time did he lock his teeth and throat shut, and the sensation was like having a red-hot dagger stabbed through his elbow. He arched like a bow. Rank sweat burst out on his back.

Oh, someone shall pay!

Had it been a mere test, though? Si-hotep essayed to think, through the pain that threatened to overturn his mind. If a test, then Mereruka must have expected a loud cry. Would he go searching for the thief on deck, or make a new trial of his accursed doll?

A red-hot spike in Si-hotep's knee gave him the answer. He could not restrain a sob. No more hesitation; he must act now! The cabin door was too strong for smashing down in a moment; the window, while a small square, had only flimsy shutters.

A ledge ran around the flat cabin roof. Si-hotep seized it in both hands, rolled off the roof, swung outward and back, lunging his feet against the shutters. They burst inward. Si-hotep, twisting like an eel, came through the violated fenestration feet first, at the cost of skin scraped from his side and a splinter-gashed leg. He noticed neither.

Landing on two feet, he let his impetus carry him to the wizard. The wrinkled fellow gaped, taken unawares. Perhaps he had seldom faced the need to think quickly. Knife in hand, Si-hotep slashed him across the chest and knew he had missed a fatal spot, but Mereruka squealed like a girl. The thief instantly struck back-handed with the pommel of his knife and stunned Mereruka with a blow to the temple. Possibly more than stunned him, he thought; that spot was dangerous.

As the wizard began to fall, Khentau opened his pampered mouth to yell. Si-hotep, trained as a gymnast and wrestler before turning to thievery, kicked Khentau hard in the belly. He subsided with his cry still potential.

Si-hotep thought, *I had better depart.*

Snatching the wax image from Mereruka's hand—the entire purpose of the exercise—he dashed from the cabin. The steersman called out, but by then Si-hotep was almost to the water in a less than perfect dive. Although not quite smacking the surface with his belly, he did not pierce it cleanly either, and came up snorting water.

He floundered a little, then realised with horror that although he breathed air, he was drowning. How? *Why?*

His left hand was in the river—and it held the wax image.

With presence of mind he later congratulated himself for having, Si-hotep raised his left hand high, and air filled his grateful lungs. He began swimming for the bank. Gods of the Nile, if he had let the doll fall—!

Not until after he gained the river-bank, and took notice of his skinned ribs and bleeding leg, did he give a thought to crocodiles. He legged it quickly away from the water then, shaking. Si-hotep loathed crocodiles more than anything alive. In some places they were reckoned sacred, but the thief felt even more irreverent on that matter than most others.

VI.

"So there was I," he remarked dryly in the dusty, cluttered back room of Ganesh's establishment. "Adrift, lacking documents, and cumbered with a wax image I dared not allow to be damaged. Believe me, worthy Ganesh, I looked after it better than some look after their swaddled infants."

"No doubt." Ganesh chuckled heavily. "I commiserate with you. That scoundrel Khentau must have decided he had told you too much once the haunting ceased."

"Now there lies the difficulty." Si-hotep feigned perturbation. "He told me nothing. Nothing. His decision, it seems, was to destroy me rather than divulge an incriminating name."

"What?" Ganesh surged bulkily to his feet, face congested, the fringes of his foreign robe quivering. "You failed? You of all men, thief, *you* had not the wit to make him speak before you eased his mind? Do you know what—the one we do not name—will do to us both?"

"I'd other things to concern me," Si-hotep answered petulantly. "There was a wealthy woman travelling in a litter; I pilfered her gems and used them to pay a magician to undo Mereruka's spell on the image. Once it could no longer harm me, I melted it and threw the wax in a privy."

"Much good that will do you if the magician makes another one! Or did you slay him?"

"Oh, most likely not. I've killed only one man, and that was in self-defence or he'd have axed me to death." Si-hotep abandoned his airy tone and grew serious. "It's two, I suppose, in fact. I may as well count myself Perkhet's slayer. I delivered him to death. Mereruka, though, cannot harm me even if he's alive. These magician's dolls do not really need some part of the victim, like hair or nails, to render them efficacious. Only the ignorant believe it. But they do have to be fashioned when the victim is close nearby. I never intend to be in close propinquity with Mereruka again." The thief sent Ganesh a sharp, heavy-lidded gaze. "I'm surprised that you do not know. You ought to. Unless you have no enemies."

Ganesh did know, and Si-hotep knew that he knew, but they were playing a game of deceit with each other.

The heavy, fleshy-faced Syrian shrugged. "It's of little importance. The anger of our mutual master makes princes afraid! How could you fail?"

"I lied!" Si-hotep moved like a mongoose pouncing on a fat cobra. His knife pricked Ganesh's throat through his great black beard. "I did not fail... let you keep still! Khentau gave me the name I sought, the name of the one who bribed him to find a jeweler skilled enough to copy the Pharaoh's heart scarab. It was *your* name, O Ganesh. Do not pretend to be amazed. What folly induced you to betray *that one* I cannot imagine. You might consider taking poison."

Within the bulky disguise of the jeweler, the most feared magician in Egypt digested this new knowledge. The thief credited it. So much was clear. Khentau had indeed told him that Ganesh the jeweler was the plotter behind him. Since Kamose himself was Ganesh—it appeared that someone else had used a like swathing disguise to imitate him, someone, very likely, who knew that Ganesh and Kamose were one. That particular secret had been discovered.

It was not overwhelmingly important. Kamose had other guises and assumed identities. As the implications sank in, he felt a sardonic appreciation of the joke. Some impudent scoundrel had made sure the trail of Perkhet would lead nowhere, and had even borrowed Kamose's own false character for the purpose. Really, it was delightful.

With Si-hotep's sharp dagger at his throat, Ganesh began to chuckle; even now, in the fruity, heavy mirth of the Syrian, not the metallic bark of

Kamose's rare laughter. He rocked with it. Si-hotep, while it required a great deal to take him aback, did feel puzzled.

"I'm glad the prospect of being changed into a crab tickles you so much."

Ganesh wiped his eyes with the back of a hirsute paw. "Put the knife away, lad! Ah, me. Ah, me. Of course I am not such a fool as to cross—the one of whom we do not speak. Someone pretended to be me to cover his tracks. A false beard and big fringed robe. You must agree it is a rare joke!"

He began laughing again.

Although well dissembled, it was enough in excess to jab the thief's wary survival instincts. Besides, it rang false; who would laugh as he received news that might displease the dread Archpriest? Ganesh did appear truly carefree on that score, though; so much did ring true, and there could only be one reason, that he knew infallibly he had nothing to fear.

An incredible surmise came to the thief's mind. Certainty followed it. The thing was more than possible; it was true. Rumours galore whispered that Kamose the Arch-priest had several identities as ordinary men which he maintained—in Hikuptah, in Thebes and other places. Ganesh himself had just said that a false beard and fringed robe would suffice to impersonate him.

Si-hotep lowered his gaze in shock and gripped his knife-hilt harder.

"Put the knife away," Ganesh repeated, and Si-hotep's skin crept at the false joviality in his tone. "We are safe. The Archpriest is not so easily fooled. He will know it was not I. Nay, I'll send him an explanatory missive at once."

Si-hotep barely listened to the patter. He was too occupied with keeping any sign of his realisation away from his face. With a brittle laugh, he put his knife away as advised. Knowing, now, that he dealt with Kamose, he thought it best—and it troubled him greatly to think that this dread figure knew him, had met him in person. It had been disquieting enough to believe that the Archpriest merely knew his name and sometimes gave him tasks from a remote distance.

"I'm glad," he said cuttingly, "you are so sure *that one* will be clement with us. Myself, I am dubious. I think I shall leave Egypt for a while."

THE SHABTI ASSASSIN

I.

Be serious, and great as to your worth. Do not speak secret matters. For he who hides his innermost thoughts is one who makes a shield for himself.

—*The Instructions of Dua-Khety*

As always during one of Kamose the magician's absences, rumors proliferated that he was dead. This time there seemed a stronger basis for the tales. He had retired to his palace at Abdu* with the scars of demonic talons raked across his rib cage, there to recover—or, it might be, perish. His most hopeful enemies said it only in surreptitious murmurs, however. They had been disappointed before.

They were disappointed again.

Bakenkhons, the urbane Archpriest of Amun-Ra, was not counted among Kamose's enemies and even rejoiced to see him in fettle. He hoped for Kamose's help. Certainly the man could give it if so inclined. More than simply restored from his dangerous decline, he blazed with vitality, and even appeared younger than before. His plans, though, or the young Pharaoh's plans for him, were known to none.

"Then perhaps you will depart for Kush, sagacious Kamose?"

Bakenkhons asked the question in a cautious tone. The temple he administered was the greatest of Egypt. Nevertheless, the god Anubis also owned wide fields, granaries, and slaves in thousands. His archpriest was a more potent sorcerer than Bakenkhons knew how to conceive. One did not offend him.

"It is possible," agreed the other. "The Pharoah disposes."

The young Pharaoh sought justice for a murdered father. Both men knew that. Moreover, it now appeared that the Kushite wizard responsible

---

* Abydos

was alive, not dead, and freely walking the soil of his own country. The Pharaoh must be ill pleased.

"One thinks of you for such tasks as this. Who else could perform them?"

"As you say, worthy Bakenkhons. I value your praise."

"If he should send you—"

Kamose gave him a considering and not especially pleasant look. Bakenkhons, as the First Prophet of Amun, wore a headdress of plumes and curled, gilded ram's horns. Beneath it showed a broad face of full jawline, flat triangular cheeks coarse with pockmarks, fleshy nose and a thick mouth held gravely straight. The mouth did not move to complete the sentence.

"If it should be?"

"I find myself in need of a favor from the greatest of magicians before he departs."

Kamose smiled, a mere curling of lips. "I'm inclined to serve the noble Archpriest of Amun-Ra by whatever means I may."

They continued to walk in the gardens of the royal palace complex. A pleasant milieu, it also offered privacy that might not be had indoors. Servants came and went on many pretexts, there, and could listen from alcoves or doorways. In the gardens they had fewer excuses.

The two archpriests followed a walkway beside an ornamental fishpond. They passed flower-beds of scarlet poppy and others of henna and narcissus. By one high white wall of the garden ran a straight row of dom-palms.

"When were you last in Thebes?"

"Seldom over the past three years. The last time, briefly—why, it was some months gone. Has much changed?"

"Three years. That, illustrious Prophet of Anubis, was about the time a noble named Ptahshepses passed away."

"I know something of Ptahshepses. His reputation did not have a sweet savor. Yes, he was prince of the sixth nome, was he not, and another man was given an office he craved, to his ire."

"Exactly so. Within months the man had died of lockjaw; an ill death. Ptahshepses replaced him."

"After which he was alleged to have diverted wealth to his own coffers."

"Yes. A subordinate scribe and an army officer accused him. The officer perished on a hippopotamus hunt. The river beast was maddened by harpoons and bit the officer's boat in two like a stick. Then it crushed him in the water. With three boats around it, half a dozen men in each boat, it slew only that one person. As for the scribe, Ptahshepses counter-accused him of being the thief, and he passed from life in a fit before hearings could proceed. He suffered from the falling sickness, but the fits had never been severe until that mortal one. A most opportune written confession was found, which may have been forged."

"It comes back now," Kamose said. "Two other instances of that sort occurred, and then—he overstepped wisdom. He conspired with Bay of despised memory to make Siptah the Pharaoh. But Siptah's reign was short. The chancellor was degraded from his post and executed. Ptahshepses survived, though he lost his position and his lordship of the Crocodile Nome, as did his family in perpetuity, by command of Queen Tawosret."

Three years afterwards, Tawosret too had died. Neither man mentioned that, nor the manner in which the next king, Setekh-Nekht, had obtained the Double Crown. In Egypt the discreet flourished, the indiscreet fell from favour.

"Ptahshepses died naturally." Bakenkhons resumed the story. "His children, a son and daughter, have been most conscientious in tending his tomb and shrine, which lies across the river here—as is merely fitting, to be sure."

"Proper," Kamose echoed. He hoped there was some point to all this. If people had been murdered—magically, it appeared—by a man now gone to judgment himself, it was hardly unknown. "Is anything other than proper? Since Ptahshepses perished?"

"Perhaps. The lovely Sitiah, daughter of Ptahshepses, wed a wealthy official much older than she. Within the year he went blind of a purulent eye disease. A month later he walked off the edge of their roof. There was a quarry taskmaster to whom the son Debhen, his sister's senior by two years, lost a great deal, gaming. I'm told that is not common. He usually wins. Shortly afterwards in the quarries, a block of stone crashed down a ramp, killing two workers—and the chief taskmaster. His heirs did not press for the gaming debt, substantial though it was."

Kamose offered no response. He thought, however, that the taskmaster's heirs had shown wisdom. These events reeked of magic and curses, as a street harlot of bad perfume. Each incident alone might have been a mishap. Taken together, with their opportune timing considered, they made a reprehensible total.

"There is more," Bakenkhons said. "Three murders in Thebes within the past twenty months. Murders without question. Each was committed after dark, at a banquet or ceremony or other public event. Each occurred when Debhen and Sitiah were present. Although they were violent deaths, nothing was witnessed. Each time, Debhen and Sitiah were together, well removed from the dispatch, with folk who could attest that they were blameless. In one instance, a *sem* priest and a high judge."

Even Kamose was moved to exclaim by that. "Teeth of the crocodile god! They chose meticulously."

"Chose?"

"Of course they chose! If, once, witnesses had been doubtful or lacking—but thrice out of three, impeccable folk each time, goes beyond mere fortune. O illustrious Bakenkhons, you think so too. Do you not? Murder... was there a method in common?"

"All were violent, as I say, and strangely carried out. One victim was stifled by having her throat packed with sand. One was found with the blade of a hoe sunk in his spine. A third was beaten to death with a peasant's wooden carrying-yoke. It was found beside him, broken. Easy to explain, if the victims had been farm workers and died outdoors, by day, but the slayings occurred under wealthy roofs, in the city. Who could bring a hoe or a basket of sand to a banquet unremarked?"

"It would be difficult," Kamose agreed. "The previous convenient deaths you mentioned might have been accidental. Not these latest ones! The manner has altered." Kamose regarded the other man from anthracite-dark eyes. "Surely this is a matter for investigators, commissions and judges? Have you a particular concern with it, O Bakenkhons?"

"You may suppose so," the Archpriest of Amun-Ra answered. His voice and look were bleak. "My son wishes to marry this young and charming widow, Sitiah. He is besotted with her."

"Hmm." Kamose comprehended now. The matter held some interest. Besides, having the head of Egypt's paramount temple in his debt would be worthwhile. The astute First Prophet of Amun had thought of that before appealing to him, obviously.

"I shall make secret and careful inquiry into these matters, if it pleases you."

II.

As for any people who shall take possession of this tomb as their mortuary property, or shall do any evil thing to it, judgment shall be had with them for it by the Great God.

          —Fifth Dynasty Tomb Curse

Kamose could enchant the sea, the sky and the earth if he desired. He understood the speech of beasts and birds, so far as they had language, and could command them also. He knew the secrets of various potions that gave one the power to walk through walls, breathe beneath water or move with a celerity beyond nature—though the first had its dangers and the last exacted its price from the body. He could even change his own face and body if he chose, though that feat called for careful preparation, and required time both to effect and to reverse.

Without resorting to magic, he employed disguises and false identities in certain places. In Thebes he sometimes appeared as a ship's captain or a vintner of repute—the latter a raucous woman. He assumed the role now. After shaving his beard, he painted his face thickly, donned a wig, and went forth as the tall, hatchet-faced widow Henut-tawy, merchant of wine and beer, established in Thebes for a dozen years.

Debhen and Sitiah made their lives an endless round of parties and public events. Bakenkhons had told the magician where they would be that evening. Thither went Kamose, in a litter and green woolen gown, long earrings swaying. Bodyguards with staves flanked the litter; flutes and dancing came behind. Last plodded three donkeys, wine-jars strapped to their useful, patient backs. When the porter at the gatehouse asked their business, Kamose leaned out of the litter, all merry, vulgar presumption.

"You ask *my* business, dear one? Who in Thebes does not know Henut-tawy the vintner, by name at least? I am she. And so, of course, I bring wine to your master's feast."

"My master's cellars abound in wine, the best vintages from the Delta. Nor has he dealt with you. Yet," he added unguardedly.

"And you, as a discriminating lad, think he should. I do agree. That is why I bring samples, to him free. These are amphorae of royal vintage from *Crete*, dear one, shipped across the Great Green at fabulous cost.

One grows drunk only from sniffing it, can imbibe all night with no headache next day!"

"She" swept past the gatehouse keeper, aided by her bodyguards, leaving a jug for him to try, and after that barged into the house by sheer presumption. The hour was late. The Theban noble and his guests were drunk, which helped Kamose gain entry, and some of those who tried to eject him stumbled or faltered—trifling magics for the Archpriest of Anubis. Besides, the wine was welcome.

Of course the vintner's pretensions before her betters were silly. Kamose intended that they should find her risible. A woman tittered, "*Where* did she obtain that ridiculous collar? And those earrings with it…"

The collar hid his masculine throat. The earrings were in character. Kamose clowned, was vulgar, and gave them mirth at Henut-tawy's expense before he left. Meanwhile he raked each room with his glance and observed everything.

He derived mild amusement of his own from the tame conduct he saw around him. One woman strutted, laughing, while she offered guests wine from between her ample breasts, and that was the most scandalous thing he beheld. If this dull gathering imagined that was debauchery, they had much they might learn from the Lady Yati's circle in Hikuptah.[*]

One seemed to share his view. An aloof young woman, gowned and painted in impeccable taste, was doing everything but yawn. This must be Sitiah. She did in fact resemble the Accursed Pharaoh's great wife, Nefertiti, as she was reputed to do.

Where was her brother, then? They were said to be inseparable.

Kamose blundered out of the main dining room, feigning to be lost, down a corridor painted with a frieze of gazelles and acacias. He resisted the guidance of polite servants, protesting that he had been told the way of egress and needed no help. On that pretext he intruded in three chambers, missing no detail in any of them, and discovered his quarry in the last.

Fumes of wine, perfume and scented lamp oil mingled beneath a ceiling upheld by six green and yellow pillars. Costly lamps burned the

---

[*] Memphis

lemon-infused oil, and two dancers in strings of beads performed to indifferent harp-music. Kamose understood their boredom. They were being ignored for a dice game which engrossed six young men.

One, slender and handsome, resembled the woman at the banquet so much that he was surely her brother. Kamose studied him, marking every aspect of his appearance, from the long-skulled head and fine features to the narrow bones of his limbs. Before he was hurried out of the chamber by servants whose exasperation now outweighed their tact, he heard someone say, "Again? There is no holding you over the dice, Debhen."

So. He was winning, as he had been said usually to do. Kamose turned and said brashly from the doorway, "Neglect not to sample my wine before it vanishes into thirsty throats, young gentlemen."

Then, all but ejected, he left the house. Returning to Henut-tawy's wine storehouse by the harbour, he felt content. This had gone well. He had beheld the heirs of Ptahshepses at a feast among their friends—if they had friends, truly. Some notions of his were now become more substantial.

Early the next morning he had himself carried in his ebony chair of office to the immense Temple of Amun-Ra that was the glory of Thebes. A long white thoroughfare led thereto between rows of ram-headed sphinxes. Bakenkhons would have carried out the sunrise rituals by now, unsealing the inner sanctuary and clothing the god in new raiment. He expected Kamose and should be ready to receive him.

He was. The two refreshed themselves with cakes and beer before they discussed their private matters. Kamose saw that Bakenkhons' composed manner hid an anxious heart; so much so that, while observant as a rule, he had not noticed that Kamose's chin-beard was false this morning. The previous day it had been his own growing hair. Well, Kamose had news to impart which ought to distract the First Servant of Amun-Ra from any such details.

"I observed Debhen and Sitiah," he revealed. "Briefly, but it was instructive. I believe a visit to their father's tomb would be more rewarding still. That is where I shall go next."

"Without their knowledge."

"Certainly. For them to become aware might make all vain. I shall be secret."

"You generally are." Bakenkhons considered him. "When did you observe those two? I know they attended a banquet last night. Perhaps you know… my son was there, mooning over that wicked little she-hyena Sitiah, as usual."

"No," Kamose answered—truthfully, though he would have lied if it pleased him. "I wasn't aware. A matter to trouble one, agreed, since it seems that she and her brother between them murdered her last husband, and others."

"Could it be proved in the vizier's court?"

"I seek evidence, and have good hopes that I will find it." Kamose leaned forward. "Master of all Khem's temples, are you informed anent the race known as the Old Dreadful Breed?"

"A legend to frighten babies." Bakenkhons looked as though he had lost some confidence in Kamose.

"Not so. They existed before the first mean graves were scraped in the sand. Their powers were terrible, among them the gift of sending their *ka* forth from their bodies by night in any form to work harm—leopard, huge snake, what they desired. The Brotherhood of Ra slew the most powerful ones and scattered their seed, long, long ago, but those with a weak and partial heritage remain. They cannot rove by night as beasts of prey, but other, lesser powers they have kept. Long heads and fine narrow bones are traits of the race."

"That was their father's appearance!"

"Not astounding."

"I heard but never credited these things. *Debhen and Sitiah*?"

"They are the very type."

Bakenkhons pondered, still doubtful, but aware that Kamose possessed a deep knowledge of hideous wonders. Fear for his son increased. He asked the pertinent question. "What lesser powers?"

"The laying of curses. Not magic as we understand it. They can—influence luck by their will, as when a man died of lockjaw. Take the hippopotamus hunt. Such are always perilous. The danger made a broad smooth thoroughfare their ill-wish might travel. Death passed by the others in the boats and smote him. The scribe was epileptic, but his fits had never been severe, until he became inconvenient to their father. The eye disease in Sitiah's husband, the quarry superintendent's death when a stone block bounded free, were occurrences of a like nature. Briefly, the more apt a thing is to happen in any case, the easier it is for these—

creatures—to cause it. Even from a distance. And I find it significant that Debhen nearly always wins a gamble."

"Your wisdom in magic is vast," Bakenkhons said slowly. "I bow to it. However, the latest murders are different."

"They are very different, and have taken place since Ptahshepses died. That is why investigating his tomb may enlighten me. At present I am baffled."

The necropolis of Thebes lay across the river on the western side. Thither Kamose took a ferry-boat, in disguise again, as a retired swordsman of the Shardana corps, with the scars of Pharaoh's battles on his limbs. He feigned a limp and mouthed obscene oaths in the Sherden tongue. When Kamose assumed a role, he was thorough.

With a paid guide and a staff, he wended through the rocky, twisting valleys where the tombs of kings and queens were cut. Nobles and even commoners who had risen to high office rested here, besides the royal dead. This was the realm over which the jackal-god Anubis presided especially. Kamose, as his archpriest, knew many dark secrets concerning burials, and revised burials, among these cliffs and valleys. Nothing, however, of Ptahshepses' tomb. It had never been a concern of his until now.

They reached it at last. A neat, finely-built structure on a limestone ridge above a ravine, its site had been well chosen. Any sudden rainstorm would pour its freshets into the lion-colored valley beneath, instead of flooding the tomb. It looked calmly innocent in the hot sunlight spilling down from Egypt's sky.

Bidding his guide wait, Kamose passed through a gateway that was a diminutive copy of the great temples' pylons. Beyond lay a walled courtyard, with the entrance to a mortuary chapel at its far end. Atop the roof stood a small stone pyramid. No longer were these forbidden to any but kings. Ptahshepses would not be interred within it, though. Kamose knew well that it was a symbol only. The inmate's burial chamber would be cut from the rock beneath the ridge, with a sealed shaft approaching it.

"Who comes?" demanded the tomb's caretaker, emerging. Kamose knew his sort, an aged, lowly priest glad of such employment. Nevertheless, it would take a certain stipend to maintain him, and the sepulchre, though small, had been well constructed. Ptahshepses had died impecunious, in disgrace. How had the cost been met? Nor did experience suggest that his son—a known idler and gambler—would be nice about meeting his obligations to the dead. No. Even at a first approach, much here was dubious.

"I come," Kamose answered roughly. "Iwoklewas of the Shardana. I come to make an offering to the lord Ptahshepses' *ka*."

"A Shardana?" the wrinkled caretaker repeated.

Kamose bristled as a mercenary soldier ought. "And proud of it, old man! I've fought more battles for Egypt than you tally years. In bygone days I was this lord's bodyguard, too. He did well by me. Now I come to offer at his tomb. I bring incense, oil and grain."

"*You* were the lord Ptahshepses' bodyguard?"

"And a good one. He knew the worth of Shardana. Like the godking Merenptah and his father preceding. I carried a sword for them all. May I enter, priest?"

With a grumble about rude barbarians, the old priest led him into the tomb chapel's dim coolness. Behind a table for offerings painted, life-sized statues of Ptahshepses and his wife, while both side walls carried murals of their domestic life. They looked admirably wholesome. The proclaimed Iwoklewas hid a cynical smile within the hirsute camouflage surrounding his mouth.

The statues were skillfully done. Ptahshepses' image showed features Kamose had expected—a long head, high cheekbones and narrow jaw. The wife by contrast had been a sturdy, round-headed woman. Of course a heritage from the Old Dreadful Breed did not always show. If she had possessed one, however slight, it might have combined with tripled force in their children.

Behind the statues, in the rear wall, the outline of a door had been cut, a normal feature in a tomb. Often they were painted only. Through this the *ka* of one who had gone beyond could return by magic, to inhabit his statue and receive offerings from his kin.

Kamose looked into the statue's painted eyes. It seemed to him that malevolence lurked there. Prejudice, or his sorcerer's awareness? He was prepared to wager on the latter.

He made his offering as though nothing was amiss. The old priest received it, and made a prayer for Ptahshepses' well-being in the beyond. A harmless, oblivious dolt if Kamose had ever encountered one.

There was nothing more to learn in the chapel. The true secrets of Ptahshepses' tomb must lie in the burial chamber itself, and the passage leading there had been sealed behind a cubit of rock. Kamose could brew a potion which gave a man the power to walk through walls, but it involved the risk of being lost in strange dimensions, and exposed one to presences it were not healthy to attract; a last resort. Kamose also knew spells that would open the earth for him, and close it again afterwards, but even the simpleton who kept this tomb would be likely to notice that.

There was a simpler way. Debhen and Sitiah visited their father's tomb regularly, like true pious children. Bakenkhons had said that on these occasions they relieved the priest of his duties overnight, and kindly gave him liberty on the eastern bank. What they did at such times should be of interest.

When you are here next, he thought, *I shall be here.*

III.

A boon which the King gives and which Anubis gives, he who is upon his mountain, he who is in the place of embalming, lord of the Sacred Land, may he give a good burial in the western necropolis, in his tomb of the Underworld, revered one, son of a local prince...
                    —The Coffin Text of Nekht-Ankh

Again, this time by night, Kamose crossed the river in a humble boat. He passed through the embalming houses of the western shore. From their premises rolled pungent smoke and steam, a reek of putrefaction, odours of spices, preservative unguents and aromatic herbs. Shops and booths innumerable sold sawdust, coffins, jars, sacred images, and grave-cloths. Statues and paintings of the mortuary god Anubis with his jackal's head abounded.

Leaving these busy, rank places behind, Kamose climbed towards the ridges and valleys from which the many tombs of western Thebes were hewn. Multitudes of stars glittered in a black, moonless sky. Kamose rejoiced in the lack of a moon, orb of his greatest enemy, Thoth, the Measurer of Time. In his renewed vitality he feared not moonlight or anything else; if the rancor of Thoth had failed to destroy him in the months when he was weak, culminating in an intricate plot to unleash the Lion of Leprosy upon him, it would hardly be effective now.

Nevertheless, he loathed the sickly white radiance of that dead world at any time.

On his breast he wore a jet amulet in the shape of a jackal couchant, on one wrist a bracelet bearing the sacred eye, on the other a *djed* pillar, each blessed by his patron god. All were potent against hostile sorceries and demons. Against more mundane perils he carried a wide-bladed bronze dagger and a hard ebony baton two cubits long.

Thus armed and protected, he followed the children of Ptahshepses to their father's tomb. Simply that they came unaccompanied and walking from the river-side, in the dark, showed that such pampered brats were on no normal errand, however believable the pretext of duty to their father's shade might appear to some. They were safe, of course. Terror of Kamose's magic did more to keep bandits away from western Thebes than the necropolis police. Tomb robbing had passed out of fashion for the first time in the archives.

They passed through the sepulchre's gateway. Kamose allowed them time to enter the chapel, then followed, keeping in the shadow of the courtyard wall. He peered around the tomb-chapel's door. The siblings stood together before their father's statue, heads bowed, murmuring prayers or spells. With their orisons finished, they pushed together against the statue's base, which turned partly around with a harsh grinding noise. A rumble ensued, and the wall behind the statue opened.

The supposedly false door was not false at all. To those knowing its secret, it allowed entry to Ptahshepses' burial chamber at any time. Debhen and Sitiah lit torches before proceeding. Kamose watched them go. Then he crossed to the square doorway himself, and followed the pair into the sloping passage beyond. Treading noiselessly, he came to the head of a stone stairway leading down.

There he paused. Orange torchlight danced and flickered up the pitch-black stair from the burial chamber. While Kamose doubted the existence of physical traps, he sensed that curses had been laid on the descent to induce missteps and fatal plunges. To Kamose they were nothing; he brushed them aside as they had been cobwebs.

Coming quietly to the burial chamber's entrance, he looked within. The young people had discarded their clothes, placed their torches in brackets and lit softly glowing lamps to better illumine the crypt. Their father's painted sarcophagus lay on a porphyry slab between them. With their palms resting flat on the lid, they leaned forward, eyes closed, and murmured invocations to the *ka* of him who was immured there. They paid their mother's coffin no attention.

Kamose scanned the paintings on the walls. They were thoroughly unlike the ones in the tomb-chapel above. *These* depicted men and women with scarlet flesh and pitch-dark eyes, a device to distinguish them; they had never been scarlet-skinned in life. But their long-skulled heads and the curious shape of their eye-orbits, with their activities, would have been enough. Sendings issued from their lithe bodies in the shapes of terrible beasts—leopards, great snakes, and some wholly unnatural creatures like the harpy. All worked destruction and harm on normal human beings, uniformly shown as their prey, to be slain, devoured, or raped. Beneath these grim friezes undulated many representations of Apep, the Destroying Serpent. A mural on the wall behind the two sarcophagi confirmed those dark and secret histories Kamose had read concerning the kings who built the greatest pyramids.

Snefru, his queen Hetepheres, and their descendants, were also depicted with scarlet skin, sending out their spirits from the pyramid tombs in the form of terrible creatures—huge carnivore bats among others. Khufu's pyramid was impossible to mistake. Kamose reflected that these paintings would have to be quietly destroyed when the whole wretched business was exposed.

He looked again at Debhen and Sitiah. Above their father's coffin a formless darkness, deeper than the tomb's shadows, had coalesced, and it swallowed the lamplight with no traces. His magician's senses perceived it as the *ka* of Ptahshepses, though it could not do the things his distant ancestors had done. It was incapable of leaving the sepulcher, or even going further than the consecrated statue in the chapel above; but here in its own burial chamber it could still work baneful magic.

Kamose watched the sister move among the furnishings and garments in her parents' tomb. She laid her slender hands on an image about two-thirds of a cubit tall and placed it on the sarcophagus lid. Kamose saw it clearly then. He knew that sort of image well. It was a *shabti*, an enchanted statuette meant to take the place of a person gone beyond, if he should be required to do field labor in the afterlife. Finely made, this one had been equipped with peasant farmer's tools to perform its duties. They included a hoe, baskets for carrying sand, a yoke to balance them across the *shabti*'s stone shoulders, a sickle, and a knotted measuring cord.

Watching from beyond the doorway, hidden in shadows, Kamose at once understood much about the murders.

Debhen began speaking. His intense tone might have astonished those companions of his who knew him as a light-minded gambler and skirt-chaser. "O shade of our father Ptahshepses, may your name live without end, grant this servant of yours the power to live and slay in the world of daylight. Grant him strength and hate! Inspire him, your children plead, to destroy the person whose death we have undertaken!"

"Bestow upon him power to gain full manly stature, strength and swift motion," Sitiah continued, her words, in a way, seeming more ominous than her brother's for the sweet light voice in which they were spoken. It came quite terribly from the face that now seemed so inhuman, like a mask above the tender and wholly human youthful breasts. "Bestow it, O our sire, from the regions outside life! Let him slay without compunction, and become a little stone image again when the deed is achieved! Let him kill the one we name!"

"Let him kill the one we name!" Debhen resumed. "Let him kill Wem! Let him destroy the Chief of Irrigation with the sickle or the cord, and become once more a diminutive stone image! Let him do this thing unseen! Let us remove him again undiscovered! Grant your children this, revered *ka* of our father!"

Wem, the Chief of Irrigation, was the next intended victim of this enterprising pair. Why? For pay, surely. Their client was someone who wished to be the Chief of Irrigation instead. Why by this method and not through their inborn talent to lay curses? Kamose presumed they liked it better because it was surer. Their curses, if that was an accurate term, had effect through weighting the dice of chance in their favour, but success remained a gamble. He wondered in passing how often they had cursed someone to death, perhaps for a mere fancied slight, and had the attempt fail. They had probably discovered the talent as children—an unfortunate thing for their playmates. Employing the *shabti* as their slayer made it certain.

He considered leaving, and with a word sealing the door into the solid rock wall it appeared, to trap these two. However, he thought again. He merely departed, mind filled with musings that became grimmer with each

step he mounted. He emerged into the tomb chapel somewhat less wary than his accustomed way.

He almost paid dearly. As he passed it, the tall statue of Ptahshepses toppled towards him in a way that should have been impossible, when it was based so solidly and soundly, but fall it did. Kamose sprang aside. Nevertheless the statue struck his shoulder with ferocious impact and tumbled him across the floor. He lurched upright and stumbled out of harm's way, gasping.

He left the chapel in considerably more haste than he had entered it. He had attained a disciplined, steady walk by the time he returned to the river-side through the reeking necropolis, though the pain had not lessened much. He cared little about that. It compared to his fury as lamb's milk to blood. By gelded and dismembered Osiris, by the knives of Anubis, he would gut the man's tomb and obliterate even his name! Yea, the man's tomb... if he *was* a man. As for his murderous children—well, their fate should be contemplated with care before it was settled. As it would be.

Kamose would have much to tell Bakenkhons on the morrow.

IV.

Then the High Priest of Amun, Menkheperre, triumphant, went to the great god, saying: "As for any person, of whom they shall report before thee, saying, 'A slayer of living people is he', thou shalt destroy him, thou shalt slay him." Then the Great God nodded exceedingly, exceedingly.

—Banishment Stele

"Sagacious Kamose, you have done well!" Bakenkhons enthused.

"I agree." Kamose's tone was acerbic. "I did well to come back from that place as a live man. I can confirm that your son is indeed in love with a woman he should not espouse. She's a murderess, several times over. She and her brother are making a lucrative trade of it."

Bakenkhons frowned deeply, his heavy face troubled. Diffuse light filtering through the fretted shutters near the ceiling made his white robes glimmer. "You are sure of this ugly thing?"

"It is ugly enough, and I am. The deceptive false door and the paintings in the burial chamber will make a believer of you when you behold them! But will it convince your son?"

"That Sitiah knew about them? No." The word fell flat and heavy in the air of Bakenkhons' house. "I said he is besotted with her. It's true as the feather in the scales of judgement."

"Then we must, as the trite words go, catch them in the act."

"Whether we can do so depends on whether they continue with their scheme to destroy Wem. Will they know that you spied on them in the tomb?"

Kamose owned that it was difficult to say. "The toppled statue may make them suspicious. The *ka* of their sire saw me, though they did not. Can it tell them they were observed by a spy? Will they understand? I think not. If they attend Wem's banquet and try to murder him with this red-handed *shabti* of theirs, we may be assured not."

"I have never heard of a *shabti* slaying men before."

"Nor I," Kamose admitted, "and where baneful magic is concerned, my knowledge extends far. But it is possible. The *shabti* is endowed with the power to do its owner's labour in the beyond. It might carry out tasks in the living world also. It is certain that images can be brought to life. Lesser sorcerers than I can do it, worthy Bakenkhons, and we know the antique tale of the wax crocodile."

He maintained an even tone with effort. His own children, long before, had been destroyed by something he had thought was a priestess of Bast, but proved an ivory image animated by Thoth's hostile magic. The memory burned him like seething oil, even now, generations of men later. It did not incline him kindly to the pair who made, as he said, a lucrative trade of such slaying.

Bakenkhons sent police across the river to investigate, on the pretext that sacrilegious rascals had damaged some tombs in the area. The agents to whom he gave the errand were expert in subterfuge. By early afternoon they had reported that the statue of Ptahshepses in his tomb chapel was standing as before, though its shoulder and part of one arm had been broken away.

"Shape of the black crocodile!" Kamose swore. "That statue is massive stone, and the base more ponderous yet!

Never could two slender young people raise it and set it back in place, unless their father's *ka* assisted them."

"If it toppled the figure upon you, it could certainly do that also."

"Just so. Hmm. Debhen and Sitiah are conceited, I think… over-confident. If they believe the tale of impious vandals wreaking damage in tombs, they will go forward with their plot."

His hope came true. The children of Ptahshepses sent no message to Wem regretting that they must miss his banquet. They would be there. Bakenkhons's wife Merit, a rounded sociable woman, placid by nature in most ways but energetic in the interests of her children, had some pertinent gossip to offer anent the Chief of Irrigation.

"O formidable Kamose," she said with a laugh, "You know Wem? He's one of those who never did a thing out of place in his youth. His career has been exemplary, his private life too. Despite his wealth, he did not even keep a harem while he was married! His wife henpecked him. But now he's years widowed and his children are grown. He has begun kicking over the traces, bless him, at that time of life one may expect it from a man who has been respectable too long."

"His feast will be an intemperate one?"

"Before midnight all will be fairly proper. After midnight there will be more licence. Some will depart, but the dancers, courtesans and young wantons will stay. Sitiah and her brother among them."

"Good lady," Kamose said gravely, "that is both interesting and of value."

Kamose did not go to the feast as himself. Instead he accompanied Bakenkhons and Merit as a Kushite attendant, with skin darkened and a great frizzy sheaf of hair adding half a foot to his stature. Having entered Wem's estate in their party, he removed to the gardens and waited. These, he reasoned, were the most likely locale for the killing. Luring her host outside to an assignation would be the obvious ploy for Sitiah to use—and, from what Merit said of Wem, the most apt to succeed.

Two little creatures within the house served as his spies and messengers—a hoopoe and Merit's pet, a black-faced vervet monkey. So he settled among the bushes with the fierce patience of the Kushite bandit he now resembled, lurking in ambush for some trader's donkey train. None of Wem's guard dogs troubled him. Sensing the aura of macabre sorcery that surrounded him, they crept away, discouraged and mute.

In time the hoopoe came fluttering through the garden on its barred wings to find him. Cocking its head, it trilled through its long narrow bill,

"Woman on rooftop. Speak with lord of house. Say encounter him. Big nest here in garden."

The hoopoe meant a latticed ornamental kiosk not far from Kamose's hiding place. Softly, in the bird's own simple language, he said, "Good. Watch if she leaves the house. Come and tell me. Many fat insects shall be thy reward."

He prowled around the ornate kiosk, but did not remain near it. Sitiah's abnormal senses might warn her of his presence. He desired her, or her brother, to come and place the fatal statuette in the kiosk where Wem would blunder upon it. Else there would be no proof of their murder scheme. Kamose's smile was wicked as he lurked in the soft, breathing dark.

Even his sorcerer's senses barely informed him when someone came briefly to the kiosk and left again. That unobtrusive silence was a remarkable thing to achieve in a garden filled with luxuriant, rustling greenery. But the person carried the *shabti* with its freight of maleficent magic under a shawl, and Kamose would have been aware of *that* from a furlong's distance. Approaching, he found the object by the kiosk's doorway, under the foliage of a blooming potted plant. He held it contemplatively in his hand for a moment before he replaced it.

The next messenger was Merit's vervet, scuttling through the soft night to find Kamose and chatter its report. Having a greater brain than the bird, and being closer to human, it was correspondingly more verbose.

"The master of the house, the fat man, the fat man, leaves his guests and comes to the garden. He comes here! He comes alone, no family, no troop, thinking to mate with the demon girl, but the demon girl is with my mistress Merit and her lord. As well go beneath a tree where the leopard waits to leap!"

The words came in an excited torrent. The vervet's white whiskers stiffened with excess of emotion and spread like a ruff around its black face. Kamose had to bring a peremptory end to its repetitions. There was little time, from what it said, before Wem would appear at the kiosk.

"Yes. You have done well, little one. Now go back to your mistress and leave the rest to me."

The monkey departed, with a deal of relief in its tiny mind at placing distance between itself and the *shabti*. It possessed an animal's sharp awareness of inimical magic. Debhen and Sitiah would be conspicuously in the midst of a room filled with folk of rank and known probity by now, conversing, no doubt, with Bakenkhons, as a way of establishing their innocence. It appeared to be their usual procedure while contriving someone's death.

Wem duly arrived, eager to meet the lovely young widow. He progressed with far less quiet than Sitiah had. He was fatter, to be sure, and driven by lust.

His fleshy shape disappeared into the kiosk, where he ignited the wick of a cat-shaped lantern. The *shabti* waited until then. Having eyes, it must need light for its murderous task, or at least prefer it.

Sudden as a bursting dam, it changed from a figurine to something as tall as Kamose and much broader, its skin a hairless powdery white. The transformed figure moved towards Wem, who stood where he was, stricken with dread. A terrible light glowed in its eyes. Blazing out of that immobile face, they were beacons on the horror beyond horrors that haunted men's souls in their worst moments of despair.

Between the huge nailless hands it held a knotted cord. The free ends trailed on the floor. A farmer's measuring rope, it could yet serve other purposes. At its waist a bronze sickle hung.

Fearfully swift, the *shabti* whipped the cord around Wem's plump throat. As it began to strangle him, Kamose plunged into the kiosk and snatched the sickle from its waist. The bronze was sharp as barber's shears. Kamose slashed through the cord in two places, and it fell ineffectual to the floor. The *shabti* turned upon him, and the magician met its gaze with barely a pang. He had dominated beings more awful than this one.

Wem, usefully, swooned in a heap.

Kamose resorted to physical attack. Why, with his great and deep resources of sorcery, he could not have explained. Perhaps it was utter loathing that impelled him. Gripping the sickle in both hands, he drove the point into the *shabti*'s midriff and heaved upwards in a gutting rip towards the breastbone. It was like dragging the blade through honey mixed with gravel. The mighty figure's torso opened, but neither blood nor entrails spilled; there was only pallid meat inside. Then the nailless hands were on Kamose's shoulder and thigh.

Kamose struck it from two sides with the bracelets on his wrists. One carried the symbol of the *djed* pillar, the other the Sacred Eye. The creature faltered, but did not release him, and bent the magician back across its knee with the manifest purpose of breaking him.

You think so, children's doll?

Either pride or presence of mind rescued him. Kamose invoked his magic and the protection of his sombre god. He roared, "In the paramount name of Anubis, be still, move not! By Wepwawet and Khenti-Amentiu, be again what you were!"

The thing froze in its position. Then it dwindled in size within a couple of breaths. The massive, solid bulk it had possessed writhed away in drifts of bluish vapour. A *shabti* manikin less than a cubit tall clattered on the floor of exquisite tiles.

Even Kamose was shaken. That being should never have been able to lay hands on him. He cursed the fatuous human emotions he had laboured to leave behind, and which had just betrayed him again. He indulged them a little further, however. Remembering the animated ivory statue that had smothered two of his children, and glaring down at the *shabti*, he spat upon it. Then he saw to the task of reviving Wem. His composure was intact again by the time the Chief of Irrigation revived.

Wem babbled wildly. He asked a number of foolish, predictable questions, among them, "What happened?" "Who was it that attacked me?" and "Who are you?" Kamose answered the last, mendaciously, glad that Wem had not seen him reduce the *shabti* by magic.

"I am Yadu, an attendant of the Holy One, Bakenkhons the Archpriest of Amun-Ra. By his command I watched to protect you this night. He suspected two of your guests intended evil, lord."

"Two of my guests? Which two?"

"The lord Debhen and his sister. Their instrument was this, a manikin from their father's tomb. See. It bears his cartouche incised upon the breast. This it was that attacked you."

Wem spluttered and disbelieved, at which Kamose shrugged, referring him to Bakenkhons. Wem returned to his house at last, with the man he believed a Kushite servant. Despite his reluctance, he had to accept that Sitiah had lured him to the ornamental kiosk, then failed to arrive, and that the *shabti* bore her father's name. He would have to accept the rest in due course.

By Kamose's advice, Wem did not have his return announced. He entered through the side vestibule and stalked into his main dining-room, unkempt, soiled, the marks of a knotted cord scarlet on his neck, but alive and enraged. Utter silence, followed by a hubbub of comment, greeted him. Debhen and Sitiah turned their heads—and Wem had the privilege of seeing their comely faces change to the colour of tainted whey. Sitiah dropped the wine-cup she was holding. It rolled across the floor to Wem's feet.

He walked to her with his rubicund features, for once, taut and harsh, and held forth the *shabti*. She and her brother found their poise again and brazened it out. Even when Bakenkhons revealed what he knew, they maintained their denial. They had never seen the *shabti*; it was spurious; the would-be murderer had tried to cast suspicion on them.

"Take them away," Bakenkhons said curtly. "I am a judge. Falsehood can be sifted from verity in the proper place, the Hall of Two Truths."

The siblings were duly taken away. Yadu the Kushite made one of their escort, lest they try to abscond. Astounded remarks from Wem's guests followed them out.

EPILOGUE

Ra hath overthrown thy words, the gods have turned thy face backward, the Lynx hath torn open thy breast, the Scorpion hath cast fetters upon thee; and Ma'at hath sent forth thy destruction.
—Papyrus of Mes-em-Neter

Debhen and Sitiah maintained their innocence with a pertinacity that would have suited purer consciences. The evidence against them mounted for all that. The murderous *shabti* matched other figurines in their father's burial chamber, and the paintings on its walls horrified necropolis police who had seen much that was impious.

The nature of those paintings was never made public. Votaries sworn to secrecy scoured the tomb featureless, and pronounced the most potent exorcisms Egypt knew. The name of Ptahshepses was made not. His coffin was destroyed, his mummy burned, the ashes given to the desert.

Debhen and Sitiah faced trial, not before Bakenkhons, but before Rameses. Wem testified, rigid and angry. "Yadu the Kushite" bore witness that he had spied on the siblings in their father's tomb, and seen them open a secret door to the burial chamber. He described what had happened therein. Bakenkhons supported his deposition. He referred to previous murders, and pointed out that each had occurred when Debhen and Sitiah were present. Now a victim had survived to incriminate the pair.

Apprised before the trial, the Pharaoh knew who "Yadu" really was. The court brought a finding of culpability. Rameses pondered long, and refrained in the end from condemning them to die. He ordered that they be mutilated by losing their ears and noses, then exiled to Dakhla for all their days, to be crushed like frogs between the stones if ever they attempted to leave.

When the pair heard it, their masks fell at last. Furious obscenities and malisons spewed from the writhing lips of both. They cursed all involved, not least the Pharaoh, as few dare curse even in private. The air seemed to roil with curdled darkness and evil spirits to gather. Before Debhen and Sitiah were manhandled forth, some court officials of long experience exchanged queasy glances and saw sweat on each others' foreheads.

Rameses maintained the gravity of a divine monarch. He did not, however, amend the sentence to death even then. It caused Kamose to wonder just how far the young Pharaoh trusted him...

About the Author

Keith Taylor was born in Tasmania in December 1946, after his father Jack came back from Hitler's War and married Fay Gourlay. Keith grew up at the foot of Mount Wellington with his three sisters, Ruth, Julie and Megan. A voracious reader from an early age (what writer wasn't?) he began writing his own stories at the age of nine. He suspects he might have been illiterate if television had existed in Tasmania then.

He also discovered science fiction and fantasy early. At fourteen he found the Ace Double Novel, *Conan the Conqueror* back to back with Leigh Brackett's *Sword of Rhiannon*. That settled his fate permanently. After six years in the Australian army and Vietnam service, he began writing again, and got his start in Ted White's *Fantastic Stories* with his yarns of the Irish bard Felimid which eventually grew into a five-novel series. His other series characters include Nasach, a fisherman's son and tough escaped slave, and Kamose the Archpriest of Anubis, whose sorcerous exploits take place in ancient Egypt circa 1180 BCE.

Various other stories appeared in British editor Mike Ashley's anthologies—fantasy, Arthurian fiction, and historical mystery.

Keith Taylor now lives in Melbourne with his wife Anna and son Francis.

CPSIA information can be obtained
at www.ICGtesting.com
Printed in the USA
FSHW01n0124171018
53054FS